BLACK KNIFE

Karl Vincent

Black Knife - Karl Vincent
First published in the United Kingdom 2007
Citation Press
PO Box 818
Bromley
G. London
BR1 9AG
United Kingdom

First edition published in hardback 2006

ISBN 0-9551238-1-X
978-0-9551238-1-8

Printed and bound in Great Britain by the
CPI Group

Here's the point: this Islamic counter-crusade is a natural dialectic of human history, and their pitiless employment of terrorism conforms to basic human behaviour. Their hate is as natural as cancer, or the plague, or locusts, or anthrax, or the exploitation of women, or slavery, or war.

Apollonia Johnson

MAX AND SUSIE

Susie was curious as to why the familiar noises of stirring or arguing weren't emanating from her brother's bedroom. Normally, Max and whoever had been his 'guest' for the night would have been eating the meagre breakfast she provided, but not today. After a few more minutes, she decided to go down the hallway and tap on her brother's door. She did so, but received no response. This was unusual but there had been times when he would sleep for thirty-six hours straight through, a result of his 'medicine' finally taking its toll, but what about the girl? Susie shrugged to herself and turned to leave, but something made her turn back; this was just not right. She knocked loudly on the door and tried the knob. The door was unlocked and she took a deep breath and cracked it open. Then a little wider, but no one was in view. Again she inched it open and so, by degrees, she opened the door, and light from the landing streamed in. Drawing in a breath she held her clenched fist to her mouth to stifle a scream. The bed sheet was drawn up over what appeared to be a body and the sheet was soaked in blood.

Reeling backwards until her back made contact with the wall of the passage she stared fixedly into the room, 'Oh… my … God,' she hissed through her clenched teeth, 'what has he done?' Gathering her thoughts, she calmed herself and stepped back to the threshold of the room, glancing inside and calling out her brother's name, 'Max, Max, where are you? What have you done?' Realizing there was nowhere he could hide in the small room she stepped back and addressed her enquiry more broadly, 'Max! Max! Where are you, you worthless piece of shit?!'

****

Max Pankow was a self-employed businessman who worked out of the house he shared with his sister and her two children. His sister, Susie, had never married either of the men who had fathered her kids. Max and Susie's mother had died shortly after the passing of their father, and brother and sister jointly inherited the house located in Hanau, Germany, a town not far from Frankfurt-am-Main. Frankfurt was Germany's financial centre and boasted a busy international airport which served as the hub for Lufthansa. It was this latter convenience that would impact upon Max.

Max was a weirdo, a computer geek who made his living building personal computers and small business systems. He would buy second-hand motherboards and cases, and then install the processor, memory sticks and peripherals which he could often secure at the flea-market in Frankfurt. He installed pirated software, and tailored each project to the needs of his client. They could get a computer from him a lot cheaper than from Media-Markt or other German retail outlets. That was his day job, but he also needed to moonlight because he had an expensive habit, his 'medicine' as Susie euphemistically referred to it.

Max was hooked on speed, and did coke when he could afford it. His sister left him to his world so long as he continued to provide for the household. In addition, she collected *Kindergeld* (child allowance) well as other provisions offered by the state for unemployed unmarried mothers, and chain-smoked while she tended to her children.

Susie was not attractive. She was thin as a winter birch, and her hair hung straight, sparse and seemed always to appear overdue for a shampooing. She was tall and flat-chested, even though she was nursing Katja, and had a long, pointed nose; all that was missing from her caricature was a pair of wire-rimmed spectacles. But she didn't wear glasses and her nose was a Pankow family trait, shared by her brother. Max was six centimetres shorter than his sister and eleven months her junior. He had been born five weeks prematurely, and the doctor warned his parents that 'statistically' this might have a negative effect on his full growth and it had indeed been the case. Like his sister, he also appeared sickly thin, but that was usual among speed freaks. When he smiled, the sight of discoloured, rotting teeth immediately repulsed anyone who noticed. If they were in close enough range, his acrid breath would further revolt them.

Susie suffered from frequent depressive moods. It was a condition of mind that rendered her a recluse, except to walk her children once a day, little Katja in her stroller and Herbie stumbling along in his harness. The weather didn't matter; rain, snow or sub-zero cold, Susie insisted on a daily outing. She considered it her maternal duty, as important as providing them sustenance; it was a German thing. Anyway, because of her reclusive nature, she paid little mind to the East European women, mostly Russian, that Max would meet at Frankfurt Airport and bring back to the house, always one at a time. Nor did she view with suspicion the screams and cries of protest that issued from behind the closed door of her brother's bedroom.

Invariably, the next day, the 'Medicine Man' would come. That was how she referred to the tall black man when talking to her brother. They were conversations Max clearly tried to avoid, and so she would sullenly withdraw. The rule was that when the 'Medicine Man' came, she and the children must retire to her second-floor domain or go out for a walk. Susie had invented the nick-name because he delivered 'medicine' to Max; that much she knew. He also retrieved the foreign girls who clung to him willingly. He was a handsome man, she granted, and didn't blame these poor girls for wanting to escape the company of her creepy brother. Although usually circumspect, on a couple of occasions Max had referred to the 'Medicine Man' as 'Black Knife'.

She suspected that this *Schwarze* (black man) worked for one of the drug and prostitution mafias that she read about in the newspaper and saw on TV. This was re-enforced by snippets of information she was able to gather from her brother. She was satisfied she knew what was going on and, although she didn't like it, she had little choice other than to accept it.

The police knew most of the Mafia 'soldiers'. If

one of these goons met girls at the airport, it would be a clear indication that all was not well. But Susie's geeky-looking brother neither fitted the Mafia profile, nor was he on police records, so he didn't attract unwanted attention and nobody was the wiser.

She didn't like the girls being brought to the house, but she needed her brother's financial support. Thus, she kept her mouth shut, cooked the extra helping at dinner, and laid an extra place for breakfast the following morning, knowing that before lunchtime the Medicine Man would collect the girl and be gone. That was as much as she knew, or wanted to know, and since these visitations occurred no more than four or five times a month, she let it be.

In fact, there was something more that Susie knew, something she had picked up from conversations with Max's 'guests' during dinner and at breakfast. These girls had answered adverts in their local newspaper. She also knew that Max didn't place the adverts; the Mafia did. They described a successful German businessman, widowed, looking for a suitable partner, and so on. Since it was Max who met them at the airport, they presumed he was the widowed businessman, and he didn't discourage that belief. She was convinced that these poor women were being hijacked into the Mafia's prostitution ring, but Susie found her suspicion more curious than

HERMAN

e highways, Herman would remi-
and sometimes even scheme. At
agine his African brothers writing
 songs about him. Unfortunately,
e burning sense of destiny that had
earlier years, but such fantasies
se boring hours on the road. In the
rman could drive from Stuttgart to
 and fifteen minutes, but morning
bably add forty minutes. Trucks
, he griped, causing chaos on the
 German trucks, but lumbering car-
ver Europe, Czech Republic and
he Netherlands and Italy, Poland,
 and so on. It wasn't necessarily

troubling.

She recognized that most of these girls were edu-
cated. Some were teachers or nurses, and some of the
youngest were college students. They were all multi-
lingual and usually spoke passable German. They
were always comely and well groomed and Susie
would chuckle to herself as she imagined their shock
when they found Max waiting for them at the airport
… their prospective suitor. She was surprised they
didn't simply turn him away and take the next available flight back home. But the routine was always
the same: the girls would sullenly accompany him,
they would resist retiring to his bedroom, but ultimately gave in after assurances there would be no
sex. She sometimes wondered if indeed there really
was any sex going on: there certainly was usually a
lot of argument and protestations coming from his
bedroom during the night.

However, now something awful had happened,
something she had never imagined might occur. She
had harboured a bad feeling from the moment she
encountered the girl Max had brought back the previous day. This latest guest was Romanian, so she
said, and spoke no German. However, she spoke
good English, which both Susie and her brother had
learned in school, so communication wasn't an issue.
It was a certain intensity in her gaze that Susie found

disconcerting, that and the fact that she tended to make unwavering and unblinking eye contact – like a predator about to pounce. She was a bit younger than most of the other guests; Susie reckoned between eighteen and twenty.

The girl insisted upon sleeping in the living room on the couch. Max insisted that either she come to his bedroom or pay him 100 Euros for the room and board. She warned him there would be no sex, and he sniggered something about a blow-job was all he required. The Romanian girl warned him again, threatening that she would defend herself, but he insisted on the bedroom or the money. He knew that the Russian Mafia had provided her airline ticket, but only one way. The letter promised that she would get the return ticket when she showed up in Frankfurt. He was used to the desperation with which these girls would insist on being given their return ticket. He would calmly inform them that they would get it in the morning, assuming that they had treated him with respect during the night. Of course, he did not hold their ticket. Once Black Knife showed up, he would never see the girl again.

Susie had got up this morning, first feeding Katja and Herbie as was the usual routine, and then prepared breakfast for Max and his guest. When they hadn't appeared or responded she'd gone to the room

and m
the sh
first in
police
arrest
foot of
favouri
kitchen
weapon
the kitc
shaking
cigarette
saucer. S

The c
Medicine
mess. He
that blood
and then
ridiculous
really piss
something
whisper, 'I
what to do.

When he drove th
nisce, daydream,
times he would in
poems and singin
he no longer felt th
gripped him in
helped to pass th
dead of night, He
Hanau in an hou
traffic would pre
were everywhere
highway. Not jus
riers from all o
Slovenia, from
Austria, Hungar

because Germany was their destination; it was because alternate routes through France, Switzerland, and Austria charged tolls or sticker levies to use the highways. German highways did not, which automatically made them the routes of choice. Maybe the German government figured that they would make their lost revenue opportunity back from the onerous taxes they levied on fuel, but these truckers were too smart for that. They would fill up in the East, and drive straight through to Luxembourg, where the fuel was hardly taxed at all.

Herman lived in Hamburg, a five-hour drive to Hanau in the dead of night, and had a pick-up from that creep Max Pankow. However, he had spent the evening and early morning in Stuttgart, not because Stuttgart was on the way – it was out of the way – but because of the oldest of motives, a woman. At the moment he was thinking about her, Apollonia Johnson was her full name, which he found amusing and at that moment made him smile. 'Polly' was a black American who spoke damn little German, so they conversed in English. He had studied it in school for three years, and picked up more English along the way. Herman was quick with languages.

She worked for the American military at EUCOM (European Command) although in a civilian capacity. She was a bit evasive about exactly what it was she did for the Americans, and he really didn't care enough to press the issue. He had more important things to press with this woman, and her response was willing in those matters. Besides which he had been far more evasive about his own livelihood and background. As was usually the case, he concocted a fabulous autobiography to impress her; Herman loved to re-create himself. To Polly he was Sam Lumumba, the illegitimate son of Patrice Lumumba, the first president of the Republic of Congo (Zaire). Although none of his identification cards would have confirmed this, Polly never asked.

Polly was a tall woman, roughly his height in the bedroom, but slightly taller than him in the street, as she usually wore medium-height heels, knowing they gave her legs a little more shape. She dressed fashionably and needed little make-up, given her unblemished *café-au-lait* skin. He was quite sure that she was not pure African, as her skin was too light and some of her facial features looked borrowed from a Caucasian side, especially her fine nose. She wore her hair shorter than most German men dared, close clipped but still Afro-style. Her large eyes seemed to dance with a mocking glee, but what he liked most about this American lady was the athletic grace with which she moved her body, whether on her feet or on her back. She claimed to be twenty-nine years old, and he saw nothing that discredited that. The fact that she was an American intrigued him.

Polly was the first American woman that Herman had dated. He'd fooled around with several Brits before, but never a Yank. She didn't seem to mind serving as a port-of-convenience for this fellow; in fact she appeared to be quite satisfied with their loose arrangement. As far as he could tell, Polly entertained no other male interests in Germany.

As Herman drove towards Hanau he reflected that the previous night she had been in a particularly festive mood, which pleased him. She was usually in a good mood but last night was better than usual and, like most women, her mood greatly affected her responsiveness. The delightful mood, she had explained, was in anticipation of a trip she would be taking in a week from this coming Friday. A bus-load of women from Patch Barracks and surrounding American bases in the Stuttgart area were embarking on a shopping spree to Milan, Italy. They would board a bus on Friday evening at Patch with a second pick-up at *Panzer Kaserne* (American barracks in Stuttgart) then stop for a leisurely Italian dinner at Da Pipo in Dagarsheim to get them in a Milanesa mood. Then, stuffed to the gills, they'd climb back on board the bus, chat for a bit, and then finally fall asleep issuing snores and pasta-induced farts as they were driven through Switzerland to Italy. They'd arrive in Milan for an early breakfast, and then have all day and into the evening to shop. There was a schedule of fashion houses they would visit, then they would have a late dinner, pile on the bus now laden with their booty, and sleep their way back to Stuttgart, arriving very early Sunday morning. Anyway, that's what Polly had breathlessly explained to him as he politely listened with the patience of a partner dutifully performing foreplay. Today was Wednesday, she complained, so she would have to grind out nine more days before embarking on this dream trip.

The party was exclusively wives of military personnel, or civilian employees of the DOD (Department of Defence) or assigned to NATO, Polly had explained. They were mostly Americans, but a few of the wives were foreign-born, German and Korean, he recalled her saying. He had never witnessed Polly gush with such enthusiasm before.

'Milan is where fashion is happening,' she said. 'I'll be in style a whole year or two ahead of my friends in the States!' Herman just shook his head, and suggested she take off her clothes; that was as stylish as it got according to his taste.

'You can leave your hat on,' he mocked, recalling Joe somebody-or-another's gravel-throated song.

She wasn't wearing a hat.

The congestion on the *Autobahn* was getting very heavy, and the morning air was already polluted with the heavy fug of diesel fumes as the trucks ground their way up the inclines. He knew the route, so he didn't need to look at the signs. It was thirty more kilometres to Frankfurt, but he would skirt the city, heading for Hanau. Glancing at his watch he calculated it was probably another fifty minutes in the stop/go traffic. 'Well,' he thought to himself as he stretched in his seat, 'I'm in no hurry.' His Mafia boss had given him the usual instruction, pick up the girl from Max Pankow and take her to Dmitri in Hechingen, hopefully about a two-hour drive further on. He'd made a lot of deliveries like this and knew the Russian never went to his office until after lunch. That was because he didn't close the discotheque he operated until four in the morning.

Hechingen would hardly have been thought of as a den of vice, situated as it was at the foot of *Schwaebische Alb* and no more than a large village. The Russians had learned that police surveillance in Germany was far more relaxed in the countryside and Dmitri's Disco pulled in party animals from as far away as Stuttgart, the university town of Tübingen and Bodensee in the south. It served as a distribution point for Ecstasy, the drug of choice for the German disco crowd.

The Russian mafia had easily gotten into the distribution of this popular drug among young professionals – 'X', as it was referred to by users. Dmitri also ran a string of 'working girls'. The girls hung around the bar or the dance floor, appropriately dressed and available for a price. Maria, Dmitri's girl friend, supervised that side of the business, but Herman always made his delivery to Dmitri; that's who paid him. Down the road about a kilometre from Dmitri's Disco was a plot with six cabins where a fellow could rent some comfort and privacy from Maria by the hour, but usually business was transacted in the fellow's car. Maria collected the full fare, the girls worked for their room and board and their tips.

Maria knew how to handle the new arrivals to her brood. They usually arrived in a state of confusion and were somewhat disorientated. After all, they had come on the assumption they were meeting a prospective suitor. Then they had been met by the foul Max and had probably succumbed to his demands before being collected and delivered to Hechingen by the handsome but quiet *Schwartze*. Essentially, it was scarcely one rung above prostitution to offer yourself to a total stranger in marriage for the creature comforts that might provide, and so the transition was usually not too difficult. If, however, a particular girl became obdurate, then the long tentacles of the Russian Mafia could usually arrange for a call on relatives back home that would soon precipitate a tearful petition to do whatever it was her newfound 'friends' wanted her to do. In all but two or three cases this had worked in short order, and for those few recalcitrants the consequences had been ugly.

As a further incentive the girls were promised a return ticket to wherever it was they called home, together with a large sum of money based on a percentage of the revenues they had generated by the end of their two-month visa. Fat chance; by that time they had usually developed discreet but expensive habits or at least a taste for goods their 'gratuity', if they ever got it, would not support for any length of time. In any event, new girls were constantly churning through the mill because of the short visa stays, and that kept guys like Herman busy. He received one thousand Euros per delivery, plus extra for any other jobs that needed doing, and paid no taxes. On a good month he'd pull in twelve to fifteen thousand Euros, and Dmitri or the others paid him cash on delivery. Things seldom went wrong, which was good because the Mafia held him responsible for his delivery, regardless of who might be to blame. He had several bird-dogs like Max Pankow and paid them in 'X' for their services, although Max was different, insisting upon speed and a few snorts of 'Charlie'.

'Well,' Herman had smugly understated to himself, 'it was a living.' His office was a new, yellow Mercedes 320 SLK replete with global navigation, a stereo system to die for and a mobile phone. Most importantly he worked when he pleased, well almost, when the *Mafioski* barked for him to jump, the only question they wanted to hear was, 'How high?' However comfortable this was, it still troubled him that it was not his 'destiny'. Delivering novitiate prostitutes and assorted life-enhancing substances would not have his legend immortalized in song or verse. At heart he was still an incurable romantic even though, in fact, he was a vicious enforcer for the Eastern European Mob.

****

OUT OF AFRICA

SWAPO (South West African People's Organisation) had been created during the early 1960s, a militant independence movement in South West Africa, nurtured and funded by the Soviet bloc through neighbouring Angola. Herman Namlos had been born in Namibia, a protectorate of the Republic of South Africa, where SWAPO waged their socialist war of independence against the 'capitalist apartheid exploiters and oppressors'. After more than two decades, SWAPO finally won and their victory changed the course of Herman's life. He had survived where thousands had not, but at a price. He had been orphaned, his mother and siblings raped, butchered and buggered as his village was attacked. He wasn't sure what had happened to his father but thought he must have been fighting on the government side and was probably also dead. There was no way of knowing.

At age twelve, along with roughly six hundred other black Namibian orphans, Herman was invited to relocate in the DDR (*Deutsche Demokratische Republik* – East Germany) as a gesture of solidarity between socialist regimes. Africa had been the most successful front for communists in their Cold War against the West, although in Africa one could hardly have characterized this contest as 'cold'. Thousands had died in sparsely populated Namibia, hence the pervasive problem of orphans, most of them living in the street. Some were so young that they had barely learned to walk but the older kids found them useful as beggars, so they lived. The older ones taught the snotty-nosed tykes how to stick out their hands while maintaining a doleful demeanour, ensuring that they were kept on a starvation-level diet to elicit sympathy. Herman had been one of these tiny *miserables*.

He was rescued from the streets by a socialist humanitarian organization and turned over to their orphanage. It was good luck for 'Sam', the name which the orphanage had given him; a name-change to 'Herman' would come later upon his arrival in the DDR. Anyway, he had learned at a very early age that luck was as important a part of life as fire, earth, air or water. Later, he would regard his journey to a new continent as a new beginning. Even though at the time he was barely twelve years old, Sam clearly considered his emigration as a watershed event in his life.

In his orphanage years, Sam had taken victories of socialism over capitalism for granted, having looked at the world through an African lens, aided by the inculcations of the orphanage staff. He had arrived in Europe in 1985 – and it might as well have been a different planet. Eastern European socialism was not what the orphanage propaganda had cracked it up to be. Nevertheless, he was a survivor. He took it one day at a time, a technique he had learned by living in Africa.

Before coming to the DDR, he had carefully dreamed up a family tree. To simply admit he was an orphan of unknown origins did not create a feeling of adequacy in the boy. And his orphanage name grated on him. It might as well have been 'Pluto' for all the relevance that 'Sam' offered him. The Namibian bureaucracy lacked a record of his family. All he really knew was that they had found him in the street as an abused three-year-old struggling to stay alive.

SWAPO had been organized by Herman Toivo ja Toivo early in the sixties. In 1968, Toivo was arrested and imprisoned by the South African government, where he remained until 1984. According to the legend which Sam had developed and periodically embellished since he was nine years old, a patriotic young Nambian lady visited the imprisoned SWAPO founder and allowed the revolutionary hero generous visitation rights. Little 'Sam' resulted nine months later. His mother, so the story continued, was killed in a raid by South African troops when he was three years old. All of this, of course was fantasy. He had no idea concerning his origins. He'd been brought to the orphanage in a state of shock and never did recall his street life, or a home life before abandonment.

Nonetheless, it was fact not fantasy that he had been picked as one of the lucky orphans for passage to the DDR, probably because he showed cleverness in the way he manipulated the teachers and orphanage staff, augmented by his relentless pledge to become a socialist freedom fighter when he grew up. But he saw a great deal more than these simple causes affecting his selection. For Sam, it was a sign which emboldened his sense of destiny. He felt certain that one day they would write poems and sing songs about him.

During his induction into the DDR, he insisted that his name should be changed to Herman Toiva ja Toiva after his 'father'. The East German bureaucracy was not easily amused. They allowed him the name Herman, but balked at his desired family name. Thus, he was simply labelled as 'Namlos' (German - nameless) and the surname stuck.

Had he been born one hundred years earlier, he would certainly not have joined the Fabian Society. Nope, Herman would have been the guy wearing a black hat and carrying a bomb tucked under his arm. He wouldn't regard any particular target as inappropriate; he would have simply liked the feel of that bomb. It gave you power, especially over intended victims. He had learned very young that survivability was twenty per cent street cunning and eighty per cent raw power.

Thus he found the failure of socialism tragic in the way a pianist might feel after having painstakingly practiced throughout his youth then, suddenly, before his very eyes the capitalist vandals destroyed every last piano in Europe. Under socialism, success had been measured in terms of power. It was an easy formula to fathom. Moreover, by the time the Berlin wall got whacked down, he had managed a fair handle on how to work the socialist system. Thus, he resented the intrusion of these capitalists who had just thrown ice cold water in his face. However, he also knew how to clean up and move on; so he grudgingly trudged into this brave new world.

It was in this respect that he admired the Russian Mafia; they had precociously adjusted to these changing times. 'Comrade', 'commissar' and 'power to the people' were no longer cool-speak. 'Business deal', 'joint venture', 'collateral', and 'return on investment' were the words and phrases dominating the jargon used by these born-again Russians. Of course, their business practices were not what professors taught in the Harvard or the University of Chicago MBA programs. Black Knife had graduated under the tutelage of a very able and sinister faculty who taught at the 'street school for mayhem and mischief'.

Observing the Russians encouraged him to employ flexibility in dealing with that ugly morning after the Wall fell. Adapt to your environment or perish. Okay, he would play the game by exploiting capitalist rules – and so by degrees he evolved a vision of his future. He wanted big money. Money was power. However, there was more to his ambition than money. He wanted recognition. He wanted lips to quiver at the utterance of his name; especially the thin, pouting lips of these white Westerners. He wanted them to tremble in the same way that the mention of Osama bin Laden caused them fear. Yes, he had a vision; but he still had no plan by which to realize it.

He had begun his last year of *Hauptschule* (High School) when the Berlin Wall came a-tumbling down on 9 November 1989 and within two years the German Socialist 'Workers' Paradise' was gobbled up by the capitalist West. Economic chaos gripped the former DDR in the early nineties and unemployment touched most young men like Herman. Chaos and unemployment, however, were not the conditions which dogged him. He was stung with the vision of his destiny. It swelled and festered. It consumed him as if God's own voice had whispered the promise into his ear. He was a brave heart with warrior blood gushing through his veins, and his spirit stirred into a restless state.

He had remained in Berlin where he joined a loose-knit organization of skinheads among whose membership were several Serbs. They convinced him he should go along with them and he 'signed up' with a paramilitary group of ruffians to serve in Bosnia. The group gave him some rudimentary military training and a few pep talks. It didn't matter that their job was to kill Muslims, nor that these Serbs despised black men. For him, the romance of war trumped all other considerations. At last, he would be a freedom fighter – a profile that conformed to his vision.

It was his Serbian connection that, in 1995,

secured him the opportunity to serve the Russian Mafia operating in Hamburg. It was a business in which one did not flaunt names. They gave him the code-name: 'Black Knife'. He had earned a reputation for employing a long, black blade to dispatch his assigned marks with ease and efficiency and it had become his trademark. The Hollywood movies would have referred to him as a 'hit man', but Black Knife was not content. The failing of socialism left him feeling more like an orphan than ever. He brooded over the loss as if history had betrayed him; but not because he was a socialist in any sort of doctrinaire way.

Black Knife took for granted that in spite of his black skin, the German ladies found him attractive – or was it because of his skin colour? Well, he moved with feline agility, his sinewy frame stood at medium height; however, what portrayed him as an intimidating fellow were his piercing eyes that peered over high cheekbones. His lips were full but not overly and had about them a mocking smirk, as if challenging whoever his gaze fell upon to knock the chip off his shoulder. He shaved his head bald while sporting a tightly clipped beard. On balance, he was an attractive hunk and the German ladies often affirmed this.

****

SUSIE

She stood in Herbie's room, staring through the window. It gave her a view of the street, the only window in her domain which did. Since finding the dead girl, well, she presumed the girl was dead, she had retreated up to the sanctuary of the second floor and waited with desperate anticipation for the arrival of the Medicine Man. What if Max came back? She viewed his return with trepidation. Why had he murdered that girl with her precious paring knife? Had Max's medicine finally cracked his mind? Was he dangerous? She didn't want to consider these questions. She was confident her salvation would be in the hands of this *Schwarze*, whom she reckoned should be coming soon.

Herbie was pestering, complaining it was time for

their walk. And she could tell from the tantrum Katja was throwing in the next room that her daughter's diapers were full, but she just didn't feel in the mood to change them; she wasn't the sort of person who could deal with several issues at the same time. Right now, the dead Romanian girl was the main issue and everything else was subservient. Susie was too absorbed in this to let the shrieking Katja or the whining Herbie distract her. She had always been good at shutting things out.

As she stubbed her cigarette out in the pile of grey ash and butts in her ashtray she saw it was time to dump the contents into the waste, but her dark mood distracted her from even this simple task. Susie was a heavy smoker, especially when she felt stressed out. Reaching into the pocket of her ankle-length skirt, her trembling hand found only the empty Marlborough packet and her shoulders slumped; she was struggling. Struggling to keep her brother from intruding into her mind, yet the fear that he might return at any minute haunted her. A tight knot was forming in her throat and she felt the first sting of tears in her eyes but she held on. Another cigarette was what she craved; smoking gave her a diversion she badly needed.

She let out a sigh and trudged back to her bedroom. Katja was still screaming, and the mother's trained nose could smell why, but she chose to pay her baby no mind. In the top drawer of her dresser she kept her precious trove of tobacco and papers, lying next to a little hand-held rolling machine. She would roll thirty or forty cigarettes at a time and then store them in empty Marlboro hard packs which she used and reused. Quickly scrabbling through the red and white packs she cursed the fact that she had smoked all her roll-ups and needed to keep an eye out for the Medicine Man. Grabbing the 250-gram tin of tobacco, she bundled the papers, filters and rolling machine together and made for the door. Her intention was to use the window ledge in Herbie's room as a workplace whilst she watched the road. As she bustled back into the smoke-filled room Herbie unexpectedly grabbed her skirt as she crossed over the threshold.

'Mummy, when do we go for our walk?!' he demanded.

It was just enough to knock her off kilter and she had to reach out to retain her balance, dropping her precious cargo. In the way that things tend to conspire to make a bad situation worse, the tin of tobacco hit the little rolling machine at just the right angle and with just enough force to reduce it to its component parts. The plastic rollers were launched out of the frame and the rubber rolling band flew off. The lid came off the tobacco tin and most of the contents spilled out onto the paper-thin carpet. Recovering her balance, Susie looked at the disaster before her and with mindless rage lashed out at Herbie with the back of her hand. It caught the boy squarely on the side of his face, spinning him around and sending him into a sprawling heap by his toy box. He defensively drew his knees up to his chest as his eyes, wide with terror, began to brim with tears. Below them, his little chin trembled as he began a heart-rending sobbing.

Surveying the scene, Susie was still too preoccupied to feel too much guilt and simply scolded him, 'Don't grab me like that! Look what you've done,' she added for good measure as she pointed to the mess on the floor. Herbie just notched his sobbing up to a baleful wail as the red welt on his face began to sting. She bent over and raised her hand threateningly.

'Shut up!' she demanded, 'Shut up! Shut up! Shut up!' she shouted as she dropped to her knees and examined the useless components of the roller. Now she needed her cigarette more than ever and picked up the packet of papers, ready to use some of the tobacco from the carpet. She had just pulled a paper from the packet when the buzzer for the door sounded.

****

34

THE BUSINESS IN HAND

Herman had chosen the *PennyMarkt* parking lot in which to leave his car. Not only because the parking was free, but because it would be far less conspicuous than to park in front of Max's house. As he had locked his car with the electronic key he had looked around for any sign of *Die Bullen* (The Bulls - the Police) and on his way to the Pankow house, he'd stopped abruptly several times, checking that he wasn't being followed. There weren't many people or vehicles about and so the three-block walk from the supermarket car park gave him adequate time to 'check his six o'clock'. Aside from the Bulls, German neighbourhoods like this one were populated with nosey neighbours. He reckoned that was because the young Germans went to the cities where there were jobs and an exciting night-life, leaving the outlying towns and villages full of older people. What else did these senior citizens have to do with their time but to watch endless TV and become curtain twitchers?

The girls from the East seldom carried more than one heavy suitcase and a cabin bag. After a long drive he actually looked forward to a bit of heavy lifting and walking to recover his feeling of fitness; what he didn't relish was having to deal with Max. Most of the 'gofers' he had to deal with were creeps, druggies and low-life scum – if they weren't, they'd be doing something else – but Max occupied a special place. Herman hated to see his rotting teeth and could almost smell his fetid breath on the street. But it came with the territory and he patted the pocket of his leather jacket with a gloved hand to assure himself that he hadn't forgotten the plastic bag filled with Max's pay-off. He deliberately hadn't taken off his leather driving gloves; when he was working he always wore gloves for a number of reasons that went beyond a fear of leaving fingerprints. They protected his knuckles in a fist fight, and his hands in a knife fight; either of which could occur at a time least expected, on or off the job. Herman had learned this lesson the hard way.

He pressed the buzzer labelled 'Pankow', and

while he waited he slowly glanced around the neighbourhood for anyone or anything that might stir his
suspicion, but nothing out of the ordinary caught his
eye. It occurred to him that an unusually long time
had passed since he buzzed, normally Max came to
the door with the eagerness of a scrambling puppy; it
was payday for the creep. He pressed the buzzer
again as a small voice of impending trouble whispered somewhere in the recesses of his mind. After
the second buzz the door was slowly opened and
Herman was surprised to see the sister; it had been
Max in the past. She had always absented herself,
except once when she had come downstairs to
retrieve something, moving like a scullery maid at a
gathering of princes. There and then he had concluded that ugliness must be a Pankow family legacy.
Now he observed the sister as she stood in the doorway white as chalk and her eyes red-rimmed and
tearful. Her thin trembling lips moved several times
before she finally spoke.

'Come in,' she whispered.

The quiet whisper in the depths of his mind now
became an alarm bell ringing and he was immediately on his guard. From upstairs he could hear one
child screaming and thought he could hear another.
Was that the problem? As he stepped through the
door Susie backed away from him like a filly not

wanting to be bridled. His eyes remained fixed on her as he closed the door with his heel. He noticed that her whole body was shaking, and that tears were now beginning to course down her hollow cheeks.

'What's wrong?' he demanded.

She turned and slowly trudged up the stairs and he followed.

'What's wrong, bitch!' he demanded, but Susie just kept her back to him as she went up the stairs and turned into the hallway. She took two more steps and then stopped, extending a shaking finger she pointed to the room at the end of the hallway, the door of which was slightly ajar.

'What?' He demanded as he took one long stride that brought him beside her. Grabbing the arm that now hung limply by her side, he jerked her around to face him; she offered no more resistance than a wet mop.

'What is it?' he insisted.

She started sobbing and dry-retched as she remembered what she'd seen, covering her mouth with her hand.

'Go see!' she finally managed to cough out before she flopped against the hallway wall and dropped her head into her hands. Approaching the door down the hall with caution Herman gently pushed it open with an extended forefinger and stepped to one side, experience had taught him he shouldn't stay framed in the doorway before he knew what was inside. Cocking his head around the door he could clearly see the bloodstained bed sheet and make out the bulk of a body underneath. Having glanced around the room, he stepped inside and took the corner of the sheet between his finger and thumb and drew it back. He didn't know what he expected, but it certainly wasn't what he saw. Max Pankow lay on his side with his legs drawn up in the fetal position. His face was a frozen mask of agony and the left side of his neck had been laid open by a deep cut of a sharp knife, probably the kitchen knife he'd already seen discarded on the floor. Herman could see the severed ends of the jugular vein and the bloody corrugations of the windpipe, 'Jesus,' he whispered to himself, 'someone's done a number on you, Maxie boy.'

Herman had a professional curiosity when it came to knife wounds and looked closer at the exposed neck of the cadaver. It wasn't a particularly professional job, but neither was it the result of a frenzied attack. He wondered if, indeed, it had been the Romanian girl, and if she'd hailed from a farming background? In which case she'd have been used to cutting the throats of sheep and calves and probably the almost daily beheading and disembowelling of chickens; she would have been no stranger to death.

Certainly, the single deep slash had been designed to sever the jugular and possibly the windpipe. About all Max could have emitted was a series of gurgles as he quickly bled to death, his brain starved of blood and oxygen he would have lapsed into unconsciousness in a few seconds. Considering the amount of blood around, Herman was puzzled as to why the killer had bothered to draw a sheet up over Max's corps, a thoughtful gesture, he mused, or maybe she was just a tidy bitch. She had been aware enough to take the clothing she's been wearing, which must have been saturated in blood, with her when she departed. Looking around the room, Herman could see nothing else that could link the girl with the dead Max.

His most immediate concern was for how he would explain this scene to his bosses in Hamburg. It wasn't his fault, but he didn't expect them to see it that way. He again wondered, dispassionately, who might have inflicted such a wound on Max? He couldn't believe it would have been the sister, although he had learned never rule out any possibility. Most likely it had been the Romanian girl they had assigned him to pick up.

'Well,' he thought to himself, 'better see what the sister has to say about it. Shit!' he cursed.

Thus, his concern was not for Max, the absentee

Romanian or for Susie; it was for himself. He needed to clean up this mess pronto and get on his way.
He was conscious that, if the girl was the killer, she
was now wandering around Hanau, or trying to get
back to Frankfurt, and she might just have a crisis of
conscience and make an anonymous call to the Bulls.
He didn't think it was likely, but he hoped it had been
the sister who had done Max in; then it would be an
easy clean-up. He'd dispatch her on a journey to join
up with her brother, but doubted that things were
going be that easy. It had to be the Romanian girl, he
reasoned, as the sister didn't strike him as having the
temperament for such things. Herman separated his
two fingers, allowing the wet sheet to slap back over
Max's grey face.

'You must've really pissed off someone, creep!'
he said. Maybe Max had tried something a bit too
perverted on the girl. He couldn't believe she'd cut
his throat for simple fuck or a blow-job. Turning in
the close confines of the room he left, pulling the
door closed behind him.

Glancing up the hallway, he realized the sister had
gone and the screaming kids were grating on his
nerves. A few long strides took him back to the stairs
where he could see the front door, and it was still
closed. Nevertheless, he went down to the small
lobby and opened the door a cautious crack. There

was nobody in sight and he closed it, turned the double lock and hooked the intruder chain into its slot. He hoped some nosey old-timer hadn't been sitting at their window and observed him arrive.

Logic dictated that if she was still in the house she was up on the second floor and his long legs covered the stairs two at a time with ease. At the door of Katja's room he saw the unfortunate child in her cot, standing and shaking the bars, red in the face and with tears streaming down her face. He also saw the yellowy-brown lines that were trickling down her chubby legs and staining the rumpled covers. She stopped screaming abruptly as she saw the tall black man framed in the doorway. Her eyes opened wide and she shouted for the only person she thought could help her, '*Mutti! Mutti!*'

Herman walked a few steps further on and saw Susie sitting cross-legged on the floor, rolling a cigarette. She appeared to be oblivious of the child in the next room calling for her, or to the little boy who sat in the corner, hugging a favourite toy.

'Tell that kid to shut up!' Herman yelled.

Susie looked up at him with a blank stare, then stuck out her tongue and licked across the cigarette paper. She gave her piece of work a quick inspection and then placed it between her lips as she leaned back and reached into the skirt pocket for her lighter.

'You shut him up, *Neger*,' she mouthed around the roll-up.

He took a quick side step towards her, as lithe as a cat, and before she realized what was coming his heel had made contact with the side of her face, almost dislocating her jaw and splitting her lower lip. She sprawled across the floor and her hands flew to her face as she went to let out a scream, but Herman was on her in a second, pulling her up to her knees by the front of her T-shirt, his face inches from hers.

'I told you to shut that fucking kid up, bitch,' he said in complete control. 'Best you do it!'

She just stared back, a pathetic collection of lank hair and skinny limbs. Herman raised his free hand to slap her again and she tried to protect her face.

'Don't hit me,' she bleated, 'I didn't kill her. I swear to you, I didn't do it! Max did it! Max did it!'

'Her?' Herman queried in his mind, 'Her?' What was the white bitch talking about? 'Max did it?' Who the fuck did she think was cooling under those bed-covers, if not her brother? The boy had crawled across the floor and onto Susie's lap as she wrapped him in a loose cuddle, wiping the blood from her split lip with the back of her hand. Herman cast him a withering look just in case he was thinking of breaking the quiet that had descended on the house; even Katja had been reduced to a barely audible sobbing

Glancing at Susie, Herman decided to go on a little fishing expedition.

'If you didn't do it then how d'you know Max did?' he growled with feigned suspicion.

She shrugged her shoulders, 'I guess it must have been Max – who else?'

He quickly put two and two together. This stupid woman believed her dead brother was the perpetrator instead of the victim. She clearly hadn't bothered to look under the sheet, which suddenly made sense to him. She thinks it's the Romanian girl that's dead, and that Max did her in. So what? Wait a minute, he sensed an opportunity and quickly thought it through as the battered woman and her frightened son stared at him apprehensively. 'Yes!' he exclaimed inside his head. He had a resolution to this problem. Well, it wouldn't bring the Romanian girl back, but she was a lesser problem at the moment. What he had to do was take the heat off the Mafia when the corpse downstairs was discovered and the Bulls were called to the scene. This woman would spill her guts to them, but to simply kill Susie would not suffice, it would only create a double murder. He had to close the loop, and he thought he knew a way to do that.

He knelt down on one knee and smiled warmly at her. The left side of her bottom lip was beginning to puff. 'Okay, okay, I believe you. You're Max's sister, right?'

'Yes,' she stammered.

'What's your name?'

'Susie,' she slurred, staring up at Herman.

He could see that the swelling lip was beginning to affect her ability to speak. It probably hurt like hell, but he felt no compassion. Herbie started to snivel again but stopped as soon as Herman's hard eyes made contact with his. Turning to Susie he switched on the casual smile again, 'Would you like me to take care of that problem?' he asked as he inclined his head towards the doorway, '… the problem downstairs?'

'Yes!' she whispered. Susie carefully touched her lip with her index finger, and then looked at the blood on it. The lip it was beginning to throb and her jaw ached.

'I'll help you on one condition.'

'What?' she finally asked in a tremulous voice.

'You must do exactly as I say. You'll do what I tell you without any questions. Agreed?'

'Like what?' she whimpered as she delicately touched her swelling lip again.

'I said no questions! Agree or I'm outta here?' he said, turning away towards the door.

'No, no, wait! Please! Yes, I agree. I agree,' she

sobbed, flinching with pain as she enunciated the words.

Again he offered her a warm smile and extended a hand, signalling that he would help her to her feet, but she ignored the offer, opting instead to struggle to her feet noiselessly except for a creak in the floor-boards underneath the thin carpet. Herbie slid from her lap and stayed sitting on the floor, eying Herman warily. Susie bent down and heaved him up onto her hip and carried him across to his bed.

'Now you stay here for a while and then we'll go for our walk,' she said to sooth the boy, 'I'll even get you some sweeties from the shop but you must be quiet for a little while and you must stay here.' For a moment it looked like the boy was going to start cry-ing again, but a second's eye contact with Herman changed his mind. Instead, he lay down, pulled an ancient teddy bear to him and made as if he was going to sleep.

'Can't you get that shitty baby in the next room to shut up?!' Herman now demanded. He had never found anything cute about babies.

'Because if you can't, I can,' he continued with a hint on menace, '… but I don't think you'd be pleased with my method.'

'She needs her nappy changed,' Susie responded.

'How long will that take?' asked Herman, but

before she could answer he raised both hands in a halting motion, 'Never mind! Forget it. I need you downstairs. Let's go.' As he took his first stride to exit the room, he glanced over at Herbie. The kid was still curled up and motionless, maybe feigning sleep; it didn't matter, at least he'd stopped making a noise.

Herman turned and led the way as she followed him down the steps at a respectable distance. They were now on the first floor in the hallway which led to Max's bedroom. She stopped two steps from the bottom of the flight and supported some of her weight by bracing one hand on the rail as Herman stood on the staircase landing appearing to be in deep thought. Finally he raised his head and turned his gaze at Susie still above him. She avoided his attention by shifting her eyes, but her face remained expressionless. He took a step back to give her space to pass.

'Go get that knife in the bedroom. Take it to the kitchen and clean it. Then bring it back to me. And while you're at it, get me a glass of water.' The woman remained motionless.

'Hey, didn't you hear me?' he growled.

'Must I go in there?' she asked.

'If you want my help, then you do as I tell you. Otherwise, I leave and you can deal with this mess on your own.'

Susie didn't pause to weigh the alternative. She hustled down the last two steps, and then slowly trudged along the hallway towards her brother's bedroom. She paused at the doorway, and turned her head back to him. The black man gave her an icy stare. He heard her take a deep breath, then she dashed inside and almost instantaneously reappeared holding the knife handle delicately between her index finger and thumb as if she were carrying a dead rat by its tail. She now stepped out more energetically as she retraced her steps down the hallway, brushing past Herman without looking directly at him. He strolled casually after her, watching her turn on the tap and feel the stream of water with her fingers, waiting for it to warm. She dropped the knife into the sink with a clatter and stepped back with repugnance as the swirling water turned red. Herman had always been amazed how the smallest amount of blood would contaminate a huge volume of water.

'Did you want fizzy water or still,' she asked, as she leaned over to the counter to where three empty glasses stood upside-down on a section of paper towel. Grabbing one she continued, 'Which do you prefer?'

'Never mind, just get some damn water in that glass,' urged Herman, '… and hurry up!' he ordered as he patted the pocket which held Max's medicine.

She moved sideways, her belly braced against the edge of the sink so as not to turn and face him. There was a small refrigerator below the work surface immediately to the side of the cupboard area into which the sink was installed. She opened it.

'No,' he said irritably, 'I want warm water. Take it from the tap.'

She looked at him, not really comprehending what he wanted. Nobody drank tap water in this part of Germany – in almost any part of Germany for that matter. Herman knew that, and so he couldn't suppress an amused look as he watched her wrestle with his request.

'T-t-tap water,' she stammered? '… w-warm tap water?'

'That's what I said, bitch. Are you hard of hearing?'

She stepped sideways again, carefully feeling the stream of water with the fingertips of her free hand. 'I think it's too warm,' she whispered and looked at him for direction.

'I want it warm,' he assured her.

'It's very warm,' she warned in a faltering voice, the pain from her lip was making it harder to speak.

'That's how I want it!' he bellowed. 'Now fill up the fucking glass – just half full – no more than half full, you hear?'

She silently complied. He could see that her hand was trembling and it amused him, as he had intended keeping her in a state of intimidation. First, she over-filled the glass, and then carefully poured some of the water back out, holding it up, squinting to gauge when it looked exactly half full. She repeated this exercise several times until she felt satisfied she had complied precisely with Herman's instructions. He looked on with obvious amusement, not only at her nervousness, but also at her physical appearance. Her lip had now swollen to bizarre proportions. Susie was no longer just plain and homely, she was grotesque. She turned and timidly offered the glass to him, the water splashed inside the glass from her quaking hand.

He pointed to the far end of the kitchen counter which had not been touched by the splashing water. 'Put it down over there,' he directed, 'and turn the water off.'

'I haven't washed the knife,' she mumbled almost inaudibly, as if she were talking to herself.

Herman sighed as he balled up his fists.

'Do what you're told, bitch!' he exclaimed. 'The knife is clean enough. Well, don't just stand there!'

She quickly reached out and turned off the water, and then sashayed sideways along the counter edge in several tiny steps so that she could set down the glass of water where he had indicated.

'Now dry off that knife. I want it completely dry.'

She side stepped back to the sink. A tea towel hung through one of the handles of the built-in drawers under the counter top and she carefully pulled it free. Susie seemed to be moving in slow motion. She reached for the knife, but her hand faltered before grasping it.

'It's still got blood on it,' she said in a quivering voice.

He craned his neck for a look. There were obvious traces of blood remaining on the knife and some stingy clots clung stubbornly to the stainless steel of the sink.

'It's clean enough,' he growled.

Suzie held the towel aloft for a moment, and then asked, 'May I use a paper towel to wipe off the knife? It will stain the towel.'

'I don't give a fuck what you use, just get it dry!' was the curt reply.

She seemed unaffected by this *Neger*'s coarse language, and carefully pushed the towel back through the drawer handle. Reaching for a paper towel on a roller she stripped off two sheets and proceeding to dry the knife. Herman, meanwhile, reached inside his pocket and drew out the plastic bag which contained Max's medicine. The speed was in capsules and there were also two medium-size rocks of cocaine, about the bulk of jelly beans, sitting at the bottom, covered in a residue of chalky powder.

He took the one step required to reach the counter top where the glass of water sat. Opening the plastic bag, he teased out the capsules onto the counter top, taking care not spill out the rocks or powder. There were thirty capsules, the usual pay-off for Max. The 'nose candy' still in the bag represented a 'tip' sometimes offered by Herman to which Max looked forward dearly.

He dumped Max's precious cocaine into the glass of water, carefully wiggling the bag to get the powder to pour. Static electricity caused some of the residue to stick to the plastic, but nearly all of it was in the glass. Most importantly, the two rocks were in and slowly dissolving.

Susie had finished wiping the knife, but continued to hold it in the paper as if it was contaminated. She cautiously offered it to Herman but he didn't take it.

'I've got a job for you, and you're gonna need that knife.'

Susie stared at him in disbelief, still holding the knife out in the paper.

'What job?' she finally asked when he didn't continue.

'See those capsules?'

She looked to where he pointed and nodded; least said less pain.

'It looks like Max's medicine,' she whispered.

'I want you to fetch a large spoon, like what you use for eating your soup. Understand?'

'Soup spoon?' she quietly queried.

'Well?'

'Don't you want the knife?'

He tapped his finger beside the capsules on the counter top.

'Put it down – here.' He backed off a step so that she had room to comply. She crept over and carefully laid it down still cradled in the paper towelling.

'Get rid of that paper,' he demanded.

She inched the towelling out from under the knife causing it to roll a turn, and the handle disturbed a couple of the capsules.

'Soup spoon,' she muttered as she balled up the paper and set it on the edge of the sink. She pulled open the drawer which had the towel hanging through its handle and noisily rummaged through the assorted cutlery until she found what she wanted.

'Will this do?' she asked, holding it up for his inspection.

'Yup,' he confirmed, 'that'll do just fine. Bring it over here and set it down next to the caps – that's it

'– good.'

He drew up beside her and pointed at the capsules.

'Now listen, I want you to do exactly what I say. Take each capsule, one at a time, and carefully cut it just enough so that you can break it over the spoon and pour all the grains out. Don't waste any! Do it very carefully. If you don't get it all in the spoon each time I'm gonna give you a second fat lip, you understand?'

'All in the spoon,' she mumbled.

'Go on, let's get started. I need all of them dumped in the spoon!'

Without turning her head or shifting her eyes from the capsules she whispered, 'Why?'

He raised hand and then with the quickness one might employ to swat a fly, he reached for her swollen lip, pinching it between his thumb and index finger. She let out a howl, and grabbed the edge of the counter as if bracing herself against fainting. He released his pinch and quickly placed his other hand at the small of her back for support in case she collapsed.

'Don't question me again,' he warned, 'just do exactly as I say.' He could feel her body stiffening again, so he released his support against her back, and made a quick inspection of the gloved hand that had pinched her lip. There was a smear of blood and something clear that he guessed was her saliva. Moving around to her other side he reached out for the balled up paper towelling she had placed next to the sink, carefully dabbing his glove clean, then dropped the paper back onto the drainer. When he turned back to her, he saw that she had obediently begun her task, emptying the capsules into the soup spoon. She glanced at him for a moment, seeking affirmation that this was what he wanted done. He gave her a nod, and so she continued.

'Do you believe me?' she whimpered without diverting concentration from her job of piercing and emptying capsules into the spoon.

'About what?'

'Her, in the room. I didn't do it,' she sniffled and he observed that a tear was running down the cheek on the side of her face visible to him.

'I didn't do it,' she repeated.

'She's not dead,' he responded very matter-of-factly.

Susie's hands stopped. She turned to him.

'She's not?'

Now he could see her full face, puffy around the hinges of the jaw and distorted with the swollen lip which had begun to bleed again, following his earlier attentions.

'Nope,' he said confidently, 'this medicine is going to revive her. That's why you're filling the spoon. So let's get cracking. We don't want her to die on us, now do we?

'But all that blood?' questioned Susie, slurring her words, 'She's alive?'

'Will you hurry up, bitch? We don't have all day!' He raised his hand as if he might go for her lip again.

She quickly turned back to her work, cracking capsules and then dumping the grains into the spoon, it was beginning to heap up. He quickly counted the remaining ones: nine. He'd let her do one more, that would be enough, the spoon was nearly full. Any more would just spill out.

'Lay down the knife and turn around,' he ordered when she'd finished the next capsule.

Her hands stopped moving.

'Huh?'

'I said turn around and face me. I have a question, and I want to see your eyes when you answer.' As he spoke he balled up the fist of his right hand, crooking the index finger so it formed a protruding anvil shape. Just as she turned to face him, he hit her squarely in the solar plexus. His other hand swiftly grabbed the lank hair at the back of her head and yanked it back while he used his body to pin her against the kitchen unit. The hand that had struck her in the stomach now grasped the spoon full of speed. She was gasping for air, mouth wide open, and before she could collect her wits he forced the spoon into her mouth and shook it vigorously. She began to gag on the granules and he dropped the empty spoon onto the counter, grabbed her jaw with his free hand and forced her mouth shut. He kept her pinned in that position, even though her whole body was convulsing, her lungs screaming for air. The thumb and index finger of the hand whose heel held her jaw closed stretched out and pinched her nostrils shut. In a matter of moments, she would be forced to swallow. He continued to hold her wriggling body in check; she was no challenge for his muscular physique, and he dispassionately watching her throat until she swallowed, once, twice. Standing back he released her and she fell to the floor like a rag doll, gagging and gasping for air.

'It wouldn't take long for the speed to start doing its dirty work,' he mused.

He had more work to do, but first things first. He had learned always to remain disciplined and methodical, no matter what the sense of urgency. He'd wait until palpitations set in and her eyes began to bulge. He knew that she would then begin to convulse, probably losing control of her bladder and bowels. At that point he could leave her and take care of the rest of his 'business'; he liked to tie up all loose ends – well, as many as he could. There was still that Romanian girl on the loose somewhere, and his boss in Hamburg wouldn't cut him any slack just because he had cleaned things up. Dmitri was expecting a girl, and Herman hadn't delivered, so that was his fault; that was the bottom line for the fucking Russians. Well, he'd worry about that later, one issue at a time. Disciplined and methodical, that's how you survive in the jungle.

Time to move on; he glanced at the glass that had been half filled with warm water and dissolved 'blow'. Somehow in the fray it had been knocked over and its contents splashed all over the counter top. As it turned out he didn't need the water as a last lethal addition to wash down the massive dose of speed. Susie was already drumming her heels on the floor as she entered the convulsive stage of her over-dose, her head thrashing from side to side. The glass would, in any event, serve as a logical piece in the puzzle for the criminal investigators. If they were to consider she had committed suicide after killing her brother and butchering her children, then what would have been more logical than that she would have washed down her chosen poison with a gulp of water? The bonus being that her finger prints, and only her prints, would be evident on both the glass as well as the knife. Even the bruised and swollen lip distorting her face would serve as a clue perhaps explaining why she might have attacked her brother. Herman hadn't exactly planned it, but things seemed to have work out that way. Yes, he'd have to take some heat from the Russians and he wouldn't get the roll of Euros that Dmitri would have waiting in his desk draw but, hey, he'd made the best of a bad job.

Susie's convulsions began to abate and his nose told him she'd entered the last, fatal, stage of the overdose. For him, it signalled that it was time to get to work, as he still had a couple of loose ends to tie up. Two, to be precise, and they were both upstairs. The boy's testimony, however difficult and time consuming it would be to extract, could screw up his carefully conceived and executed tabloid headline: 'HOUSE OF DEATH. Single mother kills brother and children in drug induced frenzy.' He delicately lifted the paring knife from where it lay on the counter-top. He didn't want to completely obliterate her prints. The blood of her two children would be on the knife and there would be substantial traces of her brother's too. Because of the blood in the sink it would appear that she's killed him, cleaned the knife and then, in deep remorse, had killed herself, having also taken the only other two things which matter to her with her.

One thing was for sure, Herman would kill the two children as easily as he would swat a fly and think no more about it. It was all part of his early conditioning, where either someone had cut the switches marked 'compassion' and 'sympathy' or they were never switched on. His prime instinct was survival and all other considerations were secondary.

Yes, Herman felt satisfied; it would be a tidy piece of work leaving little speculation for the criminal investigators. The *LKA (Landes Kriminal Amt –* Local Criminal Investigation Police - CID) would wrap this one up in short order and smugly submit their paperwork to the *Staatsanwalt* (office of the Judge Advocate) having double checked Max's room for anything the Romanian bitch might have left behind that could warrant the suspicion that a third party might have been involved, he carefully opened the door and left. Disciplined and methodical, that's how Black Knife had earned his position and reputation with the Russian Mafia. You had to be if you wanted to remain alive in *his* business.

****

BERLIN

The section of autobahn running between Hamburg and Berlin has three lanes in each direction, and is still known as *Die Schnelle Strasse*. Trucks are not allowed in the far left lane and the Germans usually get into the middle lane if someone approaches from behind, which made driving a pleasure for Herman. Sometimes you got the *Käsekopfen* (cheeseheads - the Dutch) who had no regard for the rules of the road, dragging their damned caravans down to Spain or Austria but, on balance, Herman was pleased to be making such good time. He was also enjoying the CD he had picked up in Stuttgart while he had been waiting for Polly to finish a bit of shopping. He was playing it for the first time, a collection which included the Stones, Queen, Supertramp, the Eagles and a gaggle of rock's finest. He was playing it loud and singing along to 'Hotel California' as he passed a coach full of young girls, a few of whom were making obscene gestures and holding up cards with their mobile numbers on them.

He dug rock. Even if it was part and parcel of the capitalist culture, it was music for the common man, it belonged to the world, like the air we breathe. Moreover, it had African roots and he could take pride in that. German 'techno' didn't touch his soul but, then again, neither did 'rap' which had its origins in the ghetto. The Rappers were mostly black American, like Polly, but they weren't Africans. They had the colour and the moves, but not an African soul. They didn't give a shit about Africa, except when it suited them to make reference to their 'roots'. They were nothing more than black sheep of the American family. Same went for those black dandies in England.

Herman was a fair dancer and had picked up most of his girls at the disco, but not Polly. The previous summer he happened to be in Stuttgart and was strolling by Charlottenplatz in the downtown area of Königstrasse because it offered a one-kilometre stretch of wall-to-wall shopping. The street was wide and lined with shops, but only foot traffic was allowed. He'd been at Charlottenplatz the previous year to hear a band named the 'Scorpions' perform in commemoration of the demise of the Berlin Wall. Herman didn't appreciate the celebration, but he certainly appreciated the hard rock. Three months later he had been walking past Charlottenplatz when he noticed that in the large open space where he and twenty thousand others had gathered to hear the Scorpions, there was now a collection of kiosks and tables with banners and people manning them. Some of these people were actively soliciting the passersby and he quickly discovered that they were gathered for a single purpose, to petition for contributions for Aids-In-Africa. A lot of the kiosks were selling donated wares, some new and some used. Polly was standing beside a kiosk with the banner which proudly announced: '*Deutsch Amerikanishes Institut*'. It wasn't the banner which caught his eye, but Polly. She was animated as she enticed the pedestrians milling about to come over to her kiosk. So Herman sauntered by affecting his coolest walk, pretending to be aloof. Sure enough, she saw him and beckoned him over.

He let her talk, and finally she got around to asking who he was and if he lived in Stuttgart. That's when he laid his 'illegitimate son of Patrice Lumumba' line on her. There were three girls and a guy with her at the kiosk, so she didn't seem averse to his suggestion that they go over to the McDonald's for a drink and a bite. It was lunch time and she took orders from the others, agreeing to go with 'Sam' if he would help her carry back the lunch orders for the other four. That's how he'd met Polly and ended up helping them man the booth. That evening he also ended up manning her bed.

He usually never humoured the ladies he courted; but Polly was not usual. Not only was she the first American woman he had dated, but she was also the first black woman that aroused in him the desire to continue a relationship. She was relaxed about his comings and goings and didn't ask too many questions, perhaps because she sensed that he wouldn't be forthcoming with answers. That first evening he had spent with Polly in her apartment, she had gone on and on about Oriana Fallaci, some journalist that she worshipped although she admitted never having met her in person. To read her was enough, she assured him. Yeah, Polly was a brainy girl and she had class, but she could be downright earthy when he got her between the sheets. It was an unfamiliar contrast for Herman and he had to confess that he liked it.

They'd brought a pizza to her apartment and she'd set out some paper plates and napkins. He'd asked for the knives and forks which had amused her. 'Americans,' she had explained, 'eat pizza with their fingers.' He'd given her a look of astonishment but it made more sense when she added, 'Like burgers. You eat burgers with your fingers, don't you?' He didn't have a problem with the concept and they devoured the pizza with their hands, and wiped their face and fingers with the napkins.

It was during this very informal supper that Polly carried on about her mentor, Oriana Fallaci.

'I read her book, *The Rage and the Pride*, and I gotta tell you, I was inspired,' she had gushed.

'See,' she continued, 'I've been observing the European attitudes, and she's on the money, Sam. In fact, I got so inspired, I wrote a paper. I'm a journalism graduate and I know good writing when I read it, and I think what I've written isn't all bad. I call it 'Intellectual Terrorism'. Would you like to read it, honey?'

Herman wasn't particularly fond of reading, especially when he had a hard case of seduction on his mind. He excused himself by saying that his English wasn't good enough to do it justice. She was a perceptive woman and she didn't pursue the point any further. After all, she clearly hadn't invited him to her apartment for an editorial opinion.

'That's OK,' he recalled her saying, 'it's still in rough draft and needs some cleaning up, anyhow.'

The evening had gone very well in his estimations

and he had continued to see Polly on a regular basis, something he'd never done before. He had planned to see her on his return from Hanau but the events of the day had redirected him.

He had called Hamburg on his mobile phone immediately after leaving the parking lot at *PennyMarkt* in Hanau. He'd given his boss, Andrei, the bad news, along with what he hoped would be perceived as a 'silver lining'; how he'd taken care of the problem. He had presumed the Russian would bluntly give him the nearly impossible task of finding that Romanian girl. Quite the contrary, his boss told him to get out of Hanau – but pronto!

'We'll take care of that Romanian cunt,' the Russian had barked down the phone, 'you get your black ass back here! You need to pay me, so you better return before the banks close.'

Herman had groaned quietly, and then asked, 'Pay you – for what?'

'Damages! Negligence! You lost my investment. Dmitri would have made fifty thousand Euros off that girl. I have to compensate Dmitri for his losses. When you consider the cost of my organization's expenses to advertise, scrutinize, pay off the bribes for papers, add to that the travel expense, and the risk, it shakes out that each girl costs me twenty thousand Euros. And then there is my pain and suffering over this matter, Black Knife. That must be worth at least thirty thousand Euros. So we'll make it an easy number for your dumb shit-for-brains to remember. A hundred thousand Euros, Black Knife, that's what you owe me. I want it this evening. I'll be waiting for you at the club. Come before midnight.' Having said all that, Andrei had hung up before Herman could launch a protest. There was no point in trying to call the Russian back.

He didn't have a hundred thousand in the bank; if he had that kind of money it would be in Zurich, not in Hamburg, and his boss knew it. He knew this wasn't really about money, as they'd done this to him twice before. The bottom line was that they had a new assignment, a very important assignment, for him. When he got to Hamburg there would be the expected haranguing, threats and accusations about Hanau, then they'd make him a generous offer to take the new job; adding almost as an aside that after he had successfully completed his assignment the outstanding hundred thousand Euros would need to be deducted, leaving a balance which could no longer be described as 'generous'. Instead of just asking him to take the job, the Russians always had to muscle you, and then find some excuse to re-negotiate the deal after you had done your part. *Arschlöchen*! (arseholes). In spite of this, they afforded him a living that would be impossible for Herman to achieve in any other way. He would, therefore, usually suffer their idiosyncrasies in silence.

That evening he showed up at the club, absorbed the verbal abuse his boss seemed obliged to lavish on him, and finally heard exactly what he had expected.

'You've been with me for what – eight years now, Black Knife? So, I'm gonna give you the chance to make things right.'

Herman recalled stifling his inclination to release a bored sigh and resisted the temptation to let his bored gaze wander about the club. He had learned when to keep his mouth shut and listen.

'One of my associates delivered a consignment for his client. He is an associate of some standing and the client is also important.' Herman understood that both 'some standing' and 'important' were usually a measure of the pot involved – either in Euros or dollars.

'There is a mosque in Berlin, it's called Al Nur. I want you to go there. You ask for Ahmed.'

'Ahmed?' Herman had questioned, 'Is he Turk?'

'They're all *Chornaya-zhopa*,' spat Andrei. 'How in the hell do I know who fucked his mother? What's

Chornaya-zhopa - Black Arses - Russian slang for all Arabs and Afghanis.

the difference? He's a client. That's as much as you need to know.'

The Russian then gave him the address and he asked for a pen with which to scribble the details onto a paper napkin, stuffed it in his trouser pocket and offered the pen back.

'What's the job?' he finally asked after his boss had returned the pen to his shirt pocket.

'Ahmed will explain. You do what he tells you,' the Russian ordered. 'You're doing it for me,' he added.

'What's in it for me?' asked Herman, bracing himself for the storm that might erupt. The Russian stared at him for a while and then sat back in his chair and stretched his arms above his head, 'Your life, Black Knife, that's what's in it for you. You made a mistake. We're spending a lot of money hunting down that Romanian girl, and all because you're a stupid *Neger* with shit for brains. However …' Herman knew there was always a 'however', it was just a matter of waiting for it. It was par for the course; he had to wade knee-deep through all this bullshit to get to the kernel.

'I feel in a generous mood,' continued the Russian with an elaborate sweep of his hands, 'maybe because it's only a couple months before Christmas. I'm gonna be a real St Nikolas, Black Knife – hundred and fifty thousand, if you satisfy that black-ass in Berlin.'

'Is that before or after you take out the hundred thousand I'm supposed to owe you?' asked Herman, always wary of his boss and his 'generosity'.

'Black Knife, Black Knife, this isn't fucking Africa,' said the Russian in mock surprise. 'We're civilized human beings here in Europe. When we incur a debt, we understand that the obligation must be satisfied. I didn't ask for you to screw up, did I? It was all your idea. Now I got an unhappy customer in Hechingen, and some dumb-ass Romanian bitch on the loose. You should be according me gratitude for my generosity. I don't appreciate your attitude, Black Knife. I want an apology.'

Herman didn't need a whole lot of agonizing to decide the right move to play.

'I'm sorry, boss,' he had whispered. Then in a stronger voice he had inquired, 'Will you be covering my expenses?'

'Is that a serious question, Black Knife? You are making a joke, right?' Then in a more serious tone he had added, 'You can talk to Ahmed about expenses.'

He decided to press once again on the content issue, 'Boss, can you give me at least an idea of what this Ahmed guy needs?'

The Russian produced a very theatrical yawn, and

then glanced at his large gold and diamond-studded wristwatch.

'You've a long drive, Black Knife, better get some sleep. That black-ass is expecting you by midday.' Herman understood that he'd just been dismissed.

As the Mercedes SLK ate the kilometres toward Berlin with ease, Herman had time to think. He found himself speculating as to why this guy, Ahmed, would need a hit man. They had plenty of suicide bombers, didn't they? It had to be something else, but what? It didn't surprise Herman that the Russian Mafia was cutting deals with Muslims here in Europe. The main supplier of munitions for the Chechen Islamic resistance groups were Russians. The Slavs called Arabs *black-arses* too, but they didn't mind taking their petro-dollars or opium-dollars even if it traded on the lives of Russian military and civilians. It was a business ethic they considered sustainable, and he had no problem with it, either.

However, he was curious about the nature of this deal with Ahmed. It was clear that he would become involved, but what in the devil could Herman bring to the table? It had to be a hit; that was the only expertise he offered. Or was it because they needed a black man? He doubted that; they had plenty of black African freedom fighters frothing at the mouth for jihad. On the other hand, the mosque was in Berlin and getting those guys into Germany always offered an element of risk. He was here. He was legal. Was that the angle, he wondered?

As he approached the suburbs of Berlin, he pulled into an Aral *Tankstelle* (garage). Like most petrol stations on the autobahn, they offered much more than just fill-ups and top-ups. There was a convenience market, toilet facilities, a self-serve restaurant, and this one had a motel as well. He needed to stretch his legs and grab a quick cup of coffee. He had already noted that it was ten past eleven. He could squander a few minutes without jeopardizing his timetable. Ahmed expected him at noon – which meant noonish as far as he was concerned.

He went to the WC and took care of business. After washing his hands and replacing his gloves, he walked out where a grumpy-looking old woman sat beside a little table on which was set a deep plate filling with coins. It was customary to tip the *Klofrau* with a ten or twenty euro-cent piece. Herman never tipped them; he got a kind of malicious pleasure from their dirty looks, and this old woman didn't disappoint him. She went a step further and muttered *Arschlöch* (aresehole) *a*s he passed her; that was even better.

His overarching reason for stopping at the

Tankstelle was so that he could punch the address of Al Nur, Ahmed's mosque in Berlin, into his global navigational system. He figured that he might as well get some fuel while he was at it, as he didn't know if the next step would be another long drive. He paid for the fill-up inside the convenience store and he asked for a receipt. It was his first document to support expenses for this job although, realistically, he didn't expect to see the money.

Back in the comfort of the SLK he entered the city post code for Al Nur and waited a few seconds until the female voice on the GPS instructed, 'Make a right turn.' He had named the system *Die Schlampe* – the Bitch. What else, he had reasoned, could you call something which was black, had a female voice and gave you orders all day? Following the audible instructions and sometimes glancing down at the map display he made his way through the traffic. It was just five minutes past noon when *Schlampe* informed him that he was one hundred and fifty metres from his destination and Herman pulled over to take stock. This was definitely the Arab ghetto of Berlin – not Turkish – the storefronts and the few posters he could see were all in Arabic script. Turks used the European alphabet, although they decorated it with a lot of umlauts and apostrophe-like symbols.

It was a very dirty street, strewn with discarded

paper and some heaps of dog shit – at least he presumed it came from dogs. Pulling back out and slowly driving on, *Schlampe* continued her countdown until she proudly announced, 'You have arrived. You have arrived.' He carefully scrutinized the closed-up storefront which should have been his destination. It didn't look a mosque to him; he'd expected an ornamental building towering high and topped with minarets. What he passed appeared to be no more than a lock-up shop in a long unbroken row of similar building stretching in both directions to the ends of the block. What *Schlampe* insisted was Al Nur was indistinguishable from the other fronts, except that it had no windows and a lot of Arabic script in evidence. It could have been a warehouse for carpets as far has he could see. Slowing to a crawl, he noticed that the door was secured behind an ornamental wrought-iron gate and to the right of it was a bell push. *Schlampe* was now insisting that he made a u-turn '…at your earliest opportunity,' and the direction arrow on the GPS screen had flipped around to point behind and was flashing.

There was a moderate amount of foot traffic on the pavements on both sides of the street. Unshaven or bearded men lounged at the entrances of their storefront doors, many of them dressed in the traditional Arab robes, women scuttled about all dressed in the traditional burka. To Herman it looked like a movie set, and it was hard to believe he was in the suburbs of a major European city. He had the windows of his car closed and the aircon on re-circulate but, nevertheless, a hint of the smell outside began seeping in. It was a combination of rotting fruit, putrefying meat, urine, coffee and damp carpets. He wondered if *Schlampe* really knew where she'd brought them and then again if maybe he'd entered the wrong address or maybe his Russian boss hadn't gotten it right

There was no parking in sight, and the gap he'd spotted about forty metres down the street turned out to be an alleyway access onto the street. Well, there was no chance he was going to park his fine automobile in this neighbourhood unless it remained in earshot and in his line of sight, so he parked in this gap, blocking the alleyway. If he was in the right place he'd ask Ahmed where he could find some secure parking for his car.

He got out of his Mercedes and casually leaned against the driver's door. He slowly scanned up and down both sides of the street and glanced over his shoulder into the alleyway. It appeared deserted, except for one black BMW sedan about thirty metres away. Someone was inside the car, but it didn't raise any suspicion in Herman so he slowly strode along the pavement after locking the car with the button on the key fob. There were people on both sides of the street, a few in conversation, a few taking an interest in him, but most of them seemed to just be going about their business; nobody looked like a 'Bull' or a hooligan. It occurred to him that he could phone Ahmed to confirm that he was at the right place and he reached for the Nokia in his pocket. Then he thought, 'Shit, I'm there now,' as he arrived in front of the wrought-iron gate. An Arab-looking fellow was leaning against the doorway of the entrance to a neighbouring shop and Herman looked him in the eye. The fellow smiled, but didn't appear to be put ill at ease by the attention. Herman pointed to the steel grate next door.

'Is that Al Nur mosque?' he asked slowly in German. The fellow just kept smiling with no change in his expression. Herman concluded that he either didn't speak German or was deaf, and so decided to press the ringer. Whilst waiting for some result he stepped back and looked up the street to make sure no one was messing with his car. Some guy in normal street clothes was standing beside it, seeming to look it over. No uniform, so he doubted he was a 'Bull', probably just some wannabe asshole admiring his Mercedes; that wasn't unusual. Taking more interest, Herman squinted to sharpen the image. The fellow was tall, about six feet, and looked European. 'Where the fuck had he come from?' he wondered. Was it the person he'd spotted in the black sedan parked in the alley? He turned back to the door, where was that shit-speck, Ahmed? He began to have doubts as to whether this was the entrance to Al Nur at all and impatiently pressed the ringer several times, again stepping back to keep an eye on the zoot in a suit that had now decided to park his ass on the front wing of his SLK. 'Damn!' Herman cursed to himself, 'only a Bull or some hard-faced bastard would have the balls to do that!' He turned to walk away from the gate when his phone vibrated in his pocket. He pulled it out and looked at the display, the number showed a Berlin code. Who the fuck in Berlin would be calling him? Ahmed? Maybe Andrei had given that black-ass his number. He guessed that the Arab was calling to ask when he was coming. Clearly *Schlampe* hadn't directed him to Al Nur, probably Andrei had screwed up the address.

Thumbing the button on the phone he gave a curt, 'Hullo.' A heavily-accented voice simply said, 'We're being watched. Go away. You will be contacted later.' He had no time to respond; the line dropped out. He looked at his mobile phone in confusion, 'Go where? Being watched by whom? The Bulls?' Then he remembered that tall guy by his car. Glancing up he saw he was still comfortably propping himself up on Herman's pride and joy. As he stood there wondering what his next move ought to be, a green Polizei van passed by him and pulled up beside his Mercedes. The tall guy stood up as three Bulls in green uniform got out of the van and pointed in the direction of Herman, but made no further move. The tall guy was now standing on the sidewalk in a clear line of sight and offered a sweeping gesture which clearly said, 'Won't you join us?'

'Shit!' he muttered under his breath. There was no point in running since he'd done nothing wrong. Not yet, anyway, at least not in Berlin. So he assumed his coolest saunter and walked towards them, wondering as he did so that somebody must have fingered him. Who? Why? Ahmed? Andrei? To what end? Well, he wasn't exactly looking forward to it, but he would shortly get some answers from those Bulls.

He suddenly noticed that the street had cleared. Passing the doorway where the dumb-fuck with a face full of smiles and incomprehension had stood, he noticed it was closed. The doorways were no longer propped up by men lounging against them and the few people that were now on the streets seemed to all be heading away from the Bulls' van. As he approached the tall guy on the sidewalk, he sadly concluded that the fellow was certainly not some wannabe hanging around his SLK to admire it. The three uniformed Bulls stood by the van double-parked in the street beside his Mercedes, their hands were empty, but they packed the familiar pistols on their belts.

'What's the problem, officer,' Herman asked, affecting an innocent look and faking a strong African accent.

The tall guy said nothing, but urged him to come closer with a rolling hand motion.

'Is this your SLK?' he asked.

Herman saw no point in lying and nodded.

'I was just trying to get directions,' he offered. 'I wasn't going to stay parked here. Nobody seems to speak German. That's what took me so far down the street. Really, in this neighbourhood you don't think I would leave a car like this blocking an alley, do you?'

'What're you looking for?'

Herman's mind raced ahead before he answered. They didn't send a vanload of Bulls to investigate an illegal parking incident. Worst case, they would have called for a tow truck.

'The Kus-Kus,' Herman lied. 'It's a restaurant that was recommended to me. Good North African food, they said. I thought I'd try a spot of lunch there.'

'They?' the tall guy inquired suspiciously.

'Friends,' Herman responded.

'What're their names?'

'Hey, I don't want to get my friends involved in this!'

'Involved in what?' the Bull fired back.

After a pause, Herman shrugged his shoulders and affected a really pissed off look.

'I dunno; you tell me. What's this all about? I just parked for a minute and …' he was cut short by the next question which rocked him back on his heels although he hoped he hadn't shown it.

'Is one of their names Ahmed?'

'Ahmed sounds like a Turkish or Arab name to me. I haven't any Turk or Arab friends, I'm a Christian.' He countered, trying to maintain his disaffected composure whilst his mind raced. There were only two people who knew of his meeting with Ahmed: the aforesaid Ahmed and that devious Russian bastard, Andrei. Surely Andrei wouldn't have sent him to Berlin in order to get him arrested? If he was that pissed off with him he'd already be floating face down in a Hamburg dock. So it must have been this piece of Arab shit, Ahmed, who'd fingered him, but what purpose could it serve for the black-ass?

'Let me see your ID and car registration,' the tall

guy demanded.

Herman took a step off the curb onto the street and observed the three uniformed Bulls tense up.

'Hey, where do you think you're going?' the tall guy challenged.

Herman stopped cold in his tracks and turned back, 'To fetch my car registration,' he calmly responded.

'ID first!' The tall guy extended his arm while the fingers of his hand wiggled a 'gimme-gimme' gesture.

Herman wondered for which branch of the police this fellow worked, city or federal? He was tempted to ask; an answer would at least have clarified the gravity of the issue but he refrained, reasoning that the innocent tourist he was trying to be would not ask anything so pointed. There was something about the tall guy that suggested *BKA (Bundeskriminalamt* – Federal Police) rather than the local *Kripo (Kriminalpolizei* – CID) and if that was indeed the case then something was very, very wrong.

He realized that he would have to use his real ID because the Mercedes was registered in the name of Herman Namlos. He kept it with the car registration in the glove box, but was carrying a false ID in his trousers pocket, and hoped they weren't going to search him. Herman Namlos had an arrest record and carried the false ID in case the Bulls pinched him at the pick-up at Max and Susie's. He would have claimed to be a legitimate suitor for the Romanian girl, and hope to hell that she went along with the ruse. Well, there was some truth to it from her point view. She had responded to the newspaper ad and come to Germany for the purpose of marriage. If she complained to the police about her treatment, it would be directed at Max, not at him. Of course, if they had searched him, they would have found illegal substances that would provide all the cause they needed to drag him before the *Staatsanwalt*. That would have been ugly, he conceded, but fortunately he no longer carried any of those illegal substances. They were safely ensconced in the stomach of the Susie-corpse.

'It's in the car, with my registration,' he offered innocently.

'You're supposed to carry it with you on your person!' the tall guy countered.

'Is that the law?' Herman innocently inquired.

'Yup.'

'Even when you go swimming?' asked Herman trying to lighten things up.

'Very funny,' replied the suit blandly, 'Now, go fetch me the ID and registration. Unlock the door from here and then give me the keys,' he instructed, 'and I want you to keep one hand behind your back while you're in the car. Understand?'

'Yes sir, I understand,' Herman affirmed, 'but I don't understand why you've arrested me. What have I done wrong?'

'You haven't been arrested,' replied the tall Bull. 'You're illegally parked. You've blocked an alley-way and we're looking into it. Now let's have your ID and registration before I book you for obstruction.'

'Shit!' Herman hissed under his breath. 'This is about something a whole lot more important than illegal parking, but what?' He pressed the 'unlock' on his electronic key and then surrendered it to the Bull whose hand had remained outstretched. He opened the driver-side door, and then realized it would have been a whole lot easier if he had approached his glove box from the passenger side, where he kept the documents. Oh well, he didn't feel like changing direction and annoying the Bulls any more than he had to so he put one arm behind his back and manoeuvred with one knee on the driver seat while one foot still toed the street until he managed to wrestle the documents out of the compartment. Then, keeping his head ducked down, he re-emerged, releasing the arm he'd been holding behind his back and handed over the documents.

The Bull studied each of these two documents minutely, like he was expecting someone to ask him questions later and needed to know every detail. Finally, he laid the keys and documents down on the boot of the Mercedes as he withdrew a small note-book and a pen from his jacket pocket. He jotted down several notes, referring back to the ID and the registration several times. At last, he returned the notebook and pen to his pocket but left the keys and documents on the boot.

'You're from Hamburg. What're you doing here in Berlin?' he asked.

'Well, if I tell you the real reason, you'll ask me her name. I don't want to get her involved. I don't know her that well – yet,' smiled Herman.

'Is that an answer? It didn't sound like an answer, it sounded like a line of shit to me, Herman Namlos. Now, I'm asking you one more time. Why are you here in Berlin?'

'See the sights,' he responded nonchalantly.

'Where are you staying?'

'You mean here in Berlin?' Herman replied. He had elected to play the role of a dumb-fuck.

'I don't mean in Africa!'

Herman shrugged, 'I haven't made any arrange-ments yet.'

'But you're already looking for this restaurant.

The 'Kus-Kus', is that what you called it?

'Kus-Kus,' he confirmed, 'I was hoping for an overnight invitation, but she doesn't get off work until five this afternoon, so I'm sort of killing time.'

The tall guy pointed to the keys and documents perched on the boot, 'Take them, and get out of this neighbourhood. If you don't belong here, it's not a healthy place to be.'

Herman couldn't believe his luck. As he drove off, he mulled over the very last clue which the Bull had unwittingly provided, no S*trafe* (parking ticket). They hadn't cited him for the parking violation which proved to him that the Bull in the suit was fishing in a lot deeper waters than the parking ticket warranted. He needed to call Andrei; he had a bad feeling about that black-ass, Ahmed.

****

POLLY

Polly had lied to Sam when she feigned not understanding German. As a matter of fact, she spoke passable German. Her colleagues at the *Deutsch
Amerikanisches Institut* booth, where she had met
Sam, had spoken English with her because it was
usual for them to do so. After all, they came to the
Insititut to polish their English language skills, especially the conversational side.

She could watch films and the news on German
television with fair comprehension. She'd maintained the lie with several German guys whom she
had dated. She felt that it gave her an edge which, on
a couple of occasions, had paid off. The flaunted
European racial tolerance, she had found, was largely a myth; and not only as it applied to anti-

Semitism, but they were just as racist towards blacks in Germany as many people State-side.

As an intelligence liaison officer, it made all the sense in the world for her to employ a little disinformation when it served her own purposes. Polly worked for the CIA, preparing intelligence briefings for the United States European Commander and his staff. Essentially, she was the CIA liaison to this particular military commander. Moreover, when the Command needed to reach outside their military intelligence community for local or country reports concerning force protection, she'd hustle up answers from Langle. With the focus in Europe now on terrorism, her job had gotten a lot bigger. Also, following 9/11, one of the criticisms of the US intelligence communities was that they hadn't shared information and that had to change.

She also spoke fluent Spanish; her mother had been rescued by her father from the chaos of those final days in Nicaragua when an unrestrained National Guard, loyal to Somoza, was executing political dissidents. Rupe Johnson had been a country specialist for the CIA and had been working down-range in Managua at the time, where he met the University student, Alejandra Galisteo. Alejandra was a political activist and the National Guard had no sense of humor concerning student obstruction and protest. Word on the wind had it that Alejandra was scheduled to be arrested and probably shot. So Rupe rescued her, took her back to the States, arranged the appropriate papers and, later, married her.

In due course, Alejandra had a baby girl, Apollonia, but that didn't stop the young mother from earning a bachelors degree at Georgetown, and then a law degree at George Washington, both of which Rupe had encouraged her to do. Apollonia was brought up by a series of Latino nannies and spoke fluent Spanish before she had entered first grade. 'Polly', as she became known, learned her German without the aid of nannies or schooling. She'd been working more than four years now at EUCOM Headquarters located in Vaihingen, about nine kilometres from Stuttgart Airport, and started her study of German by watching the local cartoon channel and by using every available weekend to mix with the German community. Polly could have lived on base, but she had chosen to live out in the community in order to absorb the German language and culture. Besides, housing on base was tight, so Uncle Sam encouraged off-base housing for both military and civilians by indulging them with a very generous allowance.

She leaned back in her chair, having just finished sending an alert to the Command with specific copy to Vicenza, Aviano, Naples and the other US military bases on Italian soil. A level-4 alert (two or more highly credible sources) stated that nuclear material of quality and quantity sufficient to assemble an RDD (Radiological Dispersal Device - a 'dirty bomb') had been smuggled into Italy and was in the possession of Al-Queda-associated operatives there. The material was believed to be plutonium according to one of the sources and old radiological material from the former USSR according to another. No hard intelligence on the proposed target was yet available. Italy had more coastline than California, and it offered a more porous border to illegal foreigners than West Texas, she bitterly reflected.

She had gotten the word that morning that they would not roster a TDY, a temporary duty replacement, for her while she went on her shopping trip to Milan.

'For that short duration we can handle things from here,' her 'super' had said ('here' meaning Langley). 'Let's hope they give us a quiet weekend while you're gone,' he had added dryly.

'Fat chance,' Polly had muttered to herself. Since the initiation of Operation Enduring Freedom, the operational tempo had surged even beyond the levels created by 9/11. Then, with the advent of Operation Iraqi Freedom, the tempo had gone off the charts.

She glanced at her watch. Oh shit! She had a lunch date with Leon Cole, a civilian news reporter for *Stars and Stripes*. She had promised to meet him twelve noon at the Dorint Hotel in Vaihingen itself. They offered a fairly good-quality restaurant there but, what the heck, the *Deutsch Amerikanishes Institut* was picking up the tab. Leon had agreed to give a talk at the next meeting of the *Institut*. His theme had to do with an article he had written for his newspaper which had received international attention. This lunch today was merely an amenity on behalf of the *Institut*. Arrangements with Leon for his lecture were already set, so there wasn't a whole lot of business for her to discuss with him.

However, Polly had an agenda item of her own, quite apart from any *Institut* interest, which was the reason she had immediately volunteered for the task of exchanging pleasantries with this arrogant, liberal-opinioned reporter. She had taken umbrage to his article, the methodology of his survey, and certainly with his conclusions. It reflected the pseudo-intellectualism euphemistically termed as 'anti-war sentiment'. How could this kind of guy be writing for *Stars and Stripes*, she wondered? It was a newspaper designed to promote the cause and welfare of the soldiers, like *Navy Times* did for the sailors. I guess, she concluded, it reflects the new Pentagon concept of 'embedded' reporting.

So, she pulled into the parking lot of the Dorint Hotel with a specific mission in mind. She had written a piece which she had entitled 'Intellectual Terrorism' and she wanted to publish it in one of the major newspapers as an 'opinion'. But she had questions, even if she was a journalism school graduate, mostly to do with which newspaper would be most likely to publish it – and, '*By the way*', did Leon have any connections with one of these majors that might help her get an 'in'? She already knew that she couldn't ask *Stars and Stripes* to publish it, as her piece was too politically incorrect. Anyway, she had to keep a low profile in the military community, even though she had planned to use a pseudonym. Within the intelligence community, word seemed always to get around and she couldn't afford that.

Her super would not be amused if he were to learn that she had published a controversial article in a newspaper, major or local. Thus, she had a second good reason to assume a *nom de plume*, although she hadn't yet decided what it would be. For those on base with no need to know otherwise, as well as those in the German community, she was a civilian public affairs officer; she even had business cards to prove it. Her private office was installed in the public affairs billet, and her neighbouring associates actually believed this charade. Well, it wasn't like she carried on a second life as a James Bond-type heroine. She considered herself to be little more than a glorified paper-shuffler – only nowadays you shuffled digital bits.

The Dorint was a businessman's hotel. There was an industrial park nearby full of telecom and electronics firms whose names one would find on the TecDAX (German equivalent of NASDAQ) or the most part the crowd was in suits, both male and female. So Leon Cole stood out, sitting at a table for two, alone of course, wearing an open-neck denim shirt and Levi trousers, with combat-type jacket hung over the back of his chair. He'd recently come back from Iraq, she knew that much, that's what his celebrated news article was about.

He'd gone to Iraq with a questionnaire. This two-page affair was designed to survey soldier satisfaction with their living conditions there and, most incredibly, *Stars and Stripes* had financed this junket. During his five-week tour of Iraq, he managed to survey a little over two thousand soldiers, marines and airmen. They rated things from 1 to 5: 5 meant it couldn't get much better, and 1 meant it couldn't be much worse.

'Well, if you're gonna ask opinions about living in a tent in the Iraqi boonies in the middle of a scorching dust-blowing summer, or ducking Baathist-terrorist mortar shells and bullets in the triangle, guess what kind of numbers you were gonna get?' she had scoffed. The same went for squatting in the squalor of Baghdad or any of the other cities. Then there was the food. 'Give me a break!' she had exclaimed when she'd first read the article, 'Soldiers always bitch about the food!' MREs (Meals Ready to Eat - COMPO Rations) were a poor imitation of economy-class airline food, so guess what kind of numbers their cuisine would garner? There were questions about mail service, and the availability of TV and internet service. She considered Leon's exercise to be a crock of shit. What would the soldiers of 'our greatest generation' have thought about this purveyor of such a blatantly stupid questionnaire, she wondered? Back in WW2 they idolized news guys like Ernie Pyle. How in the hell did this Leon Cole ever get hired by the staff of *Stars and Stripes*?

Nevertheless, she had not come to Vaihingen to challenge him or what she considered to be his tainted conclusions. He had compared the substandard living conditions of the enlisted men to the relative opulence enjoyed by their officers; at least that is what he claimed to have observed. He had inserted that later since a significant percentage of the enlisted came from minorities; it was a horrible message to be setting before the Iraqi people. It confirmed, he maintained, everything the mullahs were preaching about American racism. 'Oh well,' Polly had sighed, 'Leon had conveniently skirted issues like the Iraqi conventions in respect to their treatment of women, for one.'

Polly had hung up her jacket in the foyer, exposing a loose-fitting casual trouser suit. Over a shoulder she carried her sling-bag out of which was conspicuously sticking a brown envelope, sized to hold A4 paper. She asked at the small reception desk if Leon had arrived and was directed to the glass-roofed conservatory extension of the restaurant. Making her way in she was aware he was looking her over as she approached his table and awkwardly rose to a crouch, but didn't push his chair back and allow himself to stand erect. Polly reflected that he looked like a caricature of John Lennon trying to take a dump in the woods. Leon wore wire-rimmed glasses and combed his brown hair in the latter-day Lennon fashion, but his face was clean shaven. She and Leon had not met face-to-face before, just talked once on the telephone, but she had seen his photograph which accompanied the article in *Stars and Stripes* which had generated a degree of notoriety.

'Ms Johnson?'

'Yes. Hello, Leon,' she said as she stopped beside

him and extended a hand which he limply accepted and then quickly released. He seemed to harbour no doubts that she was the genuine article; of course he had heard her voice on the telephone.

'Please sit down,' he invited as he slumped back into his chair.

'What else, stand here beside you and eat lunch with my fingers?' she thought to herself. She didn't like this dude – well, she didn't like what he had written. It didn't matter at that precise moment since her object was to see if he could help her get 'Intellectual Terrorism' into one of the majors. She adjusted; 'Thank you,' she purred.

Moving around the corner of the table she seated herself across from Leon. With the back of her hand she gently pushed an ashtray to the far corner on his side of the table.

'I don't smoke,' he said defensively.

'I need the room,' she quietly responded, and then reached into her purse and retrieved the envelope, set the purse by her feet and placed the envelope at the edge of the table where the ashtray had previously perched. He watched her with a passive curiosity.

'Is that for me?' he finally asked in a tone reflecting his suspicion that it would mean unnecessary work for him.

She smiled, but didn't answer his question; she

wanted him to press the issue. Inside were the three pages of her precious opinion piece, 'Intellectual Terrorism'. They sat in silence for a few moments and she took in the surroundings. It was quiet as German restaurants went, perhaps because they allowed fairly generous spaces between tables. In Germany it was not unusual to seat two sets of strangers together at the same table when a restaurant was full. However, here she sensed that this particular restaurant was a bit too upmarket to employ that convention, no doubt because the visiting business people would not have taken kindly to discussing their affairs in such a public way. There were potted plants everywhere, she noted, giving a semi-tropical feeling and through the high glass ceiling she could see the bland grey sky.

She granted that Germany was a somber place in November; it was the month the sun usually took a holiday. Daylight saving time kicked in the last Sunday of October, so by five in the afternoon it was already getting dark. Glancing at her watch, she saw it was only a little past noon, but as Polly looked up through the glass at the sky above, it might as well have been evening for all the light that penetrated the cloud cover. A lot of Americans found this climate depressing, but Polly didn't mind. She usually worked out in the gym on the treadmill or stationary bicycle, so she paid little mind to the weather outside, except for Friday mornings when she ran with the SOPs (Special Operations Personnel).

'Is that for me?' Leon finally repeated as he now lifted a hand and limply pointed to the envelope.

'Yes, in a manner of speaking,' she acknowledged, 'but why don't we first get acquainted? Have you ordered yet?' She suppressed any outward sign of the satisfaction she felt concerning his attention to her envelope. He eyed it for several moments more as if attempting to discern what in the world might be inside. She was sorely tempted to play a little, maybe telling him it was a questionnaire, but she sensed it would be a waste of time. He had already given the impression he was a nerd with no sense of humour. She was jolted from her brief fantasy by his monosyllabic answer, 'No.'

She cocked her head and affected a puzzled look.

'No, I haven't ordered,' he said in his monotone. 'I told them to wait until you arrived before sending over the waiter.'

As if minding his cue, the waiter hustled over to their table and handed them each a menu.

'English,' he assured them while they accepted the menus. 'Something to drink?' he asked.

'I'll have a sherry on ice,' Leon immediately responded.

The waiter nodded and turned to Polly. She took a moment to collect her thoughts. 'Sherry on ice?!' She liked sherry, but not watered down with ice.

'Uhh – do you have a Merlot?'

'Of course,' responded the waiter in flawless English, 'Would you like the house Merlot? It's quite nice.'

'Yes, thank you.' She watched the waiter turn and hustle off. Most of the Germans working on base talked more like Americans, she had observed, and with a lot more German in their accent than this waiter. She resolved for the hundredth time at least to work on her German, she knew just how badly she murdered it.

'You must be from California,' Leon piped up.

'What makes you think that?' she inquired.

'Seems like everybody from California drinks Merlot or Chardonnay,' he stated with a confidence that made her wonder maliciously if he'd once done a questionnaire on wine drinking.

'Are you from California?' he pressed, seeming eager to prove his proposition.

'Nope,' Polly shrugged. 'My parents live outside Washington DC. That's where I grew up.'

'You're not military, are you?'

She let his question hang for a few moments.

'No,' she answered at last.

'So what do you do here?'

'I'm a civilian public affairs officer.'

'Oh,' he said, as his attention seemed to drift off, perhaps pondering some deep meaning to her answer.

'Yes, but what do you do?' he finally asked.

'Public affairs stuff,' she coyly responded with an impish grin.

'Mmm, can't you be a bit more specific?' he persisted, devoid of humour.

'No she couldn't,' Polly thought to herself but, on the other hand, she couldn't tell him that either. So, what story was she going make up this time? First ploy was to try and change the subject. He seemed to her to be a self-absorbed sonovabitch.

'I don't think you'll find my mundane tasks very interesting, Leon. You're the interesting person here. I'd much rather we talked about you.'

He shrugged, and then looked directly at her with a sheepish grin.

'You said we should get acquainted before you showed me what's in that envelope. So I'm trying to get acquainted.'

She touched the envelope with her forefinger, and as she did so noted she was past due for a manicure.

'It's something I've written, and I'm hoping you might give me some direction concerning getting it published. It's an opinion piece.'

'Published? Like in *Stars and Stripes*?'

'No, it's not military. I was thinking more like the *New York Times* or the *Washington Post*; you know, one of the majors. Do you have any connections?'

She watched him turn his head as his face seemed to redden.

'Depends,' he finally muttered without looking back at her.

She regarded his response with curiosity. What exactly would it depend upon, she wondered.

'Who did you work for prior to joining the *Stars and Stripes* staff,' she carefully inquired.

'A paper in Flint, Michigan,' he sighed, as if annoyed that she would ask.

'As what?' she pressed.

He looked at her with a blush now creeping up from his collar.

'As an investigative reporter, of course!' he protested, far too loudly.

Polly sat back in her seat, 'Damn,' she thought to herself, 'this bozo probably made the coffee in Flint before he somehow managed to land the contract with *Stars and Stripes*.' A feeling of disappointment gripped her as she sensed this appeal to the reporter was turning out to be an empty exercise. It remained no longer a question in her mind of what he *would* do for her, rather what, if anything, he *could* do for her. Answer: probably not much more than she could do for herself. She might as well have been asking Sam Lumumba for an intro to the *Washington Post*. Thinking of Sam at least made her smile for a few moments. She didn't think he would have liked the Dorint Hotel. He'd be pushing her to skip lunch and jump in the sack for a quick nooner, but guessed with some certainty they didn't rent rooms by the hour. God help this jerk, Leon Cole, if he were to make that suggestion to her! He and Sam were about as different as night and day, she mused, and it had nothing to do with the colour of their skin. She was attracted to Sam's type of personality because in the few relationships she'd had, men served a singular purpose for her. She wasn't looking for commitment and a lifetime's soul mate; all that could all come later. Oh, she had male colleagues and platonic acquaintances, but their gender wasn't an issue. They could equally easily have been male or female; it made no difference in the rapport or relationship, like having a gay friend. Sam, on the other hand, served a very special function, and it was essential that he be a testosterone-dominated man, in contrast to someone like Leon Cole, who struck her as being about as useful as a eunuch.

'Are you from Michigan?' Polly asked politely.

'No,' he softly answered without addressing her implied question. 'I went to school at Michigan State,' he finally added.

'Journalism?' she wondered if she should share with him the fact that she was a J-school graduate too. 'No point to it,' she decided.

The waiter arrived with her Merlot and Leon's sherry. The wine was in a small carafe and the waiter presented it an assuring way, wearing his best 'Don't worry, you're going to like it' smile. His presentation of Leon's sherry over ice was much more perfunctory. They hadn't offered it in a usual sherry schooner; no doubt the ice precluded that. She suspected the waiter had found no more grace in Leon's choice than she had. Having served the drinks the waiter stood with pen and pad poised, 'Are you ready to order?' he asked.

Leon was hurriedly scanning through the menu, but Polly already knew what she would order and went ahead.

'The Dorint salad,' she said as she closed the menu. The waiter inclined his head as though accepting the perfect choice.

'Your merlot will keep it perfect company,' he smiled.

It was what she had ordered the last time she visited the restaurant. The Dorint salad plate offered a variety of little salads partitioned like sections of a pineapple slice around the large dish on which it was served. There was lettuce, shredded carrots, coleslaw, good German potato salad, sliced tomatoes with Bermuda onion, and in the 'pineapple hole' at the centre of the plate perched a variety of soft and hard cheese wedges, and it came with a basket of crusty breads. She hadn't been able to finish her plate last time; one couldn't dismiss this salad lunch order with the comment, 'Just a salad, nothing more.'

'And Sir?' asked the waiter, a hint of accent creeping through on the 'Sir'. '*Zwiebelrostbraten*,' Leon stated, as if the final choice had been an agonizing one. He pronounced the 'w' in *zwiebel* softly, like an American, instead of the proper German 'v' sound. That's how Polly now perceived Leon, 'Kinda like a *zwiebel* with a soft 'w'.' The waiter informed Leon that it came with a salad, and requested his choice of dressing.

'Do you have thousand island?' Leon enquired hopefully.

Clearly the waiter had no idea to what he referred. Polly was tempted to intervene, but checked her impulse. It would be more fun to just watch it carry on under its own inertia. Leon glanced over at her, as if seeking her support for his right to have thousand island dressing, but her only response was to hunch her shoulders. Finally, he waved his hand through the air as if warding off a bad odour.

'Just give me the house dressing,' he sighed in capitulation.

The waiter acknowledged with a nod as he collected the menus from them and bustled off. Leon cleared his throat to get her attention, and then pointed with his forefinger to the envelope. 'May I have a look?'

She studied his face for a moment, which seemed to make him uneasy.

'To what end?' she asked, 'I don't need an evaluation of its merit, Leon. I need someone with connections to help me get it noticed.'

He slouched back in his chair and began to toy with the cutlery, apparently not wanting to make eye contact

'You were the one who brought it here,' he complained, 'I thought you wanted me to read it. So excuse me. I'm an investigative reporter, Ms Johnson. I'm not involved in the opinion business, I collect facts.'

'Yeah, right!' thought Polly, 'and I'm really Brad Pitt in drag and make-up!'

'Just out of curiosity,' he asked, 'how long is your piece?'

'Three pages.'

'How many words?' Leon pressed with a little irritation in his voice.

'About sixteen hundred, why?'

'Because the majors limit opinion submissions to no more than one thousand words, and they usually sub that down unless you're one of the big boys in the field like VDH – Victor Davis Hanson,' he expanded. 'You heard of him?'

'Heard of him?' Polly repeated back, 'I worship at his alter. Any aspiring opinion writer has to read VDH,' she declared. A sniff and a yawn told her that perhaps Leon didn't agree.

She was not happy with the way this lunch date was developing. She reached over to the wine decanter and poured half of it into her glass and, rolling it around to 'breathe', she tried the bouquet, full and round. Without bothering to offer Leon a well-wishing toast, she took a sip and her taste buds were already ahead and wanting the crisp cleanliness of her salad; the waiter had been right. So maybe it wasn't going to be a complete disaster.

He took her cue and reached for his sherry on ice, having pulled himself upright again in his chair. He took a sip and smacked his lips, which annoyed her. Then, still holding his glass, he looked up as if examining the grey sky through the glass ceiling, and airily suggested something which was as much of a turnaround as if he'd suddenly jumped up, dropped his pants and given her a moon.

'A few of us,' he began, 'are getting together over the four-day Veterans Day weekend and going to Interlaken. *Stars and Stripes* Travel Section is doing some features. We've picked the Beau Rivage Hotel in Interlaken for one of them. It's a five-star Swiss hotel. We aim to get in some skiing; I hear they've already got the first fresh snow on the *Jungfrau*. And here's the good news, the room and meals are free! The assignment comes with amenities,' he sniggered, 'We've space for a fourth if you'd like to come along?'

After a long pause, she responded, 'As what?'

'Huh?'

'Never mind, I can't. I'm going to Milan with a bus-load of ladies – shopping,'

'All four days?' he asked with a hint of exasperation.

'No, we leave Friday night and come back Sunday morning.'

'You can go to Milan any time,' Leon objected, 'But a five-star Swiss hotel and gourmet meals, all free?' he gave a boyish grin and left the offer hanging in the air.

Polly took another sip of her wine to give herself some thinking time, 'Why was he going on like this?' she wondered. 'What a jerk!'

He continued his appeal, now gesticulating with both hands, 'You don't need a four-day weekend for shopping. It's a federal holiday on Tuesday. Aren't they giving you the long weekend off?'

'Thank you, but I can go to Interlaken anytime,' she politely responded, the thought that she was expected to make up the other half of a 'couple' with Leon made her flesh creep. In any event she reflected on the reaction she'd get from her super if she informed him that she needed to extend her trip to the full four-day Veterans Day weekend. Inside her mind she heard his sonorous baritone voice on the phone and guessed the reaction, 'You don't qualify, Ms Johnson, you're not a veteran.'

At that point the food arrived, which allowed a tactical withdrawal on both sides.

****

BLACK KNIFE

Herman had gone to East Berlin to search for hotel
accommodation. It was cheaper on the east side if
you stayed away from the hotels near the museums
and avoided the Friedrichstrasse/Orionburgerstrasse
area. Moreover, for him there was a nostalgia factor
associated with East Berlin. The trump card, however, was the nightlife. Discos, drugs, and tourist ladies
looking for a good time could be found in the 'Ossie'
(East Berlin) nightlife district. It was a region of
stark contrasts including blues bar and cabarets, as
well as Hindu and Middle Eastern culture. They also
had good restaurants there, many of them vying for
which could best present the most unique eating
experience by offering fusion-type food.

It was mid-afternoon as he crouched on the side

of his bed waiting for his mobile phone to ring. He'd
expected a return call from Andrei in Hamburg and
bided his time by reflecting on recent events. He still
couldn't fathom for sure what had happened at the Al
Nur mosque a couple of hours before, well, more
specifically, *why* it had happened. The Bull had mentioned Ahmed by name. Was the tall fellow fishing
for something or was that Ahmed really a Judas?

After his encounter with the Bulls, Black Knife
had driven a few blocks and then pulled over, checking for anyone who might be following him, after
which he reached for his mobile phone and called
Andrei.

'Get your black *Neger*-ass out of there,' the
Russian exploded after hearing a breathless Black
Knife describe the episode.

'You want me to come back to Hamburg?' he
asked.

'No, go find a hotel, but not in that black-ass
neighbourhood, shit-for-brains!'

Herman sighed, 'And then what?'

'Keep that mobile phone line open. I'll get back
with you. You check into a hotel and you stay there,
hear?'

'Yeah, boss, I hear,' he griped, and then added, 'I
could use something to eat.'

'Eat your dick!' exploded Andrai, 'You stay in

your fuckin' hotel room until I tell you otherwise, Black Knife. It's not a suggestion, understand?'

'Understood,' he whispered, 'Uhh, boss, Ahmed said he would call me back. Whaddya want me to do if he calls?'

'Start by answering the phone, shit-speck,' was the sarcastic reply.

'And then what?'

'Listen to what he has to say.'

'Okay, but then what?'

'When you guys are finished talking, then hang up.'

'Come on, boss,' whined Herman, 'whaddya want me to say to the guy?'

'Nothing! Just listen, you tell him you'll get back with him. That's all you tell him, okay?'

'Yeah, okay.'

'And don't tell him where you're staying. You tell him nothing!'

Herman was getting ruffled by the Russian treating him like an idiot.

'Yeah, OK, I got that much.'

'Good. Talk to you later. Wait a minute – if he calls, I want you to let me know. I want to know immediately. Understand?'

Herman emitted a sigh of exasperation, 'Understood, boss,' he just got in before the line went dead.

So, acting on Andrei's instructions, he'd checked into the Brandenburger Haus Hotel. The name was a whole lot fancier than their accommodation; the room was slightly larger than a coffin, he moaned to himself. Ironically, the bathroom shower was of a size he would have expected from a real three star. The bed was clean and firm with spare pillows and blankets but the TV had a screen scarcely bigger than a Gameboy. How this hotel rated three stars was a mystery to him. 'Was it a reflection on bathrooms?' he wondered.

He had been cruising around the periphery of Orionburgerstrasse area, looking for a cheap bed and a warm place to crap. The location would allow him to walk or take a cab to the hot night-spots but what grabbed Herman's attention, even more than the name or the three stars, was that it offered garaged parking underneath the building. The security of his Mercedes was an uncompromising concern for Herman. He was also pleased to learn that the room offered a refrigerated mini-bar. Aside from some wine, beers, little airline bottles of spirits and soft drinks, there was a tin of mixed nuts, a pack of chocolates, two chocolate bars, and a couple of bags of crisps. He had already devoured both bags of crisps and two Coca-colas. He was now working on an Orange Fanta and the tin of mixed nuts.

So he slowly chewed the nuts and sipped Fanta as he ruminated, hardly conscious of what he was eating. He tried to work out the connection between his boss and Ahmed. It was a business arrangement to be sure, but what? What was transpiring that had caused the Bulls to stop him in the street? Or was it a knee-jerk reaction by the Bulls because he had buzzed the door of Al Nur, and nothing to do with him personally? What exactly had they suspected he might be up to? When they let him go, was it because they believed him? Or were they just slacking the line before reeling him in? He was good at spotting a tail and he didn't think he'd been followed.

Although he had no way of knowing for sure, he revisited his hunch that the tall guy was with the *BKA*, as a local Bull would have cited him for the illegal parking. Herman hadn't been cited, so it suggested to him that the guy had a Federal brief. Okay, but the question remained as to why the *BKA* was nosing around Al Nur. Then the 'T' word dropped into his consciousness and opened up a whole new can of worms: 'Terrorism'. It certainly wouldn't be the first German mosque to nest a terrorist cell. He knew that the group that had planned 9/11 had been based in Hamburg, to the acute embarrassment of the Germans. He'd heard that there were four or five

million Muslims in Germany and that would constitute a mighty big barrel in which to expect no bad
apples.

Herman didn't like Muslims; he'd seen enough of
them in Bosnia from which to form an opinion, and
so, back in Germany, he had avoided them. He
remembered once how the Serbs had raped a bunch
of young Bosnian women while their Muslim fathers
and brothers were forced to watch. Herman had
stood back from the cluster-fuck, but had to chuckle
as he watched some of his comrades lubricate the
girls with hog lard. After they'd had their fill of the
women, they rubbed lard in the men's beards and
then shot them. Evidently, the real terror was not at
the approach of what they probably realized was
inevitable death, but that these Muslims believed that
such a travesty would prevent them from going up to
Paradise. Allah wouldn't brook the pork stench. How
ignorant or primitive could people still be in this
world, he had wondered.

Herman didn't trust the motives of Islamic
activists; in fact, he didn't trust any movement
founded in religion. Nevertheless, he admired the
pluck of the jihad Arabs who thumbed their noses at
the world; it took real panache. He respected the
gutsy undertaking of a suicide bomber and the leaders who could inspire such dedication. These Arabs

were freedom fighters, not slinking jackals like those Bosnian Muslims who beseeched the Western Europeans to do their fighting for them. Palestinians went about their bloody work, killing Zionists with an unrelenting zeal. Herman respected their commitment, and he could fight alongside men of that sinew, so long as they didn't require him to carry a prayer rug.

As a matter of fact, he had rejoiced when seeing those capitalist pigs burning and jumping from the Twin Towers in New York City on 9/11. Now that was a deed worthy of poems and songs. He sorely wished he had been the one to mastermind such a heroic achievement. Yeah, Osama bin Laden and his minions had the right direction, even if it seemed to him that they went there for all the wrong reasons. As far as his regard for Saddam Hussein, well, he felt very little in the way of anything positive. Saddam was a crafty exploiter, like American President Bush and the American oil cabal that the Texan represented. Saddam struck him as a totalitarian who fashioned himself after Stalin. Josef Stalin may have matched that Arab piece of shit when it came to cruelty, but no one had squandered a national treasury with so little to show for as had that feckless Saddam; that was Herman's point of view.

He had not outgrown his orphan mentality, and

was haunted by the nostalgia of a fantasy past. Nobody admitted to being a communist anymore. They acted much like any human being who would watch their football team get their butts whacked every damn game until the disappointment of declaring themselves a fan simply became burdensome. So, if football was in your blood, you made some agonizing excuses and you switched teams. The communists he had known survived the divorce rather nicely, and remarried themselves to anti-globalization, anti-nuclear power, anti-American chauvinism, anti-war – there was a myriad of beguiling 'anti-s' from which to pick.

However, for Herman the problem of picking a new team continued to dog him. Simply put, he wanted to be *for* something, not *against* something; he was a proactive type of guy. All those 'anti-s' didn't raise his passion, but at least the Arab terrorists were fighting *for* something – their land, their liberty, their beloved Allah, whatever. That was the defining difference between protestors and freedom fighters. The protestors whined and pontificated, and marched in the comfort of a huge crowd. Freedom fighters quietly killed their enemies and slipped back into the night. Freedom fighters would sacrifice their lives to change the world while protestors seldom even chose to change their underwear.

Nevertheless, as he thought more and more about it, he realized that he didn't understand for what exactly it was that these Islamic activists were fighting. Was it really for their religion, like ridding the world of Unbelievers? That was his impression, but the fact remained that he knew one could be a freedom fighter for the satisfaction of the fight. Perhaps it was some complex psychological state, or maybe just the simple need for an adrenalin rush. He had gone to Bosnia as a freedom fighter without sharing any of the Slav hatred for those Muslims. So which was the necessary ingredient to catalyze a freedom fighter, a compelling cause or a particular state of mind? Down deep, he had come to realize that he really harboured no *raison d'être* other than his own personal gain, but he was a warrior at heart, a rebel without a cause.

Preoccupied with his thoughts, Herman had just jammed a handful of nuts into his mouth when his mobile phone chirped. Shit! He chewed frantically until finally he felt that he could successfully swallow. While the mobile continued to chirp impatiently Herman grabbed his Orange Fanta and took a cautious swig followed by a couple more hearty ones to clear his mouth and wash the refuse down his throat. He finally answered the call in a heavy breath and strained voice.

'Is everything okay?' a cautious voice quietly asked.

He was almost certain that the fellow on the other end was Ahmed.

'I've got no problem,' he grunted. 'Who is this?'

'I called you earlier, Black Knife. I promised to call you back.'

'I'm listening,' Herman snapped, recalling the advice of his boss.

'You were sent to us by your people because you are an expert in certain matters, yes?'

He had no idea what he was talking about, but he felt reluctant to admit as much, at least at this point. 'Just listen', his boss had insisted.

'Go on,' he urged with a tone of annoyance. He waited through a long a pause, until his patience finally came to an end and he demanded, 'Are you still there?'

'I think we should meet in person. This is a very delicate matter.'

'We already tried that once, and all I met was a bunch of Bulls,' said Hermann, tetchily.

'Yes, I know. I did my best to warn you away,' defended the caller.

'So you knew they were there. How'd you know that?' He realized he was transgressing the boundaries laid out by his boss, but he just couldn't resist pinning this Arab's ass to the wall.

'It was not my doing, but I think I know who may be the one. Please, we must discuss these matters face-to-face.' Another pause, perhaps he was waiting for Herman to fill it, but this time Herman held his tongue.

'If you really can do the job,' the Arab finally continued in what was scarcely more than a whisper, 'you shall be generously rewarded, very generously. They explained that to you, yes?'

Again Herman let the pause run before speaking.

'I'm listening,' he murmured, hoping the Arab would tip his hand and give him a clue as to what game they were playing.

'There is a tea shop in Neukölln,' he said and slowly dictated the address. 'I will meet you there at six o'clock. You have my mobile phone number. If you can't come, then call me. If I hear nothing from you, then I shall expect you. Tell the man in the shop that you wish to buy some Takli tea.'

'Takli,' Herman softly repeated as heard the Arab disconnect.

He laid down his mobile on the night-stand at the side of the bed where he sat. The tin of mixed nuts and his nearly expired bottle of Orange Fanta also huddled on this same night-stand. He absent-mind-edly dipped his fingers into the tin and filled his hand with a fist full of nuts, nearly exhausting the tin. He was about to pop them in his mouth when he consciously realized what he was doing. He grimaced with repugnance as he recalled his last bout with these nuts. He must call Andrei to let the Russian bastard decide what their next move ought to be. He still had no concrete idea what was going on between his boss and the Arab and that was a worry. Whatever Andrei was cooking up with him, it couldn't be good news.

So he held his fist over the tin and released the nuts back into it, brushing the palms of his hands back and forth against each other to brush off the oily refuse and salt granules. Earlier, he had taken off his gloves once he was safely alone in the hotel room. He thought about giving his hand a final wipe on his pants leg, but opted at the last moment for the bed cover instead. Taking a deep breath, he slowly exhaled, and retrieved his mobile phone. The display window showed VODAFONE D2. He hit the arrow button and started scrolling down; it was a short scroll to Andrei. He pressed the centre button and only heard the ringing tone once before he heard the familiar voice give the short salutation.

'Andrei'

'It's Black Knife,' Herman responded, careful not to let the annoyance he felt creep into his tone.

'Yeah?'

'I talked to him.'

'I'm listening.'

He related his conversation with Ahmed, careful to emphasis that what he'd done was listen. He concluded with a question.

'What you want me to do now?'

There was a pause, but when the answer came Andrei's voice was clear and unwavering, 'Kill him.'

'Huh?'

'I said, kill him, shit-speck. He's working for the fucking Bulls.'

'Okay, okay, but that's not going to be as easy as eating a pretzel, you know?'

'I don't eat pretzels.'

Herman didn't like the feel of this assignment. He wanted to know the reason behind his boss's decision to waste the Arab and had a certain curiosity as to who he was.. What kind of influence did he pack; was he a mullah or a terrorist? Or, at the bottom end of the scale, was he just a jerk who'd tried to rip Andrei off? He needed to know; but he knew better than to ask such things of his boss. The Russian would volunteer whatever he felt like telling him, and that would be as much as Black Knife was gonna get.

Realizing that the direct approach wouldn't work,

Herman decided on a flanking action.

'Hey boss, what's in it for me?'

'You're doing it as a personal favour to me, Black Knife,' the Russian responded with a mocking sweetness.

'Something personal?' he fished, 'It might help if I knew what that was, boss.'

'Ahmed betrayed our trust. We can't let that rest, now can we?' came the curt reply.

'I'll have expenses,' whined Herman, 'and there's risk. You say he's a friend of the Bulls? That makes it very risky.'

'You're angling for something, shit-for-brains!' Andrei spat, reverting to his familiar ranting. Then his voice changed back; it was just like he'd hit the button marked 'calm'.

'How much do you have in mind, Black Knife?'

Herman was taken off guard by the sudden switch back to sweetness and light and a small alarm started to tinkle. No threats, no expletives or scorn, a compromising tone, and this was completely out of character for the Russian. He concluded that his boss genuinely wanted this black-ass dead, and he wanted it badly; which made him wonder all the more why the Russian had his mind so solidly set on this. Ahmed works for the Bulls? Maybe it was true, maybe not, but so what? Why should the Russian

Mafia give a hoot? That was a problem for the Islamic activists. How were the Russians mixed up in this?

It had only taken a few seconds for Herman to run this chain of thoughts but it created one of those pregnant silences on the 'phone that oblige the other party to fill them.

'Let me help you, Black Knife. Suppose we keep the same deal, only now I forgive you the hundred thousand you owe me.'

'I get the full hundred and fifty thou in my hand?' he asked, slowly and clearly.

'Yup. Take it or leave it. I have others who can remedy this problem, you know!'

'I get the full one and a half big ones in my hand as soon as I return to Hamburg?' he repeated with a touch of incredulity.

'Done,' Andrei barked and the line disconnected.

Inadvertently, he had just sealed a deal with the Russian Mafia and you didn't back out of a deal with Andrei and his Hamburg gang; they were totally unforgiving, as numerous collections of bones in the mud of the Hamburg docks would attest. Nevertheless, he had a bad feeling about this assignment and Herman had learned never to ignore premonitions. He also knew that, one way or another, Andrei would find cause to dump the agreement for the one-hundred and fifty thousand. He'd learned to his cost that to make a contract with the Russians was, in their eyes, the beginning of real negotiations. Herman might collect fifty thousand, if he was lucky, and he'd have to be content with that. On the other hand, Andrei could make all sorts of generous promises if he intended to dispose of him after the job was done. He didn't like it when actors played a role not in keeping with their character. Andrei was definitely not a generous soul, and so his action was out of character. Herman absent-mindedly reached into the tin and grabbed a handful of nuts, popped the entire heap into his mouth and munched as he reflected.

****

THE DETECTIVE

*Today the terrorists have the will to destroy us, but
they do not have the power. There is no doubt that we
have the power to crush them. Now we must also
show that we have the will to do just that.*
Benjamin Netanyahu

Kriminal Hauptkommisar (Detective Chief
Inspector) Dieter Brückner quietly replaced the telephone back onto its cradle, Andrei had just assured
him that their 'arrangement' was in place. The
Russian had unleashed his black henchman. Dieter
had checked it out by intercepting this fellow at Al
Nur. The *Hauptkommisar* was satisfied that Andrei
had indeed sent his hit man as promised, and pulling
him right there in the Muslim neighbourhood

ensured the word would get back to Al Nur that this black man had been stopped by the Bulls; it provided Black Knife with additional bona fides. However, the overarching reason for the policeman to have done this was in response to Andrei's request that he do so. Evidently he needed a pretext on which to order his hit man to kill the Arab. Dieter accepted the premise without fully understanding the reason why Andrei felt he must justify the hit with his soldier. Dieter wondered if the *Neger* was Muslim but, notwithstanding, he grudgingly granted that sending a black man was a clever touch by the Russian. A lot of the blacks were also Muslim and the Al Nur bunch would be less suspicious of a *Neger* than of a Slav or German.

Andrei wanted once more to hear the solemn guarantee that in return for this 'favour', Brückner would engineer matters in such a way that the imminent arrest of another one of Andrei's goons, Basil, would be sufficiently impeded to allow him to board the next flight to Minsk.

'He stays put,' insisted the *Hauptkommissar* adamantly, 'until I see the results of your *Neger*'s handiwork. When you've carried out your side of the bargain, then I'll let Basil sneak out of here. He can go back to Belarus, or anywhere, as long as it isn't inside Germany, understand? Don't even think about getting ahead of me, Andrei, or I'll have your ass banged up in the Hamburg slammer.'

Since Brückner had initiated the arrest warrant against Basil with the Federal Prosecutor, he was the lead officer who had responsibility for executing the warrant; essentially meaning that he decided when to make the arrest. In this case, he maintained, he needed the results of some lab tests before he proceed, assuming, of course, that the report came back positive. He would apologetically explain to the Federal Prosecutor how the 'shit Russian Mafia' must have gotten word of the warrant through their informants in the massive bureaucracies of government. Then he would offer his most humble apology, 'I'm sorry, sir, but Basil slipped out of the country before we could spread the net. He'd claimed the capsules were penicillin for treating a case of the clap – and there's no way I could distinguish what those capsules contained, sir – and the lab didn't expedite my request for an analysis...' and so on. It was always a safe bet the lab would be slow in returning their report, more degree-qualified jobsworths.

In truth, such compromises within the *Innenministerium* (Interior Ministry) were not an uncommon occurrence. In any event, the Prosecutor would probably not be terribly troubled by this news. His office was overloaded with work, and Basil's flight removed him from circulation in Germany and didn't increase the burden on the prison system. The concept, after all, was to get these criminals off the streets, and that would have been accomplished. Basil would now have to ply his mischief in Minsk and thus the Prosecutor would smugly conclude that Basil was no longer a concern of the German justice system; Belarus could and would have her prodigal son back.

Dieter recalled warning the Russian during their telephone conversation, 'Don't disappoint me, Andrei. If you screw up, it's more than just Basil's sorry balls I'm gonna rip out by the roots. You're the *Kerl* (guy) I hold responsible.' Sometimes, police work required strange bedfellows, he mused with gallows humour. What he had schemed clearly went way beyond his authority. In terms of conventional police work it was way beyond the pale but, no matter, some of the circumstances he faced went way beyond the capacity of the 'law' to control. He comforted himself that it was 'objective-led police work'.

He had worked the Andrei connection through a colleague, Sascha, who was based in Hamburg's St Pauli district. Sascha wanted no visible collaboration in Dieter's plan, but agreed to lay some ground work for him. He understood the system; it was safer for Dieter to recruit from afar, such as in Hamburg, rather than to collaborate with the criminal element in his own Berlin backyard. It would be embarrassing in the extreme to be faced with the dilemma of arresting a goon who could spill his guts and have your badge yanked. In this particular case it would be more than just his badge, as he would serve time in *Alte Moabit* (a notorious old prison) and to be a policeman incarcerated among many of those he'd arrested would be hell on earth, or at least it would be for the brief time he lived.

The problem was *time*! He had somewhere between little and none left. Dieter recalled with a frown the moment he had made his decision and phoned Sascha. Although he had called from his office in Berlin to a *BKA* office in Hamburg, he chose not to use his desk-top telephone. Instead, he had punched the numbers into his mobile phone with an index finger stiffened by resolve. This was and would remain an 'unofficial' call to his *BKA* buddy who had worked with him for eleven years in Berlin before accepting a transfer to Hamburg on promotion. The reason he needed a favour from his old acquaintance was due to a tip from one of his informers, an Arab tea merchant doing business in Berlin and who sometimes acted as a courier for the Al Nur cell.

After the perfunctory pleasantries that quickly

degenerated into a salty exchange of insults, he had come to the point, lowering his voice into a whisper as he did so.

'I need a *cowboy* sascha. Last time I heard, you guys in Hamburg still had plenty of cowboys on the streets.' Sascha hadn't been happy to hear his request and immediately laid down the ground rules.

'I'm just a ghost in this conversation, right? You don't hear me saying anything. This conversation never happened. All you hear is a little voice inside your own dumb fucking head!'

Dieter had carefully explained the situation, as much as he felt he could over the phone, and gradually won his colleague over. Sascha knew only too well that Dieter got results, but it had worried him in the past how far 'outside the box' he was prepared to think and act – the 'box' being the law. Whilst he had patiently explained the potential gravity of what the tea merchant, Mahdjoub, had passed on to him, Sascha had interjected as possible names came to mind and were dismissed as unreliable, in prison or already dead. Just as Dieter had finished making his case, Sascha had come up with a name – 'Andrei.'

'That's the name he works under,' he'd confirmed. 'I can't remember his full handle, but I'll let you have a file number and you can study his CV. He's Russian Mafia running a gang of Slavs in

Hamburg. He owns four dives off the Reeperbahn, and one fairly fancy club in central city. Prostitutes and drugs are his game; he distributes all over Germany.'

'He's a cowboy?' Dieter had muttered dubiously.

'More like a sheriff, but he's got a whole lot of deputies. A guy by the name of Basil takes care of business for him in Berlin. If you could rope the guy and tighten a noose around his neck, then you'd have leverage with Andrei. Basil talks and Andrei goes to jail.'

'You think Andrei would send me a cowboy?' Dieter had asked.

'You're taking about hitting an Arab, right? These Russians are taking out the competition right and left. Arranging a hit on an Arab in Berlin would be business-as-usual for Andrei.'

'So, all I gotta do is put a noose around Basil's neck? If I do, will you introduce me to my new partner?'

'I'm just a ghost, remember?'

'I don't have time, Sascha. Work with me! I promise I'll keep you clean.'

'It's not you that worries me. It's Andrei. He lives in my town, remember?'

'Sascha, a thousand German folks could end up looking like *Rostbratten* that someone forgot to take out of the microwave if I don't get a little help from you!' Dieter hadn't shared with Sascha the full detail he'd received from his informant. According to a very frightened Mahdjoub, the purported target of the Al Nur cell was in fact an American military base, not a German population centre. Further, that the bomb they intended to use would be devastating.

Sascha didn't give him a 'yes', but he didn't say 'no' either and Dieter had found some comfort in that. What he did give him were Basil's details.

'He's got a rap sheet on the computer,' Sascha had added in closing.

That conversation had occurred two days before and on the same evening Dieter had cruised around the discos and lap-dance establishments to do some 'personal' police work. He got lucky; Basil was making a 'delivery'. His well-developed policeman's instinct urged him to go ahead and make the bust and he came up with pay dirt. He guessed it was 'X', fifty capsules. He told the very cocky Basil that he'd best not leave town. That the lab report would take forty-eight hours, and if it came out positive, Basil would be in deep doo-doo. Basil must have been surprised that the Bull hadn't hauled him in. Dieter was in no doubt that his first act after the policeman had left him would have been to call his boss, Andrei. Dieter's first act was to call Sascha, and beseech him to have a short conversation with Andrei.

'Just tell him who I am – you know, that I am who I say! That's all! C'mon, Sascha.' His colleague finally caved in and agreed.

He waited an hour and then telephoned Andrei with the number Sascha had given him. He was pleasantly surprised to find a very cooperative party on the other end. They beat around the bush for a while, feeling each other out. In the event it was Andrei who blinked first.

'What is it you want from me? How much must I pay to keep that ass-hole Basil out of jail?'

'Not money,' Dieter had quietly answered.

'Then what?'

'A favour, one friend to another, what do you say?'

Then Dieter told him as the Russian listened in silence at the other end. When he'd finished, Andrei voiced his doubts.

'Twenty-four hours? My cowboy will need a reason to visit the black-ass, what's his name? Ahmed? They don't let us Orthodox guys in their mosques, you know. We can't do it in twenty-four hours unless you get my man an invitation.'

'How long will it take if I don't?' asked Dieter.

'That's like asking me to predict which will be the coldest day in Moscow this winter. One must wait for an opportunity.'

'And if I get you the invitation, then twenty-four hours?' Dieter noted the pause before the Russian finally answered.

'Yes.'

'Okay, I'll get your cowboy an invitation.'

'What about Basil?' Andrei insisted.

'I'll keep him on ice until the job gets done. Do it, and I'll allow Basil to make a clean run for the border. Now, don't try to get clever with me, Andrei. It's your ass I'll come after if you double-cross me. I'll call you back when I have the invitation.' He disconnected with a flick of his thumb, set down his phone and massaged his forehead at the hairline; a bad headache was building. How in the hell was he going to get Ahmed, who ran the cell, to invite the Russian's hit man into the Al Nur mosque? He sat back in his chair and his head throbbed.

Dieter Brückner was at a dead end in his career. Wiesbaden (HQ *BKA* - Federal Police) had the notion that college graduates in criminology made better policeman that oafs like himself who had worked themselves up through the ranks. Actually, that was the German mentality which extended into almost all fields of endeavour in the country. He was a *Hauptkommisar*, forty-six years old, and that was as far as he could go. He worked for a woman fifteen years his junior; but she had a 'Doctor' in front of her name, a PhD in Forensic Sciences, and she could no more consider thinking 'outside the box' than she could fly. The fact that the team they were playing against didn't have any rules to fetter them seemed to escape her and her ilk. Dinosaurs like Dieter were a worry, even if they did get results which reflected well upon her.

Of course, he resented this discrimination, but being a German he understood and accepted it. Nevertheless, it brought out a maverick streak in him, and he couldn't resist withholding small details that he knew would have Ma'am worrying over her hot chocolate before bed. It didn't require a PhD to work the street; in fact an overly intellectual approach would probably provide a hindrance to the exercise of common sense one needed out there, not to mention a certain panache required when dealing with the hardest criminal elements. He was a tall man with an angular frame which was still well muscled and knew how to use his intimidating size to garner the 'respect' of street denizens. He'd also done an exemplary job of recruiting informers inside the Muslim community, even if the bureaucracy he served only grudgingly admitted this.

The fact was that the *BKA* had infiltrated many of the Islamic terrorist cells in Germany. Not with

Germans, of course, but with Muslim informers willing to serve the *BKA* for a variety of reasons. It might be visas for family members, or visa extensions, or the threat of criminal indictment or deportation for those who had been caught in some illegal activity; it all provided sufficient leverage to turn them. Strangely, money seldom worked as a sole incentive. Dieter had found that informers motivated purely by the prospect of money were usually unproductive, and in some cases even counterproductive. To get a worthy informer, you had to wrap your hand around his balls and squeeze mercilessly.

It was through one such informer that he had learned about the ambitious plan of Ahmed at Al Nur Mosque. Brückner believed his mole, but such a feeling would fall far short of the prerequisite evidence required by the Federal Prosecutor to arrest that little bastard, Ahmed. One turn-coat Arab's word was insufficient grounds for the Ministry of the Interior to act effectively, and it would compromise Brückner's source if he pressed the case prematurely. Yet the nature of the accusation against Ahmed and his Al Nur cell called for immediate action. Hundreds, if not thousands, of lives could well hang in the balance. This was the dilemma he faced. The 'assistance' of Andrei and his Hamburg gang exemplified just such an 'unconventional countermeasure' (essentially illegal actions) just as much as Ahmed of Al Nur illustrated one of those quandaries that the German justice system was poorly equipped to handle.

It was a dilemma facing many policemen during their careers, but no more so than now, with these Islamic terrorists nesting like a cockroach infestation throughout much of Europe. Sure, there had always been European terror groups like the Red Army Faction (Baader-Meinhof gang), ETA, IRA, the Red Brigade, and Neo-Nazi skinhead groups like Combat 18 to keep the European constabulary on alert. But since the Al Qaeda attack on the Twin Towers in New York City the tempo and the magnitude of their threat had gone off the scale.

Terrorism constituted an extreme and unconventional form of warfare. Policemen like Dieter Brückner had to deal with these terrorist groups by employing 'unconventional countermeasures'. His supervisor wouldn't brook leaving the comfort of her box, nor would any of highly paid lawyers, bureaucrats and politicians populating the Ministry of the Interior. The irony was that he did what he had to do at the peril of his pension and risking possible jail time. So, why? He felt the answer in his gut much better than he could ever articulate it in words. He had no hobbies or family, he had his work and little else to anticipate; it was a quest. That and one thing more which he had only recently admitted to himself; he was an adrenalin junkie, he really enjoyed the buzz of the chase. Sometimes towards the end of his summer vacation, he would feel the restlessness, the need to get back on the street.

He'd grown up in a small town south of Stuttgart, and his only immediate family was a younger brother, who had moved his family of four into the house left jointly to him and Dieter by their mother. She had died almost a decade ago and the brother had promised to settle with him over his half of the house, rather than sell it and split the proceeds, which is what he would have preferred. However, his brother had lost his IT job at Hewlett-Packard due to their merger with Compaq and their outsourcing of IT to Spain and India and had a family to support, whereas he had merely himself to worry about. He didn't feel, therefore, that he could insist on the sale. In any event, he had enough money for his immediate needs and was totally absorbed in his work.

He took his main vacations in the Canary Islands every July or August, and shorter stints at odd times during the year to the North Sea. He drove a BMW 328i, the SE variant which gave him nearly two hundred horsepower under his right foot when he needed it. He'd have liked an M3, which rated over three hundred of the same horses, but it was outside his budget by about thirty per cent, but then he'd promised himself he might just stump up the money when he retired. Dieter had had a string of romances which invariably turned into tedious affairs because his job left him insufficient time for the demands of a relationship. Moreover, in his police work he'd probably seen too much of life's darkest side, which probably impeded the necessary trust of a fellow human being sufficient to form a lasting relationship. Thus, he really didn't need the money. Automobile, vacation and work (emphasis on the retirement benefit it provided!) in that order were the driving forces in a German's life. Notably, marriage was often not on the short list. He realized that he was German to the core, a condition he uneasily accepted.

'Mahdjoub' was what Dieter's informer inside Al Nur called himself. It matched one of the names in the string of Arabic gibberish on his passport. Actually, the Arab was not an active member of the Al Nur cell. Mahdjoub was a tea wholesaler who, in addition to making business trips to auctions in the Middle East and the subcontinent, couriered cash destined for Ahmed and generously provided by certain Islamic 'charities'; the cell in Al Nur was one of the beneficiaries. There had been a law, the *Geldwaeschegesetz*, introduced to limit the amount of instruments or foreign cash equivalents to the value of twenty thousand Deutschmarks into the *Bundesrepublik* without making the appropriate declaration. When Germany changed from Marks to Euros, the law didn't change, it was merely amended to reflect the amount and denomination of their new currency. Mahdjoub was caught with roughly seventy thousand US dollars cash which he had not declared, a sum well in excess of the limits.

Mahdjoub, the tea merchant, had been betrayed by an informer already trapped in Dieter's network. It was in this way that a streetwise policeman could slowly and laboriously spin his web, meticulously filling in the rest of the strands once he'd secured these primary filaments. Each new informer would produce his own brood until, at last, the policeman had established for himself a respectable stable.

He trusted Mahdjoub more than most of his other informers. That's because the tea merchant was not an Islamic activist. He had been intimidated by the cell to act as a courier for them, and his only accrued benefit from the service would come from Allah. Ahmed had assured Mahdjoub that Allah would surely greet him in Paradise and present the tea merchant with the now almost obligatory seventy-two *Houris* (young virgins) well as returning the fortunate Mahdjoub to age thirty and blessing him with a hundred times his original virility that would last an eternity.

It was an interesting fantasy, Mahdjoub granted, but he didn't buy into it. Dieter recalled that having once engaged him on this subject, Mahdjoub had wondered what would become of his dear wife while he was dabbling with the *Houris*. There would be no account books or tea inventories for her to mind up there. Allah, in all his wisdom, had better not admit her to Paradise, or those poor *Houris* would be in dire jeopardy. What did compel the tea merchant to comply with the wishes of Ahmed were certain consequences to Mahdjoub, his family and his business if the cell in Al Nur was offended by a rebuff; Ahmed had insinuated as much.

Lately, in addition to carrying money for Ahmed, he would also carry messages. Nothing was ever written down; Mahdjoub was given verbal communications to pass on to the cell at Al Nur. The tea merchant had been reminded very forcefully by Ahmed regarding the sanctity of this mission. To betray the cause would infuriate Allah who would cast Mahdjoub straightaway into Hell; and Mahdjoub's family would suffer dire consequences, probably joining him there in short order. So it was with extreme trepidation that Mahdjoub had revealed to the *Hauptkommissar* this recent communication from Ahmed's associates in Florence, Italy.

Intelligence had already determined that the Russians, an entirely different group than Andrei's Hamburg gang, had provided the material for a dirty bomb, and that it had been smuggled into Italy. The new information provided by Mahdjoub suggested that this bomb was being constructed for delivery to Ahmed in Germany. The deal for the radiological material and necessary explosive core had been cut by the Florence cell, according to one of Mahdjoub's memorized messages. But this was somewhat contradicted by the mention of Milan as well. It was far from clear to Dieter whether the actual work would be carried out in Florence or in Milan and, further, his Italian counterparts had numerous locations in each city which might be used as the 'factory'. They, like all forces in Europe, were under-resourced and overstretched and Dieter knew that if they were pushed to make a raid which came up empty handed, the terrorists would have been put on notice, and Mahdjoub's treachery might be exposed as well. Further, Dieter Brückner didn't want to see that bomb smuggled onto German soil, but at one and the same time he was afraid to prematurely expose his source. He'd previously experienced enough disasters trying to work through the tortuous German legal system and was further horrified at the prospect having to coordinate with the Italians.

Thus, *Hauptkommisar* Brückner elected to launch a pre-emptive strike – to have Ahmed killed. After all, Ahmed was the head cockroach in this Al Nur nest. At the very least it would cause confusion and indecision amongst the terrorists involved in this plot. Okay, he impatiently admitted, this was a desperation move, no question, but if it could buy him some precious time, then it was worth his own personal risk. If he was indeed dealing with a 'dirty bomb' that would spread radioactivity all over the place it would be worth it. The people and the press had gasped at a train wreck two years ago that killed two people and injured about fifty. What would be the reaction to a terrorist act somewhere in Germany that killed or gravely injured hundreds, in time maybe thousands? It would be Germany's own mini-Chernobyl.

His pre-emptive action was clearly necessary, yet he had a more concrete objective in mind than to simply to buy time. He also hoped that by eliminating the leader of this Al Nur cell, it might discourage the terrorists from bringing their bomb into Germany after all. They would be faced with a disrupted command and control, and it would leave them suspicious of a leak somewhere in the organization. Let them blow it up in Rome or Florence or Milan, he coldly decided, that would be an Italian problem; his primary responsibility was to Germany.

So, the next morning he had arranged a rendezvous with the tea merchant and put the squeeze on him. Mahdjoub had met him with the information about his latest couriered messages to Al Nur which, of course, had initiated the ensuing chain of events. A seemingly innocuous conversation which he had initially let pass as not noteworthy had now become the foundation of a plot to get Andrei's hit man an invitation into the Mosque. Shafiq, Mahdjoub's contact in the Florence cell, had asked him how Ahmed would arrange to get the 'package' onto an American military base in Germany. Mahdjoub had answered that he was only a messenger, and had no idea. When Mahdjoub relayed this question to Ahmed, he had, apparently, simply raised his eyes heavenward and uttered, 'Allah shall provide.'

This was the foundation upon which Dieter had built his shaky construct, it was all he had, but his nose and experience told him it was enough. He needed to get Andrei's cowboy inside that mosque in reach of Ahmed. Pointing a stern finger, he had instructed Mahdjoub.

'Tell Ahmed that you forgot one of the messages and just remembered it. Tell him the Arab in Florence wanted him to know that the Russian who had brokered the 'merchandise' has also suggested this colleague of his in Hamburg who might be able to help with the 'delivery' of the 'package'. Then tell Ahmed they gave you his telephone number, you wrote it down, and suddenly remembered it this morning when you found it in your pocket.' Dieter again extended his finger and jabbed the hapless tea merchant in the chest.

'And Mahdjoub, you must convince Ahmed that this is a very good idea, because if they get that shit into Germany, you won't have to worry about Al Nur anymore. I'll get to you first!'

At first Mahdjoub's eyes had filled with terror, and he had wrung his hands as he began to pace in small circles muttering in Arabic and occasionally glancing heavenwards as if expecting an answer from Allah himself. Dieter brought him back to earth by simply commenting, 'Mahdjoub, how would you like me to start visiting your shop every afternoon and give you hugs and pats on the back? What would the Al Nur cell think about your having a policeman as a bosom buddy?'

He returned to his office and then called Andrei. 'You'll be getting your invite. Once my lab report comes back concerning the capsules Basil was carrying, I have no choice but to arrest him. So for Basil's sake – and for your own – I hope you act on it promptly.'

'What's the story?' Andrei had asked and Dieter had explained that he should be convincing that he had the means and opportunity to deliver Ahmed's 'package' wherever he wanted it, and that he would be sending one of his best men to make contact. That had been the day before. The call had come and Andrei had sent his enforcer, Black Knife, to do the job.

****

MAHDJOUB

Herman elected to go by cab to Neukölln. He wasn't
particularly familiar with this area of Berlin and,
recalling the slummy neighbourhood surrounding Al
Nur, didn't wish to run the risk of his precious car
getting vandalized. Moreover, he thought that
Neukölln might have been the borough of Berlin
where the mosque had been located, but he wasn't
certain. One of the downsides of using the GPS system in his car was that you tended to arrive without
too much idea where you were. At least using a map
you usually placed your destination within the con-
text of other landmarks. Also entering his calcula-
tions was the simple fact that he had no idea what
awaited him at this meeting. Not having to worry
about his car gave him more flexibility, and it cer-

tainly offered one less means of identifying him. He hadn't forgotten about his confrontation with that big Bull near Al Nur.

He had shown the driver Ahmed's address and then negotiated without a clear idea of just how far his destination might be. The cabbie refused to budge below sixty Euros and, judging by that, it was going to be a long ride and Herman now feared that maybe he had cut the time a bit too fine.

'Get me there by six and I'll give you a hundred,' he had offered. The cabbie had gunned his engine and taken off with squealing tires. Herman had opted for the passenger-side front seat. 'Safety-belt,' the cabbie curtly reminded.

'Don't need it, slow as you're driving,' Black Knife sneered.

'It's a fifty Euro fine,' the cabbie had warned.

He knew that the fellow had exaggerated about how much the Bulls would fine him, if caught. 'He must think I'm an *Ausländer*,' Herman reflected, having concluded that the driver was German and, furthermore, judged from his accent that the guy was a former East German and guessed he was about fifty years old. Every region of Germany had dialects that made it nearly impossible for a visiting German to comprehend what was being garbled in the native brogue. These dialects left an indelible inflection in the way Germans from a given region spoke *Hoch-Deutsch* (high German), the largely unaccented language used, for instance, by newscasters on the TV. The distinction of these regional dialects represented more than just a Texas drawl versus nasal New Yorker, it could be compared more precisely to Ebonics in the American language. Thus, even when one German spoke *Hoch-Deutsch* to another German, he usually gave away his geographical origins.

'Look at this traffic,' the cabbie complained. 'It's that time of the afternoon – *Feierabend* - rush hour, everybody's going home, all them lucky enough to have a job anyway,' he added with a sneer.

'Yup, he's an *Ossie*,' (a resident of the former DDR) Herman concluded with some conviction; they were chronic moaners. Of course, Herman was also an *Ossie*, albeit by adoption rather than birth, but he had retained some of the good-natured African genes, at least that is how he saw himself compared to these grim Prussians.

'Where'd you come from?' the cabbie inquired.

Herman sensed from the fellow's relaxed disposition that their six o'clock deadline seemed likely.

'Africa,' he replied as he glanced at the taxi-driver's license displayed on the dashboard. He saw his name Joachim Dresdener.

'And you, Joachim, where you from, Dresden?' he chuckled.

'*Nein!*' The driver winced as he glanced away from the traffic to take a second look at his passenger. No doubt Herman wasn't the first fare to confuse the cabby's name with his origins. He didn't see the implied joke and went on rather stiffly, 'My family lived in a village near the Oder about sixty kilometres east of Berlin. When I was twenty-four, I managed to 'cross over'. After the Wall came down, I got married and rented an apartment in Wedding; but no longer.' He paused, clearly expecting his passenger to prod him further with the question of where he now lived.

Herman wasn't sure if the man meant he was no longer married, or no longer lived in Wedding, but he definitely knew what Joachim had meant by 'crossing over'– fleeing from East Berlin into the Western Sector. Dresdener was one more renegade from the socialist cause. He and his ilk were partly to blame for the failure of socialism. He didn't want to hear any more, so he remained silent as he stared straight ahead through the windshield.

A few drops of rain had started to collect there and he glanced at the outside temperature display on the cabby's instrument panel – four degrees C. That was still too warm for snow but as he looked up at the grey sky he thought to himself, 'Oh well, it is November, a German must expect cold rain at this time.' Actually, the weather had turned unusually bitter that past weekend; it was only the first week of November but the weather behaved as if it were already the last week. 'So much for global warming!' he thought.

Finally, the driver pressed on with his Joachim Dresdener story.

'The shit-Turks took over our neighbourhood in Wedding and we finally had to move,' he spat. It would be a safe gripe to air in non-Turkish company. Herman clearly was not Turkish. Most Germans now shared a disdain for these immigrant Mongols. Officially, there were three million Turks in Germany, but everybody accepted the truth that the real figure was probably closer to five. They had been brought in during the sixties and seventies under a *guest-worker* program. In those days the West German industrial machine could not draw enough unskilled workers from their own population. The war had chewed up a huge portion of a male generation, and many who had survived were disabled or badly mentally scarred. So guest workers from Turkey, Spain, Portugal, Italy and even Greece had been invited, but the largest portion to respond to the beckoning finger of German industry came from

Turkey. Later, the majority had elected to stay, although they were denied citizenship. Even children of these workers born in Germany and schooled there did not qualify for citizen status.

Then came reunification, coupled with the ever increasing burden of the federal and state governments' 'social net' and unemployment sky-rocketed, as did taxes. With the introduction of the Euro, a stealthy inflation robbed the population of even more purchasing power. The high unemployment, ranging above ten per cent, created a lot of quiet resentment towards the 'guest workers' amongst blue-collar Germans, especially the ones out of work. Nevertheless, disdain for the Turks was 'politically incorrect' in a Germany acutely conscious of recent history, and most were reluctant to start pointing the finger at any ethnic group. However, there were still being heard the contemptuous remarks concerning the *Ausländers,* albeit through brief whispers at dinner tables, and heady discourse during the late hours inside neighbourhood bars and beer gardens.

The traditional 'enemy of the people', the Jews, were still being held to account for many of the woes of unemployed Germans. However, this time it was because they were to blame for the constant unrest in the Middle East which affected oil prices and led to world tension. Another favourite conspiracy theory was that Jews controlled the American economy, thereby wielding immense political clout. 'That's why the Americans were so pro-Zionist at the expense of those poor Palestinians,' the more liberal would carp. The theory was that the Jews wanted the Iraqi oil and they secretly controlled Haliburton, making them the chief contributors to the Republican Party's coffers. However, on balance, the poor Turks had nevertheless displaced the Jews in German *Angst*. Curiously, this time, unlike sixty years before, the outsiders threatened the blue-collar population, instead of the intelligentsia, the artists and the professionals.

Most Germans made sure they could point to an exemplary Turk they had befriended, and therefore demonstrated they weren't racists. Yet, privately, they shared a kinship with the Neo-Nazis on the issue of a growing xenophobia. It was as it always is, so easy to focus the root of all society's ills on an immigrant group. It was true that Turkish 'ghettos' were dirty by German standards and distinctly Turkish. Many of the women dressed in their distinguishing Muslim headscarves and long grey street coats, slinking behind the men as they dragged along their brood of little ones. The sight of that irritated the progressive-minded feminists as well.

The young Turkish men treated German girls as if

they were whores. Certainly their conduct towards them was of a much lower standard than their behaviour towards Muslim girls, the ones they would ultimately marry. Germans did not want to recognize this tension between themselves and the Turks, but they all shared in it. Unlike the recognized racist attitudes prevailing in America, 'Germany was free of such travesties', they stubbornly maintained. Being black, Herman knew from first-hand experience that this was a myth, but their holier-than-thou bullshit didn't particularly disturb him. He didn't give a shit about what the Germans thought of him. He made himself a decent living and he hustled plenty of native pussy, so he was a happy camper here in Germany. His dissatisfaction came from within himself; he was a dreamer who, thus far, had found his dreams out of reach. He wanted to be a warrior hero, he wanted them to write poems and sing songs about him.

'Too bad,' he responded matter-of-factly to the driver's lamentation over having to move away from Wedding. He had glanced at his watch. It was six minutes to six.

'How much longer?'

'It's not *me,*' Joachim Dresdener whined defensively, 'it's this shit traffic!'

'Are we going to be late?' asked Herman coldly.

'It depends on the traffic,' the driver stubbornly insisted.

Herman felt tempted to remind this fellow that the hundred Euros were contingent upon a prompt six o'clock arrival but thought better of it, clearly it would serve no purpose except to irritate the cabby.

'Are they predicting snow?' he asked instead.

'Tonight, yes, but it won't settle. No ice on the roads, that's what's important.'

So, the weather offered another good reason not to have driven his Mercedes, he noted with self-congratulations. His thoughts now turned to the mission at hand. What exactly was the angle these Russians were playing in this game with Ahmed? More to the point, exactly how was he going to execute the sonovabitch. He had only a knife in his arsenal and presumed they would search him. If not, then the lax security surrounding Ahmed would allow his knife all the latitude he needed.

There could be no way of planning this 'hit'. He would have to play it entirely by ear, which was not an uncommon approach for Black Knife. Plans were often more of a hindrance than a help. He knew what he had to do and he would recognize the appropriate moment to execute his brief when it occurred. However, the question as to why Andrei had dispatched him for this 'hit' remained a total mystery, but he had to admit that wasn't an entirely unfamiliar situation for him, either.

What did Ahmed have in mind when he had dangled out a significant reward if Black Knife could perform his 'specialty' on the Arab's behalf? What exactly did he consider to be Black Knife's specialty, Herman wondered? Was it simply a ruse to lull him into letting his guard down? But of what use would this be to the Arab? He suspected that Ahmed had a legitimate offer to make. Should Black Knife be disposed to even listen? That would also be something he would decide on the spur of the moment. He had settled on his familiar *modus operendi*: keep thinking to a minimum, and awareness to a maximum. Trust your instincts, and act on them without hesitation.

He glanced at his watch. *Scheisse!* It was a minute before six and they were stuck in a *Stau*, a traffic jam. He read the sign, *DREIECK NEUKÖLLN,* it was a three-way convergence of major city thoroughfares and let out a quiet moan and then demanded, 'How much longer?'

'It's not my fault,' the cabby bleated. 'Six o'clock is *Feierabend* in Berlin, you must expect such delays!'

'*Richtig*, it's not your fault, okay. How long?'

'Five or ten minutes.'

Herman shrugged and silently consoled himself.

'Well, Ahmed lives in Berlin, so he ought to know that a five or ten minute delay at this time of day is not unusual.'

They finally got there and, as he had suspected, Joachim Dresdener's estimate had been optimistic, as it was almost twenty past six. He struggled for a moment as to whether he should pay the cabby his hundred Euros, or withhold the promised bonus and pay the sixty as originally demanded. 'Fuck him,' he muttered under his breath, rationalizing that he hadn't asked the asshole to make an unrealistic promise and handed Dresdener a fifty Euro note.

'You promised a hundred,' the cabby protested.

'You're twenty minutes late,' Herman growled. 'Don't push it.'

'I said sixty for the fare!'

'And I said six o'clock, *Arschlöch,* and I don't have time to argue. You don't like it, call the fucking Bulls.' He dropped the fifty Euro note on the cabby's lap, hauled himself out of the car and without looking back, extended his middle finger in the internationally understood gesture, 'Sit on that and swivel, *Ossie,*' he muttered to himself as he took stock of his surroundings. Somewhere behind him he heard some reference to '*Neger,*' but was already concentrating on the task in hand too much to be interested.

The storefront numbered twenty-nine appeared to

be a wholesale tea distributor, he had expected a café or similar where you sat down and ordered a cup of tea; the Arabs, he knew, were into tea. The lettering on the store entrance was not in Arabic script, but in Turkish, he hadn't expected that, either. However, there was some Arabic in smaller print under the more prominent Turkish. Again, a wrought-iron grate protected the door and steel roller-shutters covered the storefront windows, which was unusual at this hour. In Germany, government offices usually close at five o'clock and at the latest six. Retail shops had, up to two years previously, had to close no later than 6.30. However, the law had been changed to allow stores to remain open until eight o'clock. The commercial aspirations of large chain stores had prevailed over the staunch objection from small retailers.

He had stopped in front of the door to number twenty-nine and paused to gather his thoughts as he heard the taxi squeal away. What was it Ahmed had said? Takli, yes, Takli tea is what he was supposed to request. He checked up and down the street, there were storefronts all along this side of the avenue. On the other side was a construction site and, by comparison to this side of the street, it looked orderly, he scoffed. Paper, cellophane wrappers, cigarette butts, discarded styrene cups and empty packages, tin cans and mounds of other, indistinguishable refuse littered the pavement and gutter on this side. He wondered if the Turks brought their garbage from the mother country to decorate Germany in a way that made them feel more at home, like a vulture's nest – all shit and sticks. 'What *Schwein*!' he thought to himself.

The orphanage where Herman had been raised instilled an almost obsessive sense of hygiene and cleanliness in the kids it warded. It was an upbringing that stuck as 'Sam' metamorphosed into Herman after his arrival in Germany. Of course, the Germans were no slouches when it came to a sense of cleanliness, other than their infrequency for taking a bath. He'd heard more than one blonde, blue-eyed *Frau* explain that soaping the hair and skin too often would have a drying effect and cause a premature aging look. Clearly, the pale European skin was more delicate than his tough African hide. He tried to shower every morning and used soap with no apparently detrimental effects. Evidently, Americans didn't share this German folklore either; Polly showered with Axe bath gel before and after their 'sexual adventures' and then again in the morning together with him. He had often reflected with satisfaction how she liked doing it in the shower.

Back in the reality of the street, Herman saw that there was a buzzer at the side of the door accessible through the metalwork of the gate, just like he'd seen at Al Nur. He took a deep breath and was about to extend his index finger and press it when the door behind the grate opened. The fellow standing in the open doorway behind the grate was short and rather portly. He wore spectacles and a knit skullcap, but otherwise was dressed in Western-style clothes. He definitely had Middle Eastern features, the swarthy skin colour, prominent nose, wide mouth, and sported a luxuriant Saddam Hussein moustache. If this was Ahmed, Herman had envisioned him quite differently. The fellow standing before him was the epitome of a harmless storekeeper.

'May I help you?' he softly inquired.

'Are you Ahmed?'

The little Arab eyed him warily before finally answering.

'No, and as you can see, we are closed for the day. Is there something you need?'

'Takli tea,' Herman carefully enunciated.

The fellow took a step back, pulled a large bunch of keys from his trousers pocket and selected one of them. Stepping forward, he inserted the key, and turned the lock releasing the grate. As he swung the heavy metal grate open, he gestured with his other hand that Herman should enter. Stepping into the badly lit interior, Herman's senses were at their highest state of readiness. The first thing they detected was the unusual smell; he'd already encountered the usual stench of the ethnic areas outside but this, although pungent, was a cleaner smell, difficult to qualify. It was too subtle to be characterized as spicy, but too vague to call it musty. He didn't find it a particularly pleasant aroma and guessed that it came from the vast array of teas, gathered in open bins which he could now make out in the low light. The bins formed four rows, two to each side of him and extended to a counter top, perhaps twelve or fifteen metres away. A woman sat behind the counter, seemingly attending to ledgers, either affecting or practicing disinterest in the visitor. She wore the typical Muslim headscarf which completely hid her hair and most of her forehead and face and didn't even glance up.

What little light there was came from some dusty and poorly maintained fluorescent tubes which were suspended from the ceiling and which were festooned with ancient cobwebs. Several of them flickered for the want of a new tube or starter, which added to the alien scene. As Herman patiently waited for the Arab to close the grate he continued scanning the area he could see, gleaning what information he could. The wrought-iron gate was swung closed, but Herman noted that he didn't lock it, another small piece of information which he filed away. 'Who might come through the unlocked gate whilst he was distracted by this fat little shopkeeper,' he wondered, 'Ahmed?

The little fellow now approached Herman as he glanced at his watch.

'It is almost time for *Isha*,' he said, 'our evening prayers,' he clarified. 'You will have to excuse me for a few minutes please, my wife can bring you some tea, yes?'

'How about coffee?' asked Herman, never having been a lover of tea.

'I'm sorry, none is brewed here,' the little Arab offered apologetically, 'This is a *tea* warehouse,' he said as he gestured about him with his hands.

'Who are you?' asked Herman bluntly.

'I am Mahdjoub, but that is of no consequence to you. You will be taken to Ahmed. He is at Al Nur to perform *Isha*.'

'Then why the fuck did he tell me to come here?' he asked, not disguising his irritation.

The shopkeeper shrugged apologetically, 'You shall be taken to him.'

'Are you taking me?' asked Herman, taking another precautionary look around the gloomy interior.

'No. Others are taking you,' replied the little fellow, 'Please wait. Are you sure you won't have some tea?'

Herman shook his head decisively. Mahdjoub glanced at his watch impatiently.

'Then you'll excuse me please. I must go to pray.' He turned away and briskly paced towards the counter, slipping sideways through the raised flap between two sections. His wife glanced up at him and, although Herman discerned no gesture or other expression from the man, she grunted to her feet, retrieved her ledger book, and followed him as he opened a door positioned behind where she had been sitting, and the pair passed out of sight, closing the door behind them.

Herman was immediately on his guard, every instinct told him there was something wrong with this picture, but what and why? Why had Ahmed instructed him to come here? He looked for other entrances into the store other than that through which he'd entered and the one through which that Muslim pair had just exited. He sensed a set-up; he could smell it through the pungent odour of the tea which surrounded him. Backing into a gap between a couple of the bins he positioned himself so he couldn't be easily jumped. He checked the ceiling: nothing caught his attention, no hatchways, no holes. Still the basic question haunted him, 'Why the fuck would he be a target? Into what kind of intrigue had Andrei delivered him up and why? You could never be sure what those devious Russian motherfuckers had up their sleeves.

Then he heard it, but by the time he saw what caused the faintest rustle, it was too late. The guy had apparently been huddled behind the row of tea bins to his far left and Herman was now staring down the barrel of an automatic. 'Shit!' he rebuked himself for obligingly walking into something so easy. Then a second noise came from his right side and he slowly turned his head, no sudden movement. What he saw didn't surprise him; there was a second guy with a handgun in the classic double-handed grip. The thought immediately crossed his mind that if he ducked below the tea bins and scurried away, their line of sight would be obstructed and their chances of scoring a fatal hit somewhere between slim and none. But scurry to where? The front door was closed but he didn't think it was locked and then, behind it, was a closed grate. They could empty their ten-round mags at him in the time it would take him to swing both these obstacles open. Then again, he could make a run up front and try to get through the door where that storekeeper and his woman had exited, but there was a chance they had locked it. Besides, where would he go from there? No, the sensible option was to stand fast and see how it played out. Maybe they were his escorts to Ahmed.

The nearest of the two gestured with his gun that Herman should raise his hands, and he duly obliged. Then the gunman indicated that he should come forward out of the protection of the angle in the barrels he'd chosen, as he himself stepped around to the open aisle in the middle of the shop. Herman took a few moments to study them as he slowly and carefully complied with their directions. He didn't know if he was dealing with a pair of nervous amateurs who'd blow him to hell if he farted unexpectedly. They were both of some form of Arab extraction and were dressed in black sweatshirts and wore the floppy Afghani hats, Pakols, not traditional headdress. Herman had seen those hats on the newsreels and wondered if these two had seen any action. They were clearly used to working together – nothing said, just eye contact and posture were enough. The guy in the aisle shoved his pistol into the back of the waistband of his trousers whilst the other retained his steady two-handed grip, his weapon aimed unwaveringly at Herman's head. He felt an ease and experience about these two and was, in a way, relieved. They wore dark beards, in both cases generously streaked with grey; they were no spring chickens, but they each had a weapon which made up for any physical deficiency. They didn't appear nervous, which gave him peace of mind. A nervous trigger finger was what made neophytes more dangerous than their professional counterparts.

As Herman waited for the next move he continued to size them up. Neither one of them appeared very robust. They both were a good four inches shorter than him, he guessed, and probably twenty pounds lighter. They could have been brothers, and in that light it was hard to distinguish them with certainty. The guy approaching him stopped about three metres in front of him and smiled, exposing several missing teeth. The smile was a very good sign, Herman thought, but remained alert.

'We have been told to take you to Ahmed,' he said in reasonable German. His intonation sounded like those man-on-the-street Palestinians sometimes interviewed on the German TV documentaries. It had always puzzled Herman as to why any Palestinians would bother to learn German. English, yes, but German? He glanced sidewise to confirm the other Arab was still covering him. It would still be a bad time to make a move, even though he was sure he could take the Arab nearest to him in seconds.

'We must search you for weapons,' the affable guy in front of him said, almost apologetically. 'We're taking you to Al Nur. It would offend Allah if you were to bring a weapon into his house of prayer.'

'Not to mention offending Ahmed,' Herman added in his own mind as the little guy took a step forward, and then stopped.

'Do you have a weapon?' he asked.

Now Herman had to make a split-second decision. He carried his blade on his left forearm in a lightweight breakaway sheath. He'd installed it while in his hotel room and the sleeve of his leather jacket dutifully hid it to all but prying eyes. However, under the jacket he was wearing a short-sleeved T-shirt, so if they asked him to remove his jacket, the knife would be exposed. The arm of his leather jacket was flexible enough for him to slide it up to the elbow and retrieve his knife in one fluid motion. His conclusion was that these two probably weren't formally trained in the art of the body search and, secondly, if they did find it, he could always plead that he thought they meant a handgun, not the knife.

'*Nein,*' he answered without further hesitation, 'I left my heat in the hotel room. I wouldn't offend Ahmed by bringing a gun here.'

The Arab standing before him looked over to his colleague and gestured with a subtle nod of his head, then turned back to Herman and broke into another Gap Tooth smile. In his peripheral vision, Herman caught the motion of the other Arab moving. He mentally tracked his quiet footfalls, the guy was moving down the aisle so that when he came back it would be from the direction of the front door, now behind Herman. 'Gap Tooth', as Herman had named him in his own mind, wasn't going to frisk him until his partner was behind him and at very close range. No doubt the muzzle of his handgun would still be pointing unwaveringly at Herman's head.

In the event their plan was a bit different than he had surmised. As he stood there with raised arms staring at Gap Tooth, his colleague came up from behind and patted Herman down. He started at the calves and worked his way up the thighs, butt, torso, chest, back – but, not the arms which Herman had fully extended as high as he could stretch them. When he'd finished he spoke to his colleague and Gap Tooth indicated that Herman could lower his arms.

'Thanks, Allah,' Herman silently muttered, feeling a heady relief.

****

THE BLACK KNIFE

The weapon that had become Black Knife's trademark hadn't been his idea at all and its discovery had just been one of those chance encounters. He had been in a bar in Remscheid, in his early days working with the Russians, having come south from Hamburg with Andrei to deliver some goods and to collect a particularly stubborn debt. Andrei was to talk to the small-time dealer that owed him the money and if he paid up it would be the end of the matter. If he didn't, or continued prevaricating, then Andrei would withdraw to a place where he'd have a solid alibi and Herman would do what he was paid for. Andrei would have to write off the debt but word would spread, particularly if the murder was brutal, and would save him some problems in the future.

Herman was quietly enjoying a *Viertel* of white wine with a bratwurst and potato salad when a bit of a commotion broke out at the bar. An elderly man, Herman guessed he was about eighty, was staggering back as a big fellow in a leather jacket poked him in the chest and shouted abuse at him. It looked like a very uneven match and Herman wondered if he should intervene. After one last stream of abuse, the big fellow balled up his fist and it was clear he was really intent on inflicting some damage on the older guy. In the blink of eye, Herman saw the old guy slip his right hand up the left sleeve of his tweedy jacket, and then his hand moved as fast as a cat's paw. With a scream of pain the big fellow fell back, holding his hands to his face. The older guy followed him and Herman could see he now held a blade lightly in his right hand. It was about seven inches long and it was clear the older man was familiar with its use. His erstwhile assailant now had his back to the bar and was staring in disbelief at the blood on his hands and feeling gently at the gash across his face that started at his right nostril and finished near his ear.

'You old bastard!' he had shouted, 'You've cut me.'

'I'll do more than cut you if come near me again,' the old man had grumbled as he stopped advancing towards the bleeding protester. What he didn't see was that one of the younger man's friends was sliding his hand around the neck of a bottle of Dortmunder Union beer, with the clear intention of going for the old man from behind. As he made a step forward, he felt a strong hand grip his wrist and another wrap itself around his wind pipe, the fingers digging deep into his throat. Gasping for breath, he dropped the bottle and tried to struggle free, but Herman held him and pulled him backwards off balance. In a few moments he was unconscious slid to the floor. The old man had turned, realizing what had happened and how close he'd come to being whacked from behind, a silly mistake.

'Thank you, friend,' he had said as he slipped the blade back into the sleeve and motioned for Herman to join him for a drink. Herman was fascinated by the knife and asked his new-found friend to show him how it was sheathed. The old man reluctantly drew up his sleeve to expose the neat sheath which was secured to his arm by two soft leather straps. These had small elasticated gussets which allowed the muscles of the forearm to flex whilst still holding the sheath in place; the straps were fastened by flat buckles. It transpired that during the last war he had worked for the knife and sword makers Eickhorn, in Solingen, producing the ceremonial edged weapons the Nazis so enjoyed. When, in 1940, he had finished his apprenticeship his skill had been recognized and he had been commissioned to make some special hunting knives and daggers for Herman Göring. This brought him into contact with a leading figure in the Gestapo who had asked him to design the knife in the forearm sheath. It had been a simple adaptation of the *Fliegerkorps* dagger, with the tang flattened out instead of the rounded grip and the wide cross-piece of the original modified. In the end, he had made several and retained some after the war. He had told Herman his special skills and contact with the likes of the Gestapo and SS had served him well; after all he'd never been drafted into the army and, consequently, had not perished on the Russian front like so many of his peers.

Herman was so taken with this knife that he'd asked the old man to make him one. At first he had grumbled that he'd lost his skills and that his arthritic fingers wouldn't allow him to do such fine work but in the end he couldn't resist the challenge or the premium sum Herman was offering him. Thus it was that Herman acquired the first Black Knife that was to become his trademark. The buckles of the original were superseded by modern Velcro but, ostensibly, it was still the weapon that had been designed all those years before by a German craftsman. In the end, he made Herman five knives, which he cherished.

EUCOM – WAITING FOR THE WORD

johnsona@eucom.mil was Polly's 'business' e-mail address at work. It was provided by the government for unrestricted messages, and personal correspondence could masquerade as business so long as it didn't involve abuse of privilege. You didn't need a judge-advocate lawyer to distinguish the difference between a note from a friend and a naughty co-ed's dormitory room video-cam website or the 'Texas Hold'em' tables at *Paradisepoker.com*. For her serious business, the government had provided an entirely different signals platform. Nobody sent her chatty messages on that set-up. It provided 256 bit encryption, which were one or two orders of magnitude above what most secret Swiss banking transactions used.

It was six o'clock in the evening and her digestive system was beginning to send her nasty e-mails informing her that gastric juices were standing by and blood-sugar levels were dipping. She was waiting for the signals platform to send her some serious business from Langley. The Command Staff here at EUCOM wanted more information on the alleged nuclear material smuggled into Italy, which one source had speculated was intended to construct a 'dirty bomb'. She had forwarded the request to Langley and had already received two impatient calls from EUCOM INTEL wanting to know how soon she could prepare a briefing.

This was not the first grim 'rumour' to hit the European intelligence community; some dastardly plot loomed almost daily. Therefore, she suspected that military intelligence knew more than they were telling her. With all the big howdy-do about having opened up the intelligence-sharing channels between agencies, the reality was that little had really changed from pre-9/11. Access was still a commodity you got by networking the good-ole-boy system. More than a question of need-to-know, it was grounded in the reality of who-you-know. Polly wasn't one of the good-ole-boys (or girls), but nonetheless she felt obliged to ignore the gripes from belly and continued to maintain her vigil, waiting for Langley to send her the information on which she could construct her briefing. After all, that was the whole reason she was there: she was CIA liaison to EUCOM.

To wile away the time she had read the *New York Times* on-line, followed by perusing the Fox News site for a 'fair and balanced view', and then went back to several links her Dad had forwarded to her. A lot of ladies her age considered it *chic* to call their fathers by first name or nickname, but for Polly her father was not Rupert or Rupe, he was Daddy or Dad, and her mother was Mom. She was sometimes amazed at how solidly the marriage between her fire-brand Mom and apparently easy-going Dad had endured. Her admiration and wonder had nothing to do with the racially mixed marriage they shared. It had to do with the little bags of truth they carried in the pockets of their minds. They were so different in their culture and temperament and especially in their political views.

Rupe was a political conservative to the bone and Alejandra had been a leftist revolutionary during her university days in San Salvador, opposing the Samoza regime. Although her views had ameliorated once she came to the States, she would nevertheless qualify as an unrelenting liberal. Dad was obsessed with politics, whereas Mom was far more concerned with social and humanitarian issues. Naturally, these two spheres could not be juxtaposed without generating heat. Nevertheless, most of the heat the Johnsons shared was of mutual respect and love.

Rupe was very proud of Alejandra. After he'd brought her back to Washington DC from San Salvador and married her, she had earned a degree in law and for the last eighteen years had been a senior partner in a consulting firm for off-shore business enterprises and foreign joint ventures. Her specialty, of course, was Latin America.

Dad was also very proud of his daughter for following in the 'old man's' footsteps. He'd retired from the CIA two years before, but although he didn't express his pride in so many words, she could feel the warmth he felt towards her. Mom was not so inhibited in expressing her emotions towards loved ones, and she could exhibit an outrageous passion about ideas. Currently, her pet peeve was George Bush & company. Not so Rupe; he loved Donald Rumsfeld. He had sent her a quote by 'Rummy' which had won the prestigious 'Foot in the Mouth' award offered annually by the organizers of the Plain English. It was apparently something he'd said at an intelligence briefing and went:

Reports that say something hasn't happened are always interesting to me, because as we

know, there are known knowns; there are
things we know we know. We also know there
are known unknowns; that is to say we know
there are some things we do not know. But
there are also unknown unknowns – the ones
we don't know we don't know.

Yup, she knew that it made all the sense in the world to Daddy, if for no other reason than that Rummy had said it. Almost every day Daddy would send her a selection of links written by conservative political opinion writers. His favourites clearly were Ann Coulter, Jonah Goldberg, and, of course, Victor Davis Hansen. Polly read these as often as she could and felt deeply indebted to him for having prodded her into reading Oriana Fallaci's *Pride and Rage* treatise. Fallaci had affected her in ways that no other author had ever moved her.

Oriana had inspired her to write her piece, 'Intellectual Terrorism'. It suddenly dawned on her as she sat in her office waiting for Langley to respond that she ought to e-mail 'Intellectual Terrorism' to her Dad. See what he thought about it before she tried any further pursuit towards publication. He'd probably tell her it was good writing, but bad professionalism. 'You work for an organization that keeps those kinds of thoughts to themselves,

Polly!' That was the response she anticipated from him, which was probably why she hadn't sent it to him sooner. Well, the piece was in her laptop at home. She would send it to him one of these evenings, but not this evening. It looked like being a long night. EUCOM wanted that briefing.

Poor Daddy, she reflected. She sensed that underneath that cast-iron veneer, he wasn't taking retirement well at all. Mom was still busy and productive and, lately, she had persuaded him to join her on some of her business trips. For as long as Polly could recall, Alejandra had been the major breadwinner in their family, although it could hardly be said Rupe worked for a pittance or that his pension which he now drew wouldn't keep him in bourbon and cigars. Alejandra made serious money; she was good at what she did. To his credit, Rupe never showed resentment. He had always been totally supportive of her and Polly respected him for that. More than anything else, it demonstrated for her the strength of character of her father. He was quite a guy, she sighed. She missed him.

****

AHMED

It proved to be a short ride from the tea warehouse to Al Nur, Herman recalled. He had been invited into the front passenger-side seat of their elderly Volvo. The man with the gap tooth smile was the designated driver, the other sat behind him in the back seat. In order to frisk Herman, he had also 'holstered' his gun in the back of his pants, a signal to Herman that he was no longer a hostage, although he did not have sufficient confidence to put it to the test. In any event, he needed to get close to Ahmed. It would serve no purpose for him to arouse suspicion, so he moved obediently and without hesitation to their gestured commands.

His thoughts went back to the scene in the tea merchant's warehouse. No one other than these two

henchmen had appeared from behind the bin coun-
ters, but Mahdjoub had returned from the inner sanc-
tum into which he and the woman had disappeared
just as Herman was about to step out into the street.
The chubby tea merchant bustled towards them as
one of his escorts opened the storefront door.
Mahdjoub had, in that moment, flashed Herman an
unusual look; he had no idea what it signalled, but it
seemed to lean towards the sympathetic. As soon as
they had emerged from the storefront door onto the
street, he heard the tea merchant swing the heavy
metal grate closed with a clank, followed shortly by
the rattle of his bunch of keys.

He obediently proceeded down the street, chilled
by the moist cold air, following in the company of
those two motley Arabs who led him to the Volvo.
They didn't appear to be adequately dressed for this
near-zero temperature, but showed no signs of reacting to the cold. Not what one would expect from
guys nurtured in a torrid desert climate. Maybe they
were Afghani mountain men? As a matter of fact,
their hats looked more like what he'd seen worn by
Afghanis in the evening news than the flowing
Keffiyeh that he had seen Arabs like Arafat, Qaddafi
or the Saudis wearing.

Outside Al Nur, they double parked the Volvo
opposite the wrought-iron grated door. Nothing had

changed since his earlier visit at noon, except there were fewer people on the street and most of the storefronts were closed up. The driver motioned for him to get out, and he was followed by the guy from the back seat. A new face stood in the street in front of the now open grate and door, having opened them on cue moments after the Volvo had pulled up. He was clearly feeling the cold and was dressed in ordinary German street wear with nothing on his head other than his neatly clipped black hair; again, there was no doubting his Middle Eastern origins. He hustled over to the off side of the car from whence the driver was emerging and they had a short exchange in Arabic, after which the new boy scrambled inside the car, gunned the engine, and it screeched away. The two henchmen had, in the meantime, adopted positions on either side of the doorway and urged Herman inside.

It was pleasantly warm inside Al Nur and surprisingly spacious. He was led to a very large room, more like a hall to be precise, certainly big enough to hold a reception for fifty or sixty people. If it had been a Christian gathering place, that's exactly what this hall would have been used for, Herman speculated. In the past, on two different occasions, his Serbian freedom-fighter buddies had gotten married and he had attended the receptions. They were both held in a hall similar to this.

Several women, most with broods of children, had been sitting at one of the long tables lined with folding chairs which were arranged around the room. The Arab with the Gap Tooth smile barked something in what Herman guessed was Arabic. The women immediately hustled to their feet, rounded up the little ones, and then obediently bustled out of the room. Herman took the opportunity to look around and familiarize himself with his new surroundings and saw there were no religious symbols which he could discern. There were some stacks of reading material on several of the tables which lined the wall to his right but most of the floor space was empty and uncarpeted.

If this was Al Nur mosque, it didn't fit his preconception. He had already been disappointed by the scruffy, run-down façade and now inside he stood looking at four very ordinary walls and a mostly bare floor. He'd expected tiles, mosaics, colour, Arabic script, sumptuous carpets, lavish decoration, the sounds of their high-pitched prayers and the smell of incense. The only times that he had ever entered a mosque before were in Bosnia, and that was for the purpose of hunting down certain Muslims, and then having a bit of juvenile fun desecrating the place. He shook his head in disbelief as he considered that even in a backward dumb-fuck place like Bosnia the mosques had way more class than this one – and this was Berlin!

Once the women had left, Gap Tooth motioned for him to sit down at the table where the women had previously sat. He complied, seating himself with a quiet sigh. He was beginning to tire of this 'meek as a little lamb' masquerade. They had positioned him so that he could only see one of the two henchmen in the blur of his peripheral vision, about five metres away. Finally he turned to see if Gap Tooth was behind him; he wasn't. Evidently he had left the room, perhaps to fetch Ahmed? He glanced back at number two who, in turn, stared back at him quite impassively although Herman noticed that he had retrieved his weapon from the back of his pants and had stuck it in the front of his waistband. 'Hope it goes off and blows your heathen dick away,' Herman thought to himself and smiled to the Arab. It was met with stony indifference. 'How in the fuck can Ahmed do business with me if he has to hold me at gun-point?' Herman wondered. On the other hand, what possible reason could Ahmed have for bringing him there, if not to negotiate business?

'Where is Ahmed?' he demanded, in an effort to break the stone silence and to test the mind-set of his guard. The henchman responded by answering in

Arabic and placing his hand on the butt of the pistol. 'Well, that's sorted that,' thought Herman and fell to speculating how he would be able to kill Ahmed with all these goons watching his every move. Clearly, he would have to take this henchman out first and now would be as good a time as any, before Gap Tooth and Ahmed returned; always presuming that he had in fact gone for Ahmed and not for a piss. If he had gone to get the target then, with this guy out of the way, he would have the element of surprise on his side. When they returned, he could take the other bodyguard down with his colleague's pistol, and then deal with Ahmed one on one.

However, he immediately realized that there were several flaws in his plan. First and foremost, that Ahmed would be returning with only Gap Tooth in his entourage, and even if that were the case, how was he going to get out of this mosque after killing three Arabs. The front door and grate were locked, and he had no floor plan whatsoever to guide him to any other possible exits. Nonetheless, the real reason he hesitated was due to none of these obstacles. He wanted to hear what this Ahmed had to offer.

Out of the corner of his eye, he caught movement from the henchman. Then he heard the sounds that helped to explain the man's stirrings. While remaining seated he turned awkwardly, craning his neck in the direction of the door behind him from whence the sounds had come. Three men had entered the hall and, glancing at the guard, Herman realized this must be the boss man making his entrance. The goon had taken his hand away from his pistol butt and had made a barely perceptible bow, hands by his sides. Gap Tooth had not returned with these three new figures. It was safe to assume one was Ahmed, but which? All three wore the *Keffiyeh* but the one who was slightly behind the leading pair wore a business suit. The other two had on paramilitary olive-drab uniforms with black braiding, the like of which Herman had seen in Bosnia, each with a webbing belt and pistol holster around his waist. It was fairly clear that the suit was his man, but Herman had learned nothing if not never to make assumptions.

Whilst waiting for the first move, he quickly scrutinized the two uniformed guys, and concluded they were bodyguards. Their clean dress, alert eyes and military bearing gave them the appearance of competence many orders of magnitude greater than the two mountain men who had brought him. The pair had well clipped beards, were short but broad-shouldered, and wore sunglasses which seemed to Herman unusual because the lighting in the room was dim and he knew that outside, darkness had fallen some time before. 'Triumph of style over substance,' a little voice in his head piped up. One of them jerked his head almost imperceptibly at the guard, who reacted by tugging his sweatshirt over the butt of the gun, still wedged in his waistband, bowing once again, and slowly retreated from the group without turning his back to them, making his way out of the door by which they had just entered.

As Herman stood up and turned to face the trio, his chair made a momentary squeal against the floor. The three Arabs approaching him halted, although they were still a good five metres away. The two uniformed guys instinctively closed ranks, shoulder to shoulder to obstruct any sightline to what was clearly their master, and their hands dropped to the flaps of the holsters on their belts. There was a moment's silence whilst they came to terms with the fact that there was no threat. The tension was broken by their master who quietly parted them to step forward and greet Herman.

'So, you are the Black Knife of whom Andrei has informed me,' he said in a tone that carried no menace. Two things surprised Herman: the first was the tone and the second was that he had addressed him in English. Whilst the two bodyguards remained at parade rest, no weapons to hand, the now-smiling Arab offered his right hand as he strode confidently forward. 'Why has he spoken to me in English?'

Herman wondered. That afternoon on the telephone he had used German, admittedly a very heavy accented and clumsy use of the language. Herman replied in German.

'Wie, bitte?' He saw no reason to give away anything more than he had to, particularly his knowledge of English

The Arab dropped his hand to side and his smile gave way to a more serious mien. The two body guards hustled forward to take up station on either side of him. Things were looking ugly again and he thought he might have been too clever by half. He'd have to see what panned out and react accordingly. Ahmed cleared his throat and spoke in his rather poor German, 'I am Ahmed. You are Black Knife, not so?'

Herman nodded his agreement, 'Yes, I am Black Knife,' and now extended his hand but Ahmed ignored it.

'You speak no English?' he queried suspiciously, 'But then you can not possibly serve me as Andrei promised. I do not understand. Why he has sent you to me?'

'Whoops,' Herman silently groaned, 'definitely too clever by half.' There was no alternative, he had to come clean and changed to English.

'I'm sorry. Yes, I can speak English. It just surprised me that you do. It had made me suspicious.

After all, I couldn't be sure who you were.'

Ahmed's smile did not return.

'Suspicious of what?' he softly inquired.

'Well, you know, what happened this afternoon. I came to meet you, and was pinched by the Bulls.'

'Ah yes, I apologize for that. On the other hand, it also made me suspicious. How did they know you were coming? And now you are here again. What did they want?'

'I convinced them that I was looking for a restaurant.'

'But why did they stop you?'

'You tell me! It could have been the parking violation but they didn't slap a *Straffe* on me,' Herman said impatiently. 'You were the one that picked this place to meet. Is this really a mosque? It certainly doesn't look like one.'

'Yes,' replied Ahmed, 'this is Al Nur Mosque. You are in the women's room. It is customary for us to invite Unbelievers into this room. After all, we are in a house of prayer and worship and one must be sensitive not to offend Allah, great be His mercy.'

One of the bodyguards muttered to Ahmed in Arabic and he reacted by taking a small step backwards, away from Herman but at least he smiled again.

'Would you please remove your leather jacket?

My colleagues insist on our security protocol being followed. Anyway, it's rather warm in here for a jacket, don't you agree?'

Herman's mind raced whilst he maintained his cool demeanour, because he was now faced with a chilling dilemma. If he took his jacket off it would expose the knife he literally had up his sleeve, yet not removing it didn't appear as a viable option.

'I thought it would be irreverent towards Allah to stand here in my shirt-sleeves,' he tried lamely.

Ahmed smiled again, but it was a calculated expression not suggestive of warmth or compassion.

'Allah won't mind. After all, he brought us all naked into this world.'

'I thought a Muslim had to cover his head,' he tried as a last throw. He knew his stalling was only putting off the inevitable, but it bought a few seconds for him to make a decision on his next move. There seemed to be only two choices: pull up his sleeve, rip the knife from its scabbard, and go for the two body-guards, or quietly take off his jacket with panache and expose the weapon on his left forearm as if it were no more unusual than a tattoo. After all, Black Knife was a hit man; Andrei had surely told Ahmed that. Carrying the knife would be in character, and in fact serve to solidify his identity. The only interest this Arab could possibly have in Black Knife would be in his 'professional' expertise.

The two bodyguards stiffened as he slowly took off his jacket, first exposing the right arm which felt awkward, but he intended to leave the best for last. Finally he pulled away the left sleeve and exposed his blade hugging the forearm. To his surprise, the two uniformed Arabs, already at high alert, didn't flinch as the weapon came into view. Ahmed softly spoke a few words in Arabic, then smiled at Herman.

'My colleagues would like you to please put your knife on the table and then step away from it.' Ahmed paused, as if measuring the impact of this demand on Black Knife. He then added, 'It will be returned to you after our meeting.'

He sighed audibly as he slowly and deliberately complied with the Arab's demand. It may have sounded to Ahmed like an expression of displeasure, but in truth Herman was expressing enormous relief. 'Thanks again, Allah' his delighted mind's voice declared as he carefully laid his blade on the table. Herman then straightened up and turned to him as the expression on his face gave a clear, 'what now?' Ahmed gestured to the other end of the table.

'We will sit there. They will bring tea.'

He thought about countering with a petition for coffee, but then killed the impulse. Frankly, he felt damn fortunate that his throat could still swallow.

'What in the Devil did this Arab want to discuss with me?' he now wondered as he moved down the table to the spot.

As he sat down, he watched Ahmed pace briskly around the end of the table and then pull out the chair opposite him. The Arab sat down effortlessly and Herman didn't have to look over his shoulder to know that the two bodyguards stood close behind him – he could feel it. One developed that sixth sense in his business. Again Ahmed smiled, it was the sort of smile you would trust about as much as if you had seen it on a salivating crocodile. It annoyed Herman and he began to relish the idea of wiping it of his face. The Arab was of slight build, and easily three inches shorter than Herman. His face was typically Arab in features, but quite handsome with a neatly clipped beard. He had the dark, Middle Eastern eyes that watched with the intensity of a hawk, and Herman had to exercise some control to maintain eye contact. He didn't want to appear cowed before this man as had the guard who had brought him to Al Nur.

He speculated that if this were a Hollywood film, Ahmed would immediately impress him as a petro-dollar magnate, or the eldest son of an emir. He had class, Herman granted grudgingly because he admired quality, and Ahmed had it in spades. From the Armani suit to the handmade shoes, he oozed class. Herman had long since realized that affecting a classy act didn't come naturally; it had to be bred into your bones. But, he reasoned, if one could garner respect from people of quality, some of it might rub off, at least enough to ratchet up your own esteem. Like some of his own African roots which dictated that an enemy's strength and spirit could be absorbed by eating their heart and liver. Polly had class; it was probably what turned him on to her so strongly, but he didn't want to eat her liver. To hear her moan and feel her body throb as he exercised his prerogatives also bolstered his self-esteem; a person of class was submitting to his will.

As Ahmed watched Black Knife sit down, his usually crisp grasp of a situation was muddled by conflict. He wondered how much this Black Knife had been told by Andrei. Well, Andrei did not know the whole story. The Russian knew only that Ahmed was willing to pay for someone who could sneak a bomb into one of the American bases here in Germany. Andrei didn't know that this bomb would be filled with highly radioactive nuclear debris and that it was to be a 'dirty bomb'. One worrying problem was that according to his colleagues in Florence, who had brokered the deal with the Russians for the nuclear material now secreted somewhere in the

Tuscan countryside, the German Federal Police knew that something of this nature was in the planning. The Americans had passed their information on to the Italian police and also to the Germans, but so far as his colleagues could tell there was nothing specific, just rumour. They had concluded that the leak had come from the Russian side. Nevertheless, Ahmed considered it might also have come from a leak somewhere in their organization. Like Herman, Ahmed was careful and was never given to presumption and trusted no one, not even his closest colleagues.

Then there was the incident that afternoon. How had the police known to intercept Black Knife? They had to have been tipped off by someone. He now had two points upon which to construct a line and, thus, he had drawn a conclusion. It pointed to one person who could have passed on both the non-specific information concerning the bomb and the information about Black Knife. He ruled out Andrei, because although he, of course, knew about Black Knife, and knew about a planned terrorist bomb attack, he did not know about the nuclear material. The Russians who delivered the material had known nothing about Andrei or Black Knife. Yet Florence had their informants in high places at the Italian Interior Ministry and they claimed that the presence of their nuclear material in Italy had been compromised. Assuming their source was the Americans, how had those infidel American dogs learned of this? On the other hand, even his Italian colleagues did not yet know about Black Knife. So, unless this Black Knife worked for the police, Ahmed had to grudgingly concede that the leak stemmed from his own Berlin organization; it had to be one or the other. If it was his own organization, he believed that he had just deduced who it could be. He must be sure. 'Allah give me the wisdom,' he silently pleaded.

As if in answer to his silent prayer, he was suddenly struck by a flash of inspiration. 'He could both ride the camel and drink its milk. Allah is great!' Allah had graced him with insight. His strategy crystallized in this very moment as he stared across the table at Black Knife but, first, he needed to understand how this black man sent by the Russian could smuggle a bomb into one of the American military bases. He was aware, however, that by asking the question he would be disclosing more than he was willing to offer until he had a more positive feedback from this stranger. It called for a test. Yes, Black Knife must be tested. 'Allah be praised for Allah shall provide and His will must be done!'

'We shall chat for a while and sip our tea. It is the Arab way,' Ahmed explained as he continued to hold eye contact with his guest. 'This is a proud man,' the Arab mentally noted. 'He has courage. Perhaps Allah has sent this infidel for a purpose, after all.'

'What's your proposal – and what's in it for me,' said Herman bluntly, clearly ignoring his host's suggestion that they first engage in some small talk.

'Patience,' Ahmed insisted, 'Even the revelations by Allah to the Prophet were not delivered in an instant. I must go at my own pace. Are you not familiar at all with Islamic ways?'

Herman shook his head in the negative.

'Is that a requirement?'

'In order to gain access to Paradise, yes, but it is not required for serving *me*.' The word 'serving' didn't sit easy with Herman but he held his tongue.

'Good, I'm listening.'

'What are your feelings towards the Americans?'

He shrugged his shoulders.

'I guess it would depend on which American.' He immediately thought of Polly, but knew better than to bring her into this conversation.

'The man Bush, for instance, their President?'

He didn't understand where this Arab was taking him and, frankly, he couldn't be arsed to try to work out what was going on in his sick black-ass mind. He held the Muslim religion in no special esteem; from what he'd learned in Bosnia, they were dupes just as were Catholics and Evangelicals. The Bosnians smoked and drank and did their share of rape and pillage, same as the Orthodox Serbs. However, it seemed to him that those Muslim guys were a whole lot more ignorant than Christians, and therefore took their religion to extremes. Islam wasn't an opiate as Marx had professed religions to be – it was more like speed or angel dust.

'Bush? He's a capitalist,' he replied. 'He took Iraq for the oil, and he wants to make the Middle East a piece of the American Empire.'

'Is it wrong to be a capitalist?' Ahmed prodded.

'It's trying to fly in the face of the inevitable. Bush can't stop it, and America can't stop it. The capitalist West is only a meddlesome obstacle that will be overcome, Socialism is the future, Ahmed.' Herman felt a bit awkward addressing the Arab by name, but he felt he must establish parity in their status. No black-ass was going to be his boss; moreover, he had taken umbrage at him saying earlier that Herman would 'serve' him.

It appeared that the Arab was suddenly distracted. He was looking away to the distance behind Herman, and smiled with what appeared to be satisfaction.

'They are bringing us tea,' Ahmed finally said, but did not re-establish eye contact. Herman could now hear the shuffling footsteps approach as an old, bent fellow delivered the tea. The cups looked small and did not have the traditional handle and Herman could see a mass of tea leaves steeping in the bottom of the cup. Vapour steamed from the vessels, but the fellow's fingers did not seem affected by the heat as he grasped the cups and set them before the two of them.

'It's good tea,' Ahmed assured, 'It comes from Mahdjoub. You know him. My colleagues met you at his tea warehouse.'

'Little fat guy with glasses and a moustache?'

'Yes, it's good you remember his appearance,' the Arab said with a clever smirk.

'Yeah – why?'

'Because I shall pay you to kill him.'

Ahmed had added two and two together and coming up with a very ugly zero. Mahdjoub had told him belatedly that Shafiq, the head man in the Florence cell, had suggested an infidel Russian from Hamburg could help get the Al Nur package into an American base. Ahmed had, upon hearing this, considered it very strange that the tea merchant would have temporarily forgotten such an important detail. That was out of character and, moreover, he had seemed extremely nervous. Was this a set-up? If Mahdjoub was a traitor, then this Russian was working for the police, which meant that the African opposite him also worked for them. The message had apparently come from Shafiq, but he moved about a lot and was no longer in Florence. Within the time constraints, there seemed no way for Ahmed to verify Mahdjoub's story unless this Black Knife killed the tea merchant. Then he could at least believe that he and this Russian, Andrei, were the genuine article.

****

THE PACKAGE

Herman was back again in the 'women's room' of Al Nur. He'd gone to Mahdjoub's warehouse, taken care of business and returned, all in less than forty-five minutes. Now, he sat at the same table as before, but in a chair on the opposite side of the table from where they had originally installed him. It felt more comfortable because he could observe the entrance to the room without having to twist his torso and crane his neck. Ahmed had been waiting as Herman followed the bodyguard inside while the other stood beside his boss. Ahmed greeted Herman by offering him a brief smile and a nod of acknowledgement, but seemed pre-occupied with the mobile in his hand. After taking his chair, Herman watched Ahmed, who stood across from him on the other side of the table.

The Arab had pressed a series of numbers on his mobile and talked softly into the tiny mike on the state-of-the-art Bluetooth earpiece as he began to pace around restlessly, the two bodyguards maintaining a respectful distance.

Many thoughts ran through Herman's mind as he watched the Arab in animated conversation, but the overarching question was whether or not he would get paid for killing Mahdjoub? The Arab had promised him fifty thousand dollars for the job. On the one hand he was extremely pleased with this potential gratuity but, on the other hand, it seemed unduly generous. Any Berlin thug could have managed a hit like this for a tenth of what Ahmed had promised to pay him. He might have felt more comfortable if they'd forced him to negotiate the sum; it was unlike the Arabs, it was too easy, it wasn't natural.

This really set Herman thinking, to earn the same fifty thou with Andrei would have involved a hit many, many times more risky than 'slotting' the helpless tea merchant – like killing Ahmed. That would require a more careful plan and a far more substantial arsenal than simply coming at this Black-ass with a knife, that was if he intended to survive in a condition to enjoy the money he hoped to get from Andrei. Then there was the promise this Arab had dangled of an even more lucrative job to follow. Life was getting complex. Herman therefore resolved there was no immediate need for him to formulate plans, and he would follow his instincts, reacting to events as they unfolded; it had stood him in good stead so far.

Forty-five minutes before, he recalled, Ahmed had arranged by telephone for Mahdjoub to hide Black Knife in his tea warehouse for the night; at least that's what the Arab had explained after jabbering away in Arabic. The two men who had originally brought him to Al Nur then led him outside to the same Volvo to complete the return journey. As far as Herman could recall they travelled the reverse route back to the tea merchant's warehouse, but this time they parked up the street from the warehouse near a Turkish *Imbiss*. Gap Tooth motioned for Black Knife to get out and to his surprise both henchmen remained in the car; clearly he was on his own. His second surprise was that he found both the grate and the storefront door of the warehouse unlocked. That caused warning lights to go off inside his head as it reeked of a set-up, but set-up for what? His instincts urged him to proceed, so he opened the door and walked in as if he owned the place.

Inside, Mahdjoub was standing near the door, hands at his sides and a nervous smile on his face. Herman quickly scanned the place. No one else appeared to be present, not even the woman who, during his first visit, had been sitting behind the counter. Black Knife did not believe in overtures or ceremony.

'Where am I to stay?' he asked.

Mahdjoub didn't answer but beckoned for Herman to follow as he turned towards the counter and the door which led to the rear of the building. As he did so, Herman quickly slid the sleeve of his jacket up and with one smooth action withdrew the blade from the sheath and dropped it into his left hand. Two quick strides brought him up silently behind the hapless Mahdjoub, his powerful right forearm whipping around his neck, his right hand taking a firm purchase on the collar of Mahdjoub's jacket. In one fluid movement Herman increased the pressure with his forearm, beginning to crush the windpipe, as his left hand pushed forward with power and accuracy. The black blade passed easily through the clothing and penetrated the body with practised ease, passing between two ribs, left of the spine and just below the shoulder blade. Using his overwhelming strength, Herman continued the pressure with his forearm to ensure no sound emitted from the victim and that he was tilted backward and least able to exert himself in any form of defence. In any event it would have been too late, the blade had already penetrated the heart from the rear producing a massive internal haemorrhage and, after a few more beats, failure. Holding Mahdjoub hard against himself, Herman felt first the tell-tale relaxation of the muscles, followed by some brief spasms as the muscles and brain became starved of fresh blood and oxygen. After a couple of minutes he was just holding dead weight and allowed the body to slide down onto its knees and then to crumple forward, face down. Leaving the knife in place until he was certain there was little or no residual blood pressure, he carefully withdrew it and wiped it, using Mahdjoub's clothing. He was forensically aware, although that wasn't how he thought of it, he just called it 'keeping clean' and resolved to shower as soon as he could, to thoroughly clean the knife and sheath, and to buy himself a new jacket and gloves at the earliest opportunity. A dark stain spread around the point of entry through Mahdjoub's jacket as some blood seeped out and was absorbed by the surrounding material, but there would be no pooling around the body, dead hearts don't pump.

The Volvo was still parked near the Turkish *Schnelly* and the two guards had remained in it waiting for Black Knife. As he approached, the one sitting in the back-seat jumped out of the car and opened the passenger-side door for Herman. As they whisked him back to Al Nur, he sensed an improved attitude towards him by them. It could almost, he observed with a touch of bewilderment, have been characterized as deference. The Volvo double-parked directly in front of Al Nur and, once again, the guard in back jumped out and opened the door for him.

One of Ahmed's bodyguards had met him at the doorway into Al Nur and had taken him back to the women's room; Herman had noted he was still wearing dark glasses. He wondered if that was a common Arab affectation or if he just thought it was 'cool' – no matter. Ahmed, along with the other bodyguard, stood in the room, clearly awaiting his return. Ahmed gestured for him to sit down and the bodyguard who had remained with his boss had indicated which chair Herman should use.

Ahmed had pressed a button on his phone and removed the earpiece and tiny mike from his ear, then added sardonically, 'I just called Mahdjoub. Apparently he must be pre-occupied. He doesn't answer,' he chuckled. It appeared to Herman that he'd been expected to respond positively to this cynical remark; however, he just sat with a poker face.

'Would you like a basin of water and a towel?'

'Nope,' Herman had answered coolly. 'I don't make much mess,' he'd added, showing Ahmed his gloves. Ahmed raised an eyebrow as he clearly recognized true professionalism.

'Nonetheless, I expect you would like to wash. I will arrange it,' said Ahmed. Herman shrugged his shoulders in indifference.

'What I would like is my fifty thou,' he said, but any further conversation was put on hold as Ahmed's phone gave a quiet warble and he re-introduced the small headset into his ear. For a few moments he concentrated on what he was hearing and then, on a signal from him, one of the bodyguards left the room and returned a few moments later with a sealed envelope. Ahmed gave a nod in Herman's direction and the guard put the envelope on the table and slid it across to Herman. He eyed it carefully and found the dimensions to be encouraging. Sitting back in his chair he waited for a signal from Ahmed that it was his, since it would have been bad protocol to grab the envelope and rip it open. The next time the Arab paced slowly past he glanced at Herman and caught his eye, a clear hand gesture indicating he was to take it. It would also have been bad manners to open it and to start to count the money. Ahmed casually waved his right hand in a circular motion which clearly said, 'it's nothing'. Moments later he pressed the button on his phone and walked back to the table.

'Your wages, Black Knife,' Ahmed said as calmly as if he had just passed Black Knife the vegetables.

'You are free to count it. I will not be offended,' Herman nodded as he slowly used his right hand to methodically tease at the fingers of his left glove, and then grasped it by the middle finger and slipped it off. He carefully laid the glove down on the table and repeated the same ceremony upon his other hand; it just said, 'I'm in no hurry, what's fifty big ones to a man like me?' Having set down the second glove he flexed his fingers like a magician about to pull a rabbit out of a hat and carefully slid the left sleeve of his leather jacket up to expose the knife now nestling back in its sheath. One of the guards stiffened and took a step forward, but Ahmed stood his ground, looking on unperturbed. Herman cast a mocking smile at the bodyguard and then, with one practiced movement, he drew the blade and with a casual flick of his wrist he used the tip of it to slit the end of the envelope open. Easing the blade inside he lifted the side of the envelope high enough to see the bank-sealed plastic bag inside full of greenbacks. He didn't need to count it. It was obviously very unwise to try to cheat someone you'd just employed as a killer; never try to short change your lawyer, doctor or hit man – it was sound advice. Still completely at easy, and acutely aware that Ahmed and his goons were watching his every move, he lifted the envelope on the blade until it was nearly vertical and the plastic bag fell out. Catching it in his left hand he smoothly slipped it into his inside pocket, flicked the envelope off the knife, and returned the knife to its quarters, slipping the sleeve down to hide it. During the whole process his eyes had constantly flicked to and from Ahmed and he knew he'd made the impression he wanted.

'I have some business to attend to,' said Ahmed to break the heavy silence that had followed Herman's little act. 'I shall return so that we may discuss your next assignment.' With that he turned on his heel and strode off with his minders. This time it was Herman who was surprised; they were leaving him alone in this room. He hadn't expected that. The prospect of an escape attempt flashed briefly in his mind, but escape from what? He'd just been paid and, according to Ahmed, he had another paying job lined up for him, he'd hit pay dirt here and without all the damned arguing and hassle he usually got from Andrei.

Herman had a dollar account at UBS in Zurich, and it was from there he made his cash withdrawals, usually in banded bundles of one hundred dollar bills. Thinking about the money reminded him of when his account executive at the bank had warned him, shortly after 9/11, that he ought to consider transferring his dollars into a Euro account. He'd had two hundred thousand dollars and change sitting in his dollar account at the time. However, Herman had embraced the dollar with an implicit trust, and had viewed with suspicion the integrity of the Euro. His disdain of capitalism did not distract him from appreciating the steadfastness of greenback Benjamin Franklins. Thus, he watched helplessly as the value of his dollar account, relative to other major European currencies, diminished by roughly thirty per cent. Oh well, the dollar would make a comeback, he consoled himself, as it always did. It was merely a capitalist game being played by the G7 nations, so that they could make money on their currency speculation at the expense of little guys like him. It offered him yet another reason to hate America and the capitalist West.

His thoughts now turned back to Ahmed's parting remark, that when he returned they would discuss a new assignment. He sorely wondered what the assignment could be. He had a second issue relating to this promised project, wondering how Ahmed might be disposed if he were to refuse the mission? Would the black-ass let him walk away from Al Nur with his fifty thousand dollars? Maybe it was just the bad karma he had learned to endure whilst working all these years with Andrei and the Russian Hamburg gang. It had just been too easy, do a job and get paid handsomely and no hassle; it was alien. Weren't Arabs renowned for their tendency to haggle? Anyway, he suspected there was a link to this bundle of dollars and his willingness to accept Ahmed's new assignment; a kind of part-payment on account – but account of what? He further suspected that if he refused to accept, his account executive at UBS might never hear from him again.

He was distracted for a moment as he contemplated the obscurity of what would happen to his money in the secret Swiss bank account if he never came back to claim it. There wasn't a single person in the world to whom he could bequeath his treasure. He'd have considered Polly, but that wouldn't have worked from her side, he guessed. Anyway, it was a little late for estate planning, he mused.

So, returning to the dilemma at hand, if he refused Ahmed's offer, they might simply dispatch him back to Andrei. Certainly, the Arab harboured no clue that he had been sent here by the Russians to kill him. Ahmed seemed to believe that this hit man, Black Knife, had been sent to do a job. However, it remained a mystery to Herman as to why Ahmed had solicited Andrei for a helping hand. Nevertheless, if Andrei's treachery were discovered, surely these Arabs would have killed Herman, not paid him. The rub was, of course, that if Ahmed turned him back over to Andrei, then the Hamburg Russians would kill him anyway. He'd been sent to assassinate the Arab, not to do a job for Al Nur and collect fifty thousand. At that moment he felt as though he sat between a rock and a hard place but, as usual, Herman was prepared to wait and see what hand he would be dealt.

It was clear that as things stood he would be wise to accept Ahmed's assignment, no matter what it might entail. Agree to whatever he must in order to get his sorry butt out of Al Nur. Once out, he would probably have three choices: kill Ahmed, accommodate Ahmed, or phone for an appointment with Michael Jackson's cosmetic surgeon to undergo a complete identity makeover. Continuing in the employment of the Hamburg gang would no longer be a realistic alternative with anything but option one.

His ruminations were interrupted by the appearance of that bent old Arab man who had earlier brought tea. He was now carrying a basin and had a clean linen towel draped over one arm as if he were a waiter at some swanky restaurant. The gnarled little man needed both hands to carry the basin as he shuffled towards the end of the table where Herman sat and carefully placed it before him, not splashing a drop. Finally, he offered the towel with a degree of formality, then withdrew a few short steps to stand with his arms at his sides and eyes cast down.

Herman wasn't certain during the first few moments whether the old man had paused before him in readiness to retrieve the polluted basin and soiled towel when the clean-up was finished, or if he was expecting a tip for the delivery. There were some essential oils floating in a film on top of it that mixed with the steam misting up from the basin, assailing his nostrils with a strong herbal smell. He plunged his hands in and immediately withdrew them, issuing a curse through his gritted teeth, it was damn near boiling! The old man didn't flinch or look up; he just stood still, looking like the knotty old stump of a tree that had been the victim of some fatal disease.

Gently patting his hands dry with the linen towel Herman was relieved to see there was no obvious damage, no reddening or blisters but his hands still stung. Reaching over, he picked up his gloves and checked them for obvious blood stains. Wrapping a corner of the towel around the index and middle fingers of his right hand, he carefully dipped it into the water for a quick soak, then began to scrub at a couple of discoloured spots. Then he slipped off his jacket and treated that to the same inspection and process but, fortunately, his technique with the knife was good and there was little to show for his butchery.

Whilst exposed, he took the knife from its sheath and gave it a thorough cleaning although he was aware that he couldn't clean the inside of the sheath and so both weapon and sheath would require urgent attention later as well as his change of clothes

He stood up for a final inspection and discovered a couple of blemishes on one leg of his trousers and, lastly, one more spot which had splashed upon the toe of his right boot. It took several minutes, but in the end he felt satisfied that he had done an acceptable clean-up. At last, he tossed the soiled towel onto the table near the basin, the water in which hardly steamed any longer and which had been turned into a reddish-brown pool. He then inserted his hands, one at time, back into his gloves and took one more look at his clothes before sitting down again and stretching his long legs out under the table.

Evidently, the old Arab fellow took that as his signal to retrieve these toiletries. He reluctantly picked up the towel, regarding it as if a leper had used it to dry off festering scabs. He dropped it into the water, then leaned forward and picked up the basin, turned, and slowly shuffled away. Meanwhile, Ahmed had evidently been alerted to the conclusion of Black Knife's ablutions because his two minders stepped back into the room, followed by their sheik. Ahmed had taken this natural pause to carefully think through exactly how he would communicate his thoughts to Black Knife. The mullah in Florence had arranged and paid for this delivery of the 'dirty material' for their package. His Tuscan cell would make a bomb with the material and explosives they had procured from various sources, through the Russian Mafia. It had apparently been these self-same Mafiosi who had, according to Mahdjoub, referred them to Hamburg Andrei as someone who could help Ahmed and his Al Nur cell to get their package into one of the American military bases on German soil – if the price was right, of course.

Higher authority in Al Qaeda had urged the Tuscan Islamists to cooperate with Ahmed, but offered no assistance concerning the implementation of his plan to explode a dirty bomb in Germany. Why not Italy, the Florentines had wondered? There were American military installations there as well, but theirs was not to reason why. The Florentine cell could offer Ahmed no guidance on delivery but apparently Shafiq had passed the Hamburg connection to the late Mahdjoub, who could no longer confirm or deny it. Shafiq, Ahmed's contact with the Florentine cell, was out of touch and so there was little alternative, for the time being, but to proceed; albeit that his gut feeling was that there was something wrong somewhere.

The Al Nur mission had been tabled in conjunction with a call from Al Qaeda to attack worldwide American and Zionist interests. In a separate communiqué, it was stressed that the German people needed to be mobilized against the presence of American soldiers stationed on their sovereign soil. The German bases had played an essential role in the exploitive wars against Afghanistan and Iraq. If the Germans were to deny them these bases, the Americans would find their further exploitation in the Middle East far more logistically complicated.

A major blow against the American military establishment was required. Lessons had been learned from the American reaction to casualties in Lebanon and Somalia. Despite the belligerence of this cowboy, George W. Bush, if the United States were slapped in the face by a sufficiently catastrophic event, the American press would demand an immediate re-assessment of his anti-Islamic Crusade. Defence of Zionism would suddenly take on a new and costly price-tag for the American public and the families of American servicemen would no longer feel safe living in foreign lands. It would constitute another shot across the bow of the American ship of state by Al Qaeda. As in the past, the pampered American public would wretch at the sight of blood and quiver in fear of such threats. This so-called superpower had a soft underbelly and a low tolerance for pain. The Will of Allah would prevail.

Considering this, Ahmed conceived of the notion that a dirty bomb exploded at an American base in Germany with its collateral consequences for German citizens ought to be a powerful incentive for the Germans to demonstrate their discontent with the American presence. By clearly targeting an American base, as opposed to a German population centre, Ahmed believed that the German people would overlook the reality that it was an Islamist initiative and quickly blame the Americans for the German Federal Republic's predicament. That would soon be followed by organized demands that the government reconsider 'American occupation' and NATO commitments.

The Islamic jihadists had learned from liberal Western moral relativism that guilt was not measured objectively; it was assessed in qualitative terms. Soft-spined European sympathy for the 'Palestinian victims of Zionism' over the last four decades had made it clear that such transfers of anger redirected from the terrorists to the 'causes of terror' were easily spawned in the Europeans. They delighted in championing the underdog and, after all, anti-Semitism was a Christian invention.

The time for Al Nur to act was now, given the

German–American rift over the Iraq War. Furthermore, Ahmed was convinced that the Greens and Ultra-leftists would foment violent nationwide demonstrations in Germany if he could motivate them with his 'dirty bomb' plot and had fiercely argued the competence of the Al Nur cell to carry out this battle in the Holy War. Yes, Ahmed had made his pitch to the leadership and, evidently, they had found his arguments compelling. Al Qaeda provided the expertise and directed Florence to assemble the dirty bomb for onward delivery to Germany, care of Ahmed's Al Nur.

However, as Ahmed sat down opposite the man they called Black Knife, he searched for a way to discuss his project in such general terms that no details concerning the nature of the plot would be disclosed. Before revealing any of the essential elements, Ahmed needed to hear what resources this man could offer to smuggle his package into an American military base, and what price this service would require. If the plan or the price Black Knife offered was unacceptable, he would probably have him killed. Certainly, Allah would guide Ahmed in these decisions, he humbly re-assured himself.

'I am prepared to listen to your proposal.' Ahmed said.

Herman maintained his best poker face whilst

bewilderment swam in his brain.

'What proposal?'

The Arab responded with a grin while he cocked his head, as if to compliment Black Knife on his cleverness.

'I'm sure Andrei must have discussed my particular needs with you before dispatching you here.'

'No, he didn't. Andrei said you would discuss your assignment with me,' Herman fought back the urge to smirk at this irony. If Ahmed only knew the true reason for Andrei having sent him here!

'That's it?' Ahmed queried, now becoming concerned that this Black Knife really didn't know what he was supposed to be doing. He tried again.

'Come now, Black Knife, why did he choose you? Surely you have some expertise that Andrei thought would be of use, setting aside the obvious,' he added as an afterthought. 'Were you not at all curious?

'Yeah,' replied Herman as he interlocked his fingers behind his head and stretched. 'I wanted to know how much you'd pay.'

'I see. What exactly did Andrei say?' asked Ahmed, now clearly less than at ease. Herman paused a moment for effect before answering.

'He said that you were a very generous man.'

'But pay for what, Black Knife? He must have

given you some general idea.'

'He said you'd explain.'

'That's it,' Ahmed huffed, 'that's all he said?'

'That's it,' Herman affirmed as if it made all the sense in the world for Andrei to have done so.

The Arab slowly rubbed his hands together as his eyes cast heavenward. It seemed to Herman that he might be appealing to Allah. Finally Ahmed's gaze focused back on Black Knife. 'I need to transport a package.'

'I'm listening,' Herman prompted.

'The package must be transported to an American military base here in Germany.'

Herman's mind raced, what was this black-ass going on about? A package? Give it to FedEx or to some woman to stick in her baby's nappies. Why the fuck did he need him on this?

'Which base?' he inquired. 'What sort of package?'

'I leave the choice of base to you and the package will weigh several hundred kilos, but can be assembled in the most accommodating shape. It could, for instance, be a casket.'

'A casket?' Herman confirmed. Ahmed nodded.

'Will it have a body inside?'

'No, no, no!' Ahmed fired back. 'It will be something like the size of a casket, a reasonable-sized box and quite heavy. So it will need a van or a lorry or something like that, you understand?'

Herman kept his cool although he could see that Ahmed was losing his.

'I'm not in the logistics business. Why do you need me? There's any number of companies who can deliver your casket to the Americans.'

Impatience and frustration were now clearly gripping the Arab. His two bodyguards seemed to sense this because they stiffened and looked directly at him.

'It's a very special package, a very valuable package, and we will pay handsomely for its delivery,' Ahmed said, clearly finding it difficult to keep his temper. He had expected this Black Knife to solve his problem, not to create new ones. 'The package must not be left unattended and it would not be welcomed by the Americans if they inspected it. It has to come from Italy.' Once more Ahmed wrinkled his brow and leant forwards. 'You truly know nothing about this?' he asked.

Herman gazed back at the Arab who stared at him intently, then swept a momentary glance at the two bodyguards who appeared to continue their state of high alert. Fuck it, he hadn't a clue what this black-ass was talking about but he thought he might as well tag along for the ride. There wasn't a realistic alternative. All he knew was that some kind of deal had been cut between Andrei and Ahmed, but what deal?

'Am I working for Andrei, or do I work for you?' Herman asked flatly. Ahmed was clearly taken aback and took a few moments to consider his position.

'You work for me, yes? Assuming I have confidence in your plan.'

'Good,' replied Herman and emphasized it by slapping the flat of his hand on the table, which made the minders even more twitchy, and one even made a move towards his holster.

'You tell me what it is you want. Whatever Andrei has told me is of no consequence. You tell me exactly what you want; and how much you offer me for the job. I can only serve one master.'

Again silence reigned as Ahmed sat back in his chair and cast his eyes heavenward as though seeking inspiration. A full two or three minutes passed as he completed his meditation and then he sat forward and placed his elbows on the table, his chin resting on his intertwined fingers.

'One week from today the Americans celebrate a holiday they call Veterans Day. It is dedicated to the soldiers who have served their country's causes. It would be an appropriate day to punish the American Army here in Germany, don't you think?'

Herman only offered a noncommittal shrug of his

shoulders, 'Any day would be good for me.'

Ahmed smiled indulgently. He understood Herman's socialist perspective, even if he didn't agree with it. 'Yes, but this day is particularly appropriate, you see.'

'Okay, so where do I fit in?'

'I mentioned a casket. What does the image of a casket bring to your mind, Black Knife?'

Herman frowned, his simple hand gesture signalled that he waived the right to reply. Ahmed filled in the blank for him.

'*Death,* Black Knife. Death lies inside this casket, enough death to fill hundreds of American bodies. Horrifying deaths which would make even a leper shudder with dread. Our casket must be transported into one of the American bases the weekend after this, or at the latest on Tuesday which is their Veterans Day. It must be slipped under the noses of the gate guards and it must reach a vital part of the base where there is a concentration of military people and their families. Can you do this for me?'

'Yes,' was Herman's automatic response. He had already resolved that whatever this Arab would ask of him, his reply must be in the affirmative. If Ahmed had asked for him to steal a nuclear submarine or shoot George W. Bush, he would have responded positively; he knew it was his only ticket out of Al

Nur alive, because Ahmed had told him too much. If Black Knife was not with him, then the Arab would ensure that he couldn't be against him. There was no question in his mind concerning this issue and, equally, there was no doubt that he hadn't a clue as to how he might achieve the task offered by Ahmed.

The Arab raised his face heavenward again, as he clasped his hands. Herman watched Ahmed's lips move as if the Arab were silently reciting a prayer, maybe 'Allah be praised'. Finally, he returned his hands to the table and his attention back to Black Knife. The bodyguards seemed to relax a bit as they saw the tension drain away.

'So, I am eager to hear your plan, Black Knife,' Ahmed softly urged.

'Yes,' smiled Herman, 'and I am eager to hear how much you will pay me for this service.'

After a thoughtful pause, Ahmed replied, 'I cannot assess the value of a service which has not yet been disclosed. You've given me no details. You must be the one to name your price since only you know what your plan entails.'

Herman carefully weighed the options. He had to ask enough to establish credibility, but not so much that Ahmed would immediately reject the offer. However, the overarching necessity was to propose a scheme which allowed him time to come up with a plan of some sort. His immediate requirement was to stall and hopefully get his own black ass out of Al Nur.

'I want one hundred thousand dollars transferred to my Swiss bank account,' he began boldly, 'then I'll tell you the plan. When the plan has been executed, I want another transfer of two hundred thousand dollars.' His reasoning was that it was too late for the Arab to arrange a transfer that evening and, likewise, too late for Herman to call UBS in Zurich to confirm. Therefore, the transaction needed to wait until the morning and, this being the case, he hoped that Ahmed would allow him to return to his hotel room. It was the best shot Herman could conjure on the spur of the moment.

'That is a formidable amount of money,' Ahmed objected.

'It's a formidable job,' Herman countered.

'I can not pay you one hundred thousand dollars for something so obscure. You are selling me a camel, but refusing to let me see it first. At least I should have the right to look at its teeth, Black Knife. Let me please see its teeth. Tell me something about your plan so I can feel confident that I am doing the right thing.'

'No,' replied Herman firmly. He knew he was pushing his luck but he felt that at least for the moment he held the high ground. 'One answer will bring two more questions,' he continued. 'I can arrange for your package to be smuggled onto an American military base here in Germany. I will tell you the how of it when I see the colour of your money.'

Ahmed brought his hands down to the tabletop and balled them up into fists. Clearly, he was riding on the horns of a dilemma. He wasn't used to being spoken to like this by such an upstart, and a *Neger* to boot. But he was out of ideas as to how he might execute his grand plan and this infidel claimed to be able to do it. He had, therefore, to play his game for the moment but he resolved that if this African dog was lying he would have him put to death in a particularly painful and humiliating way. The thought calmed him once more and he looked up calmly and held Herman's gaze.

'You must tell me something. Which base do you have in mind?'

Herman relaxed back into his chair; he had weathered the first storm. It bought him a fraction more time as his mind again raced for a plausible answer. The only American military installation he had even a passing familiarity with was Polly's, having picked up titbits of information during their conversations.

'It's located in the vicinity of Stuttgart.'

'Which one?' Ahmed immediately challenged.

'There you go,' teased Herman, 'I answer your question and you ask another.' Again Ahmed tensed but relaxed again, he'd decided he'd play this *Neger*'s game for a while longer before he had him killed.

'There are several American military bases in or near Stuttgart.'

'Patch Barracks.'

'Why that one?'

Herman was surprised how convincing his answer sounded and wondered where it had come from.

'It's EUCOM Headquarters. It's where the Americans maintain their European Command. If we are to shoot a bullet at the creature, we should aim for the head, don't you think?' Raising both hands as he finished, he added, 'No more questions. First I want to see one hundred thou' transferred to my bank account, then I'll detail the plan.' Herman felt he was on a roll so continued, 'Right now I'm bushed. I need a shower, a change of clothes, some food and a drink. And if there's one thing you good Moslem boys won't have here is a stiff drink.'

Ahmed sat back in his chair and again raised his eyes heavenward. The two bodyguards shifted their weight nervously. He returned his gaze to Herman and his eyes blazed, Herman thought he might just have gone too far.

'Fifty thousand dollars is all I will give you in a blind advance. Another fifty after you have detailed the plan.' The Arab squinted his eyes as he continued, 'Do not quibble with me over this matter. I am being generous. I am showing you trust. I expect you to reciprocate in kind'

Herman had no intention of quibbling.

'I accept. I'll need a taxi to take me back to my hotel room.'

'Why? I can put you up for the night and we can find you anything you need, even alcohol.'

He understood that his life now depended upon his ability to come up with a suitable answer to the Arab's question.

'My computer's there,' he lied. 'I must have my computer to verify your deposit into my account.' He had seen how this was done in the movies. Of course, in reality, he would simply call his broker for the confirmation, but this was not reality; it was fast approaching being a black farce.

'I see. Very well, I will have you driven to your hotel. It would be rude to coldly dispatch you in a taxi,' Ahmed cast him a chilly smile, 'We do not treat our colleagues with such disregard, Mr Black Knife.'

'Thank you,' Herman said, feigning gratitude. He realized that they would not only drive him back to the hotel, but would remain on station, see to it that he didn't leave. Well, he had better chances in the hotel for escaping from this nightmare than here in Al Nur.

Ahmed acknowledged with a smile, and the bodyguards relaxed again.

'But first, you must write down your wire transfer information.'

****

THE PLAN

Herman was sitting on the edge of the bed in his hotel room. Glancing up at the illuminated red numerals on the clock radio he saw it was 1.30 in the morning. The bed was still made and he hadn't turned on the TV, evidently the hotel staff had refilled his mini-bar. He'd finished a new can of salted nuts and was midway through his third bottle of soft drink as he ruminated over his predicament. He'd 'sold' Ahmed on the idea that he had a plan for which he was to be paid a very generous reward. The only problem was, of course, he didn't have a plan. How would he be able to smuggle a 'casket' into Patch Barracks? Moreover, what exactly was Ahmed referring to when he used the terms 'casket' and 'death'? What was going to be in this box of indeterminate size and proportions? Would it be biological shit? Was it a bomb? It was coming from Italy and Herman felt he could be reasonably assured it wouldn't be marble or spaghetti!

The Arab certainly wanted to make that delivery to an American base bad enough to pay three hundred thousand dollars, which brought him back to his immediate problem, how the devil was he going to accomplish it? Realistically, he hadn't given any thought to the consequences of what he was doing, that an indeterminate number of people could and probably would die as a result of his involvement. If he had thought about it he would, no doubt, have dismissed it easily by the comforting fix-it-all thought that if he didn't do it they'd find someone else who would – as if that was ever a valid excuse. His mind plodded in slow circles, drifting off the subject from time to time and he found himself scratching his crotch and thinking of Polly. There was a little voice deep in his mind that was whispering something about a connection with Polly that would solve his problems but, frustratingly, he couldn't quite hear what it said.

He was also contemplating the awkward combination of events which had brought him to this impasse. Why did the Russian want him to kill Ahmed? Initially, he had accepted the insinuation by

Andrei that Ahmed was to be eliminated because he appeared to have been a traitor – traitorous to whom or to what? That no longer made sense; he'd been inside Al Nur and met the man. No way was this guy, Ahmed, working with the Bulls. He was an Arab, probably a terrorist, and certainly no friend of the German constabulary. After all was said and done he'd had Herman murder the hapless Mahdjoub because he had suspected *him* of just such a 'crime'.

So what was Andrei's motive? Ahmed did not appear to suspect Andrei of treachery, which made this entire situation all the more perplexing. Was the tea merchant a piece of this puzzle? Herman had a generous measure of questions, but a dearth of answers. However, one thing was patently clear; he was balancing on a razor's edge. There was no room for a single bad decision. Either he must kill Ahmed, or somehow neutralize Andrei. Either option offered Herman scant odds for survival. For the moment the best, and certainly the most potentially lucrative, option was to come up with a plan to move Ahmed's 'casket of death' from Italy to Patch Barracks; but how?

He looked over at the guard who had been ensconced in the room with him. Gap Tooth had refused to accept either food or drink from the mini-bar, he just sat nearly motionless in a chair wedged in the corner, spending most of his time staring into space and occasionally flashing Herman a cross between a leer and a smile. He seemed completely relaxed but his right hand hardly ever left the butt of the automatic pistol which was wedged in the waist-band of his trousers. Herman had his own hand-gun, an Italian Beretta, but he had made what now looked like a very poor last-minute decision to leave it in his car when he left the hotel to meet Ahmed. Being apprehended with an unlicensed handgun carried severe penalties in Germany and because he'd been stopped by the Bulls during his first attempt to rendezvous with Ahmed, he felt disinclined to take the weapon with him. So now he sat in this room with an armed black-ass; he had literally brought a knife to a gun-fight. The other man had remained in the car and, he presumed, was still outside. It seemed like just about every fifteen minutes Gap Tooth would call on his mobile and jabber something in Arabic, Herman supposed it was an 'all's-well' signal to his colleague.

****

What neither Herman nor Ahmed knew was that at that precise time *Hauptkommissar* Dieter Brückner was on the phone roasting Andrei's sorry ass.

'What's your fucking *Neger* doing working for Al Nur?!' was his opener. He went on to explain in the roundest terms that Herman had, in all likelihood, been responsible for the killing of Mahdjoub. What he couldn't tell Andrei was that Mahdjoub had phoned earlier to say that he was expecting a visit from the one they called 'Black Knife' and that he was supposed to accommodate him for an unspecified time.

'Now, I went out to Neukölln and saw the body. It was a clean, professional hit and I've no doubt it was your man. What the fuck have you told him to do or has he gone native? Are we looking at a loose cannon, Andrei, or what?'

The Russian had blustered and claimed he'd didn't know anything about what his man had or hadn't done but promised on all he held as holy to get some answers.

'You do that,' Brückner had hollered down the phone, 'or I'll grab that son-of-bitch Basil here and send my man in Hamburg to feel your collar. Depending on what Basil tells us when we put his balls in a vice, coupled with conspiracy to murder, you won't be seeing much daylight for the next few years. Now get your sorry ass in gear and tell me where that homicidal bastard, Namlos, is roosting.' Andrei wasn't allowed the right to reply, all he heard was the line cut as Dieter pressed the button on his mobile and considered throwing it across the room.

'Damn!' he shouted at thc blank wall, 'Damn, damn, damn!' He slumped back in his chair and winced as he tried to massage his temples with his fingertips. His headache was now well established and he couldn't remember when he'd taken the last medication. Groping around in the draw of his desk he found the aspirin pot and washed down two more pills with cold coffee and dropped the pot into his pocket. He'd no doubt it wouldn't be the last dose he'd need.

****

Herman breathed in deeply and then slowly exhaled, making a soft sound as he controlled the escaping breath. His eyes were closed and thus he didn't observe Gap Tooth come to immediate attention and stare at him with misgiving. As he repeated this breathing exercise, the Arab finally relaxed, slumped back in his chair, but kept a wary eye on his charge. This was a technique Herman used to reduce tension, as on each exhaled breath he mentally ran through the litany, 'Out goes the stress, out goes the stress.' He had learned the yoga technique from a young teacher he'd met in a Hamburg disco. Now he needed to relax and get back in touch with his instincts, with his reflexive self and, sure enough, as he continued to breathe according to his formula, the connection between Polly and his plan suddenly materialized. Yes! It was like opening the door on a bright spring morning, it was all there in one great leap. He slowed his racing mind down and started to run through the details, just as he felt his phone vibrate in his pocket.

Herman opened his eyes and was suddenly dazed, even by the low light level in the room. Although he'd thought he was just a layer below complete consciousness he had clearly descended to a much, much deeper level and was having trouble coordinating his limbs. Clumsily fumbling for the phone, he thumbed the pick-up button and held the small miracle of modern technology to his ear. He immediately recognized the voice on the other end.

'Did I wake you?' Andrei's voice purred disarmingly and Herman was immediately on his guard. Andrei was never pleasant and especially at this God-forsaken hour.

'Yes,' he lied, and decided to let the Russian play his cards first.

'Where are you, Black Knife?' he asked innocently.

'In bed,' Herman replied and waited for the

explosion at the other end of the line. The fact that it didn't happen made him even more suspicious. Andrei cleared his throat and continued in strained good humour.

'Yes, that is a good place to sleep.' He was managing to keep control whilst at the same time beginning to resolve which of the vile options he had on hand he would visit on Herman as and when he got his hands on him. 'And where exactly is this bed you are sleeping in located?'

Herman concluded that this game he was playing might be too clever by half. He wanted to know why Andrei was calling and why he was acting so unusually civil.

'What's up, boss?'

'Answer my question!' The thin veil of graciousness behind which Andrei had previously spoken suddenly lifted. The Russian growled in full throttle and Herman felt relief in familiarity, but he was still suspicious.

'I'm in Berlin. You sent me here, boss.'

'Yes, Black Knife, quite right, and I sent you there for a purpose. Have you accomplished that purpose?'

'I'm working on it, boss.'

'Where exactly are you staying, Black Knife?'

'In a hotel.'

'The *name* of the hotel,' Andrei demanded in a

voice of exasperation still tempered by control.

This was a test question. Herman knew exactly what his boss had in mind. He would immediately verify his answer by calling the hotel and asking to be connected to whatever name Black Knife had registered under. It made no sense for Herman to add to whatever suspicions Andrei was harbouring by playing cat and mouse. He and his goons were in Hamburg, so Herman had time. Then he remembered there was a contingent in Berlin – Basil. Never mind, he still needed to know what was on the Russian's mind. This would not be forthcoming until Andrei had called back to the hotel and confirmed that he was telling the truth and not worried about revealing his location.

'The Brandenburg House. Would you like the address?'

'Under what name did you register?'

'Herman Namlos.' He heard the disconnect click loud and clear.

He stared at the display of his mobile for a moment before dropping it onto the bed. Why was Andrei calling, he wondered. Well, for one thing, he hadn't phoned Andrei with either an update or a deal-done. It seemed natural that the Russian would finally lose patience and call. However, what made him suspicious was that if that had been the case Andrie's opening would have been a broadside, not an obviously restrained enquiry as to whether he'd been asleep. His instincts warned him that there were more sinister forces in play and Herman never disregarded the good counsel of his instincts.

The hotel telephone rang – two short riffs followed by a long pause and then two short riffs again. It huddled next to a lamp and the digital clock radio, all squeezed together on the sparse surface of the nightstand near the bed. Gap Tooth had straightened up at the sound of this ring and he eyed Herman suspiciously. 'My God, that was quick!' Herman thought to himself, as it could only have been a few seconds since Andrei had disconnected.

Picking up the handset he said, 'Hello,' and expected to hear Andrei's voice in full flow.

'It's the desk, sir,' said a pleasant female voice. 'There's a gentleman asking to visit your room.'

'Who?' Herman asked. He couldn't believe that Andrei had already known where he was staying! But how? Only Ahmed could have told him. What in the Devil was going on here? Was it one of Andrei's goons in the hotel lobby? If it was, then he wasn't there on room service and he wouldn't be coming through the door with flowers or chocolates.

'I'm sorry, sir,' continued the receptionist. 'The gentleman's German appears to be rather limited. He just repeats your name and then points to the elevator. He looks to be Middle Eastern, sir.'

Herman let out a sigh of relief, 'It's the other mountain man,' he thought. Herman immediately concluded with a sigh of relief. 'Is he wearing one of those woolen floppy hats like you see them on the TV in Afghanistan?'

The hotel clerk giggled. 'Yes, sir.'

'It's okay, send him up,' he said without enthusiasm. 'And thank you for calling first. If anyone else turns up to see me will you ring again, please.'

'Now what in the devil does asshole two want?' he wondered to himself. Andrei would be calling back, of that he was convinced. The last thing he needed at that moment was to play host to the Islamic Brotherhood. 'How did that he know my name,' he suddenly wondered, and then he recalled that he'd given Ahmed the *Herman Namlos* ID as part of his wire transfer information.

His own built-in early warning system was on high alert, he'd run into a tunnel and no light had yet appeared at the other end. Well, one tiny glimmer perhaps. He'd now got a plan for Ahmed, at least the beginnings of one but he needed to think it through. He'd have liked to confirm certain points in his tentative plan with Polly, but that wasn't an option; it didn't matter, the bare bones would do. What troubled him was the Hamburg gang. He needed some-how to prevent Andrei and the gang from cashing in their chips, one of those chips being his sorry ass. That would require a clever turn, one which yet escaped him. He relished the prospect of three hundred thousand dollars being added to his Swiss bank account, but he certainly didn't relish the path he'd have to tread in order to acquire the booty. He began to feel like Frodo carrying the ring. He'd seen the first two movies of *Lord of the Rings* and was eager-ly anticipating the third instalment due to arrive in Germany the following month around Christmas time. But, as matters were currently panning out, he did not exactly rate his chances of living that long too highly.

A knock on the door caused Gap Tooth to leap out of his chair. Herman stood up and took the three strides necessary to reach the door. When he opened the door, it came as no surprise that standing before him was the other guard. The fellow cast a weak smile as his right hand lay over the bulge in his sweat shirt that was undoubtedly the butt of his 'Tan'. There was no question in Herman's mind as to whether he was there to deliver pizza.

'What do you want?' Herman asked quite brusquely.

The Afghani stared back blankly but Gap Tooth

piped up behind him, 'It is his turn. He comes, I go.'

'Does he speak German?' asked Herman over his shoulder.

'A little,' Gap Tooth said half-heartedly.

Herman read 'little' to be 'damn little' but further speculation was cut short by the hotel phone. He turned and sat back on the bed, grabbing the handset and holding it to his ear.

'Black Knife?' barked Andrei's tobacco hardened voice. 'Are you spending a comfortable night in Berlin?'

Herman pondered for a moment as to whether he should respond with a wise-ass crack, or just defer to his boss. As he framed his answer the two Arabs performed their changing of the guard and Gap Tooth pressed past him on his way out as the asshole two brushed by him on his way in. They apparently found nothing disturbing about the telephone calls. He needed to get some idea of what was fomenting in that devious Russian bastard's mind. He decided he'd let Andrei do the talking and set a direction for their dialogue.

'Not very comfortable, boss. You didn't tell me that black-ass was the big chief surrounded by bodyguards.'

'Is that your way of saying that you need my help?'

He could have interpreted this remark as sarcastic if it hadn't been offered in a tone which Herman judged as sincere. Then he immediately wondered why the Russian was apparently being sympathetic. It sounded like he was amenable to sending Black Knife re-enforcements. Back to maximum alert; what brief would these goons have? To kill Ahmed, or to kill Black Knife – or both?

'What's your hurry, boss?' Herman tried to stall, 'I just need time to come up with a new plan. My first plan was to take him out with a knife. That wasn't good, but you're always telling me there's more than one way to skin a cat.'

'I'm in a big hurry,' Andrei fired back, devoid of sympathy, 'I need the fuckin' black-ass dead tomorrow. Can you arrange for him to meet with you tomorrow?'

'I'm listening,' Herman urged without answering the question.

'Yes or no!' Andrei demanded as Herman held the phone away from his ear.

'Yes.'

'Where?'

'Al Nur.'

'Mmm, that's going to take some manpower. Okay, when can you meet with him, what time tomorrow?'

'How's tomorrow morning?'

Andrei paused. Herman could hear him breathing. 'What time?' the Russian finally asked impatiently.

'I dunno; first I gotta call him. I'll do that first thing tomorrow morning. Is that my job, to set him up? Do I still get my fifty thou'?'

'You'll be lucky to walk away with your scrotum intact, Black Knife. Why'd you kill the tea merchant? How much did Ahmed pay you for doing the job?'

Herman felt an icy hand grip his gut. How the devil did Andrei know about that? It was only a second or two's silence but enough for Andrei to start shouting down the phone, 'Hello? Black Knife, are you still there?'

He didn't have the luxury of time to sift through the options he might employ in this chess game he was playing with Andrei. Should he try to bluff it out? Or accept it as a matter of fact. No time!

'I had to get his trust, boss,' Herman said in a hurt tone.

'Whose trust?' Andrei fired back suspiciously.

'The black-ass... Ahmed,' Herman explained.

Again there was a pause before Andrei responded.

'You believe that he trusts you now?'

'Yeah, I think so. I did the job.'

'How much did he pay you?'

Was this idle curiosity? Herman wondered or did he actually know? He decided to quote a reasonable figure, 'Ten thousand.' Again there was a pause as Andrei digested what he'd said. It gave Herman time to think as well. He was confident that fabricating a much lower figure had been the correct decision. Andrei was measuring his loyalty in terms of dollars and cents. Andrei's offer of fifty thousand dollars trumped the Arab's weak bid of ten thousand for Herman's loyalty.

'I have considered your suggestion, Black Knife, I think it's good. Inside Al Nur is better than on the street, less likely to attract the Bulls. Yeah, that works much better. But I need you to open the door and finger the black-ass for my fellows. How're you gonna do that?'

'How many guys are you sending, boss? Are they already here in Berlin?'

'Tell me about this Al Nur mosque. What will they be up against once they get inside?'

He shot a glance at the guard who had sat down in the same chair which Gap Tooth had previously occupied. 'I'm … I'm, with someone, boss. It's not an ideal time to talk.'

'Is she sucking on your black prong, or what?'

'You might say I'm under house arrest. They have

me under armed guard.'

There was the typical pause from Andrei before he responded, 'How many?'

'Two.'

'Sounds like you sure as hell have won Ahmed's trust,' Andrei laughed cynically, 'I keep all my best friends under armed fucking guard. Now recite to me one more number. How many guns do I need to clean up this abortion you've left me?'

Now it was his turn to pause. He was reminded of those times when they were trudging through the muddy fields in Bosnia where the muck just kept caking up on your boots until it felt like each foot weighed ten kilos, but you had no time to stop and clean them off just like he had no time now to take a break and figure things out.

'Five or six… *six*, just to be on the safe side.'

'You call me with a plan first thing in the morning, you hear?'

He heard loud and clear, but he said nothing. His mind was whirling with alternatives. Frankly, the strategy for this chess game had gone beyond his ability to predict the next three or four moves. He knew he was way over his head, but realizing this didn't help or make the issue go away. He was brought back from his reverie as Andrei began to growl down the phone again.

'I don't hear no enthusiasm on your end, *Neger*. As a matter of fact I don't hear anything at all!'

'Yes, boss, yes,' Herman stammered out. 'I'll call you first thing in the morning, once I've talked to the black-ass. How long will it take for your boys to get here?'

'My boys will be in Berlin before breakfast.'

'Who's in charge?'

'What's the difference?' Andrei gruffly challenged.

'I think I ought to know who's in charge,' he asked.

After a moment, Andrei relented. 'Basil,' he said.

That seemed logical to him, Basil knew Berlin, and he was already here. He had met Basil. He was a genuine asshole, from Belarus. Actually Herman had never worked with him; Basil didn't like *Negers*, nor did he hide the fact. Finally, in a soft voice which chilled Herman to the bone Andrei added, 'Oh, and Black Knife …' he paused as Herman waited for the Russian to continue with something which he knew would be less than pleasant, '… don't double-cross me or I'll reach up through you black asshole and pull out your heathen heart.' There was an abrupt click on the line as Andrei finished his one-way conversation.

Herman let out an audible sigh as he hung up the

phone and then glanced over at the guard. The fellow was eyeing him nervously while one open hand rested on his thigh so that the outstretched brown fingers perched close to the bulge in his shirt. In spite of this, Herman felt confident he could take down the asshole, but not just yet. Let him get more acclimatized and lower his guard a bit more. Then he'd cut his throat before he could fumble under his shirt for the gun. 'Fucking amateur,' he thought.

He didn't like the odds of his surviving either way, whether he threw in with Andrei, or betrayed him and rode with the Arabs. Nevertheless, if there was a third choice, it escaped him. Of course, he could simply kill this black-ass and run, but run where? Moreover, it wasn't in his warrior nature to retreat. They wouldn't sing songs about him if he just legged it. One question now perplexed him more than any other. 'How the devil did Andrei know about the hit on Mahdjoub?' he wondered anxiously, 'And how could he know I did it?' Only Ahmed could have told him, he concluded. Who else? 'So, why does Andrei want to kill the black-ass?' Nothing made sense.

****

WAITING FOR ANDREI

It was 5.30 in the morning and Dieter Brückner's mind wandered as he sat in his office, his headache still pounding. There were somewhere between forty and fifty thousand Jews in Germany, most of whom had come from the former Soviet Union and Eastern Bloc countries. In the German synagogues, aside from Hebrew of course, Russian was the first language. So why build a Holocaust Memorial here in Berlin, he wondered? Why don't they build it in Bavaria or Poland? That's where most of the victims had burned. He didn't place much stock in the argument that the Jewish influence in the press and academia had caused the Holocaust to be greatly exaggerated. On the other hand, he didn't much care. It had been a great human tragedy, he granted, but so had the genocide in Rwanda, and he wasn't losing any sleep over that misfortune either. Neither of these travesties had touched him personally, any more than bubonic plague in the Middle Ages or flu in 1918 had stirred his compassion for its wretched victims. These events were markers in history to him, and nothing more.

Lately, the news was full of 'latent European anti-Semitism', especially in France, Germany, Belgium, Italy and Great Britain, all of whom had large Muslim populations. Strangely enough, as far as he could determine, the Neo-Nazi Germans and the militant Muslims never cooperated in their vandalism and hooliganism, even though they shared a common theme of anti-Semitism. In fact, Eichmann and Hitler would appear to be a couple of guys 'soft on Hebrews' when he compared their Nazi Jew-baiting speeches and super-race propaganda to the rabid hatred spewing from the pulpits of mosques, and printed in the Arabic school texts by the Muslims camped in Germany.

Every Muslim school child was made aware of the 'Twenty-four protocols of the elders of Zion' which outlined how the Jews would take over the world. He had observed as well that 'Holocaust denial' had become a matter of fact to Muslim children, as well as to their teachers. He had once read an explanation concerning the reason it was necessary for anti-Zionists to warp history in this way. The Muslims reasoned that the 'so-called' Holocaust was a lie which the Jews had perpetrated to justify their spurious State of Israel. They had created illegitimate sympathy among the Western nations in order to acquire their bogus homeland. Arab archaeologists had apparently scientifically determined that the Jewish tribes originated from Ethiopia, and settled in Palestine as refugees from Egyptian slavery.

He further marvelled that unlike most Germans, the 'True Believers of Islam' were keen admirers of Adolf Hitler and felt unabashed at expressing their esteem. What any German, or Westerner for that matter, dared not utter was admiration for National Socialist Leaders and, consequently, the anti-Semitic rhetoric that would naturally follow, but the Muslim world could crow it with impunity. Yet he knew that Neo-Nazi groups in Germany had little use for these Islamic foreigners. They viewed the Arabs as half-breed Jews, bastards from the seed of Abraham.

The mullahs blamed the Jews for spreading the AIDS scourge throughout Muslim countries. Jewish whores purposefully infected with a host of venereal diseases had been sent into Egypt, Gaza and the West Bank where they seduced young Muslim men. Jews were the chief architects of the 'globalization' that impoverished tens of millions of Muslims, and no doubt, he chuckled, the mullahs would soon contrive an argument blaming the Jews for the gases gathering in our atmosphere and apparently causing global warming.

Thus, the Americans were regarded harshly by Islamic activists because they were seen as a nation controlled by the 'elders of Zion'. America had become a nation of 'useful idiots' hijacked by the Jews to further their conquest of the world. The American presidents had been 'bought off' by the Jews while the greedy American capitalists were keen to cash in on the spoils as they impoverished the Muslim peoples.

In the Cold War days, terrorism had been practiced in Germany, mostly against the perceived reactionary forces of capitalism. Although the rationale offered by Red Army Faction or Baader-Meinhof-Bande was that American greed perpetrated hunger and oppression in the third world, even a foot-weary detective like Dieter Brückner knew that their real quest was for political power. Likewise, anti-Zionism served the Islamic terrorists as a provocation which justified their acts, it had never been their reason. No, it was all about regime change in the Muslim world – and Islamic fundamentalists intended to be the new regime.

In the case of the German radical left, the party line was that America made it impossible for a socialist revolution to prevail in Western Europe. In fact, Brückner privately held that most of those radical misfits fighting in the trenches were searching aimlessly for a purpose, for a cause. There was no ideological imperative to which they had dedicated their lives; rather it was an exercise in narcissism. After all, if you had a good idea or solution, hey, you lived in a democracy. Go convince your fellow citizens in the arena of ideas and finally at the ballot box. Blow their minds with your logic, not their hapless bodies with C4. Even Joschka Fischer had been forced to conclude this.

Anyway, those days were gone. Now Germany was entering a new season, at least that is what Dieter sensed. The Americans would be targets of these terrorists, the Jews would be targets, and that didn't particularly trouble him, except that they would sometimes be targets on German soil, and German citizens would become innocent victims of the collateral damage.

A stark example of this lay in the alleged plans of Berlin's Al Nur cell, led by Ahmed. The previous evening he had sponsored a pre-emptive strike against this impending calamity. He had done so without hesitation. He had done so with righteous indignation. He had been gratified by the rush of adrenalin it produced. That was yesterday. Earlier, in the wee small hours of this morning, he recalled having felt drained right down to his nerve endings. His head had throbbed, his eyes had burned, and if he could have gotten his hands on Andrei at that moment, the world would have witnessed the instant transformation of a balding baritone into a new Russian mezzo-soprano.

During the evening, the first shoe had dropped when he had a call from Mahdjoub a little after seven o'clock. The little fellow was anxious, and his fluency in German suffered during such moments. Finally, Dieter had verified that what the tea merchant wanted to tell him was about a call he had just received from Ahmed. The leader of the Al Nur cell needed to use Mahdjoub's warehouse to hide Black Knife for the night. After requiring the tea merchant to repeat what he had said a second time, Dieter grudgingly came to grips with the news. This not only raised a flood of questions in his mind, but also underscored a stark reality – Ahmed was still alive.

'Did Ahmed ask you to hide a breathing *Neger*, or a dead one?' he had asked.

'I cannot be sure,' Mahdjoub answered breathlessly. 'It is my impression he comes alive. Maybe they are holding him prisoner?'

'Shit!' Dieter had spat down the phone. 'When are they bringing him?' His impulse had been to get his ass over to the warehouse. If he could intercept that Arab and his entourage, he just might decide to kill them himself if he could engineer some kind of shoot out.

'They are on their way,' the miserable Mahdjoub had replied.

Dieter had been at the *Revier* (Police Station) in central Berlin. He'd quickly calculated that he needed to have left about thirty minutes before if he'd wished to intercept Ahmed at the warehouse. His only hope was that they might have lingered. Well, no matter, first he needed to call that Russian asshole, Andrei, and see if the pig-dog knew what had gone wrong?

'Let me know when you find out what the fuck's going on,' he'd instructed Mahdjoub, then had added, 'Keep your door unlocked so that I can get in there. Do you understand?'

'Yes, of course,' Mahdjoub had weakly responded, and then inquired in a tremulous whisper, 'You are coming?' The response he'd received to his question was the unmistakable click of a telephone disconnect.

Dieter had tried to raise Andrei, punching the buttons of his telephone with a stiff index finger that would have been poking him in the chest if he'd been in range. No answer. Frustrated, he tried once again, but to no avail. He had no more time to waste on that Slavic piece of shit. He considered a strategy as he patted his government issued Glock 19 pistol which he wore in a shoulder holster. The plan hadn't take him long to conceive. He'd gone to his locker and pulled out a roll of lightly oiled canvass, and its contents were definitely not government issue. This was his private arsenal, a South African-made 'street sweeper', a specialized semi-automatic shotgun. The name fairly well described its effectiveness. He had acquired it during a drug bust a year or so before and at the time had wondered if it 'might come in useful one day'. From the back of the locker he'd also retrieved a box of heavy-gauge shells for the gun and a leather pouch which contained two reserve magazines for the Glock. Pushing the shells into the shotgun, he'd filled the magazine to capacity; it could deliver devastating firepower at close range.

Having finished pressing the heavy shells into the street sweeper, Dieter had clipped the magazine pouch onto his belt and sat down to try to raise Andrei once more, but still no reply. Again, for a few moments, he had massaged his temples and along the hairline, it hurt like hell but he knew it would bring some relief. It was the inevitable result of lack of sleep, overindulgence of stale coffee, and the tension caused by the developments of last few days. He had given up smoking four years before and it was at times like this that he regretted having done so. Standing up resolutely, he'd hooked the loop sling of the shotgun over his right shoulder and pulled on a trench coat that hid its presence. Cramming the remaining shells into his pocket, he had grabbed the keys to his car, left through the back door of the station and retrieved the black BMW from the car park and set off alone. He couldn't call for backup; this was a private war. Anyway, he couldn't afford witnesses, not even his colleagues in the *BKA*. He intended to kill that mullah or whatever kind of Muslim title Ahmed held. No doubt that meant he would have to kill Ahmed's partners at the scene as well, and what about Black Knife? Well, he'd take that as it came. If the Hamburg *Neger* got in the way he'd resolved to cut him in half, too.

Having cut across town at high speed he had slowly driven by the warehouse. The curbs had been fairly free of parked cars, given the lateness of the hour and this not being a residential area. The lights of a Donner Kebab *Imbiss* were shining at the far corner; otherwise this street had been deserted. Mahdjoub's storefront was all buttoned up and it was impossible to tell what was going on inside, or who was there. It made no sense for him to maintain a vigil outside the place because the probability was that Ahmed and his entourage had beaten him there. Either they were inside, or they had come and gone. He felt a strong temptation to pick up his mobile phone and call Mahdjoub, but his instincts cautioned against it. He needed the element of surprise. There was no telling how many of these hooligans he would be up against, so surprise and all out firepower were the only things that would give him an edge.

If he waited for them outside, and took care of business in the open as they left the warehouse, it would appear very much like he'd ambushed them without ever calling for backup. What grounds could justify such action? He needed to have his shoot-out inside, to make it appear he had been confronted and reacted accordingly. He hoped that Mahdjoub had left the door and grate unlocked, otherwise he had no other way to get in. So, how would he explain the street sweeper? Good question, but he intended to take it one worry at a time. The first things first, he had to waste that bastard, Ahmed, and provide him with a permanent transfer to the care of Allah.

Dieter had again pressed the tips of his fingers against his temples and then got out of the darkness of his car. He'd long since removed the bulb from the courtesy light, no point in letting everyone know you're around on a dark street when you open the door. Similarly, he had locked the car with the key, rather than arm the alarm with the ultrasonic key fob, as it avoided the momentary flash of the hazard lights and the muted beep as the alarm set. Hugging the shadows he had made his way towards the door of the store, unbuttoning the trench coat as he went. At the door he had stopped and listened before his right hand felt for the pistol grip of the shotgun and swung it clear of the coat, flicking off the safety as it emerged. He had felt his heart pounding in his throat as he nudged the door through the grate with the muzzle of the gun; it had easily swung open a crack. Stepping back, he had eased the wrought-iron grate open and taken up station on the hinge side of the door. The last thing in the world he had wanted was to be standing framed in the doorway by the light from the street, the perfect target. He'd eased the door open another crack and stopped as it emitted a squeak. Listening again he had heard nothing, so took a deep breath and shoved hard at the door as he moved forward quickly through the gap and pressed his back against the wall inside the doorway. His finger on the trigger, he had swept the room quickly but thoroughly in the dim light. Nothing. Relaxing a little, he checked behind the door and then began to work his way around the walls, peering into the gloom, shotgun at the ready.

His progress was halted by the chirp of a mobile phone. He froze thinking it might be his own, and his sphincter muscles clenched with such energy that it could have chopped off a length from a broom handle. However, he had quickly realized it wasn't his phone, the noise bringing his attention to a bundle on the floor, which he approached with caution. It was quickly apparent that it was a figure lying on the floor in the straight aisle to the left. The chirp of the mobile had been coming from that bundle on the floor. As he approached, he knew who it was before he was close enough to verify it. The nightmare just kept getting uglier; it was Mahdjoub. The little man had lost his glasses in what seemed to have been a scuffle. It was equally clear that Mahdjoub had not only lost his glasses but his last fight too. Dieter used the muzzle of the shotgun to flip open Mahdjoub's jacket and saw his shirt was bloody but he couldn't see a wound. Closer inspection had revealed the neat penetration through the left shoulder, clearly a professional job, not a frenzied attack.

He had speculated whether he should answer the mobile, but by the time he decided to do so the chirping abruptly stopped. He'd checked the window of the phone for a caller ID by pressing on the 'detail' for the display 'one missed call'. It'd shown a number which he memorized. Where was Black Knife? According to Mahdjoub, they had been bringing him there to spend the night. He looked around the warehouse for a second corpse, but found none. He had then decided to extend his search to whatever spaces lay behind the door on the other side of that counter. He'd taken a small Maglite from his coat pocket and by its thin beam he'd ventured through the door behind the counter. All he'd seen had been rows of pallets supporting large plywood tea chests which were stacked three and four high. He had listened carefully and then conducted a cursory search of the premise – nothing.

Back in his car he checked out the telephone number which had called Mahdjoub. It belonged to a name clearly Arabic, but not specifically Ahmed. Nonetheless, it told him what he had needed to know, and it also posed a question. If Ahmed had killed Mahdjoub, then why in the devil would he ring up the fellow?

Dieter was a self-taught criminologist and he was able to do the arithmetic. The telephone number was assigned to an Arabic name, although it was not necessarily Ahmed. It didn't have to be, it was just Arabic. Conclusion: Black Knife had killed Mahdjoub, and Ahmed had called to verify that the tea merchant was no longer able to answer his phone, meaning the hit had been performed by Black Knife under orders from Ahmed. The *Neger* was now working for the Arab. A new string of invective involving the name Andrei had streamed through his mind as he realized the sleazy Russian pimp had apparently double-crossed him.

Finally, at 1.30 that morning, the thoroughly frustrated police detective heard Andrei answer his phone. At first the Russian professed shock at the news which Dieter Brückner had to deliver, which was soon displaced by consternation.

'I will take care of this *Chornaya-zhopa*,' he spat, 'this black-ass Ahmed myself, I promise you.'

'When?' the policeman had asked. 'And remember it's your neck on the line, Anrdrei,' he added menacingly.

'Within twenty-four hours – it is a promise.'

'How can I be sure?'

After a pause the Russian made his best offer, 'I will deliver Basil to you myself if I fail.'

'What about your *Neger*?'

Another pause, 'He is my *Neger*, my problem.'

'Yeah?' said Dieter scornfully, 'Well, Ahmed is my problem. I want to know what you plan to do about solving my problem, where you plan to do it, and when. I'm listening!'

Dieter had again waited patiently through a long

pause. He knew the Russian was making it up as he went along but he had no choice but go along with it, even if it was bullshit. He could only comfort himself that he would inflict a terrible retribution before this Slav could escape to his roots. Finally Andrei responded.

'Give me a few hours.'

'It better be damn few hours, and it better make sense!' That ended the conversation between the Russian and the *Hauptkommissar*, which had taken place four hours earlier. He still had not received a return call from Andrei, nor had he been able to contact the slug. However, the headache he now suffered at this hour of the morning had less to do with any of these aforementioned events, and far more to do with his agonizing over the report he had laboured on for the past four hours. It wasn't such a long report, but he continued to re-read and to revise it. He wanted to include as much detail as possible, and reflect as much of the truth as he could, but he needed to take care that he didn't compromise himself in the process.

Mahdjoub was dead, so there was no longer any necessity for him to shield his source. Nevertheless, how and why the fellow had died was a delicate matter that could reflect adversely on *Hauptkommissar* Brückner. The policeman had not exactly been forthright in sharing information with his superiors. Thus, he had to carefully tidy up the report, and check it from several different angles. That's what was causing him such a God-awful headache. This report could put his neck in a noose if he allowed it to reflect a speck of the unfiltered truth. However, he felt compelled to get his report out concerning the Al Nur cell activity as soon as possible so that his superiors in Wiesbaden could pass it on to the European and American agencies with which the *BKA* routinely shared intelligence involving terrorist activities.

Of course, his initiative to unleash Andrei against that black-ass Ahmed could not be included in the report, nor could he dare to mention the complicity of Andrei's henchman, Black Knife. He had coloured the facts to reflect a strong suspicion that Mahdjoub was murdered by the Al Nur cell for having compromised their trust, although he made it clear that this was purely speculation on his part.

The central theme remained that according to Mahdjoub, he had acted as a courier bringing information from an Islamic terrorist cell in Florence, Italy, to the Al Nur cell in Berlin. That message had indicated very strongly that the Florentine Islamists already had enough nuclear material in their possession to construct a 'dirty bomb', and that was precisely what they were doing. He had played down

Mahdjoub's credibility, which served as an excuse for his reluctance to act immediately on the information and pass it along. Anyway, according to this weak but usually reliable source, the bomb was being prepared for onward delivery to the Al Nur cell, but it remained unclear if the delivery point would be Berlin or elsewhere in Germany. He left out the intelligence that the true destination was an American military base. That would surely have put his neck in a noose for not having immediately passed it on to higher authority.

Concerning his pre-emptive strike, Dieter would worry later how in the devil he could explain why Ahmed was shot in a drive-by, assuming of course that Andrei delivered on his promise. But putting that aside for the moment, he seriously doubted there would be any pressing inquiry into the matter. Nevertheless, there was a worrisome risk which he could not overcome. The *BKA* might downgrade the importance of his report concerning Ahmed and the Al Nur cell activities. After all, the report was based solely on the hearsay of an immigrant tea merchant, for whom the *Hauptkommissar* had offered only a weak endorsement. It was a delicate balance to strike, hence the headache and the burning of copious amounts of 'midnight oil'.

Headquarters in Wiesbaden had become inured to

the flood of imperative field reports concerning terrorist threats. He knew that they would want corroborative sources. Mahdjoub was dead and Ahmed would soon be dead, so there was little chance of verifying this intelligence. On the other hand, with Ahmed slain the likelihood was that Al Qaeda would abort the delivery of their bomb to Al Nur. They would suspect that their operation had been compromised, certainly on the German side, anyway. Frankly, that was the premise which had guided him to negotiate with Andrei for a 'hit' on Ahmed in the first place. Law enforcement, like public health, relied on prophylaxis as their primary procedure, and resorted to treatment only when the former failed. Killing Ahmed served as an inoculation against the Florentine dirty bomb spreading to Germany, at least that's how he viewed it.

Well, the conclusion of this episode depended upon Andrei. The next twenty-four hours would tell the tale. Thus, Dieter considered whether or not he should hold off submitting his report. If Andrei were successful, the report might become more troublesome than helpful. However, if Andrei did not succeed, then the tardiness of *Hauptkommissar* Brückner's report would surely raise uncomfortable questions with his immediate superior, who so liked everything tied up, no loose ends, no outstanding questions unresolved – a pain in the arse. He pressed the tips of his fingers against his temples again, massaging them painfully. The headache would not go away.

****

SELLING THE PLAN

Herman once again glanced at the digital clock sitting near the hotel telephone; it was 5.32. He stole a quick peek at Gap Tooth who had relieved the other guard about ten minutes before. The motley Arab looked reasonably alert for having endured the fatigue of this all-night watch. He wondered if these two guys used some chemical aid to help them get through their appointed rounds. He hadn't needed any chemical stimulus to stay awake, good old stress and adrenaline was enough for him. Rather than fatigue, he felt elation because at last he had come to a decision.

The one thing he had not yet resolved was at what time this morning it might be appropriate to call

Ahmed. The black-ass certainly was the trump card in the deck. He understood that he must use whatever fast shuffle was necessary to ensure this trump card fell into his hand. The dealing would begin when he dialled up Ahmed and set his scheme in motion. Clearly, the earlier the better in order to coordinate with the Berlin gang, but what time in the morning would be judicious from the Arab's point of view? On the other hand, his message was sufficiently urgent to excuse making the phone call any time of day or night. So why not do it now and be done with it? Weighing the decision, it seemed reasonable, even propitious, giving a sense of urgency at this early hour, making his improvisation all the more credible to Ahmed. Yes, now was not only as good a time as any, it was in fact the best; Herman's faithful instincts confirmed his decision.

He tugged the mobile off his belt and viewed the tiny screen while he thumbed the right arrow to scroll for Ahmed's number. Having selected it, he looked at the screen where the next question presented, 'Call?' Herman actually grimaced as he took in a deep breath like someone about to dive into ice cold water, then thumbed the 'Go' button.

Ahmed answered promptly and his voice was crisp, not fogged by sleepiness, this first signal gave Herman heart. He related a scheme to the Arab which he had began concocting, following his inspiration and conversation with Andrei four hours earlier. Furthermore, he hoped this scheme would prove beyond any reasonable doubt to Ahmed that Black Knife could be trusted, that the Al Nur cell could transfer a full hundred thousand today, accepting with confidence the plan Black Knife would outline for smuggling their 'package' into Patch Barracks and that Black Knife would see it to a successful conclusion. As Herman had anticipated, the fellow was acutely suspicious at first, so he patiently endured the Arab's intense grilling. After twenty minutes of gruelling cross-examination, Ahmed warmed to Black Knife's scheme and agreed to make the monetary transfer.

'If what you say is true and you do as you have promised,' the Arab stated, 'then I shall regard you as a blessed intervention by Allah in our Holy War against these Infidels. Do not let Satan tempt you into betraying the cause of Allah, for Allah is great.'

There was a long silence before he asked, 'Let me speak to one of my colleagues, please.'

****

PLANNING TO GO TO MILAN

Polly had set her alarm for 5.30 in the morning because of the briefing paper on the 'Italian intelligence' which she had been 'requested' to produce for EUCOM staff. She hadn't put her head to her pillow until one o'clock, only four and a half hours before. As it turned out, the report was disappointing since Langley hadn't been particularly forthcoming with details, probably, she guessed, because they had damn few. It wasn't like pre-9/11 when the Agency would often withhold information from the Department of Defense for fear of compromising sources. At least that was her judgement of the new tone at Langley, although she only had a ground-level perspective. Anyway, she had passed what Langley had given her on to EUCOM staff.

Whilst she had got to bed late, she nonetheless opted for this early rise because each week on Friday mornings she would rendezvous at oh-six-thirty with the Special Operations Staff members for a six-mile run, a mix of Army Special Forces and Navy SEALs. One would have thought that they maintained a physical fitness out of her league but this SOP head-quarters group at EUCOM was comprised mostly of senior enlisted personnel. Coupled with this was the fact that she had been a premier cross-country runner in high school and college, so she was able to keep up with the pace of this 'elite' group, if not lead it from time to time. It was recommended that military personnel stationed in Europe always run in groups. This particular group challenged her stamina, and she liked that. Moreover, she got on really well with them. They were intelligent folks with an earthy sense of humour, her kind of people. Most of them had a fair idea about who she worked for, but they were professionals who understood protocol and never asked the question, so she never had to avoid it.

Once she hit her 'second wind', usually about five minutes into the run, she would sink into automatic pilot and let her mind float in a day-dream state. This morning at roughly mile two into the course, as they ran on a packed earth path winding through wooded environs, she conjured up her friend, Hay-wan. The young lady had a Korean-born mother who had remarried to an Air Force Master-Sergeant now serving at Aviano Air Base in Italy. Hay-wan was active in the *Deutsch Amerikanisches Institut*, which was how they had became friends.

Hay-wan's step-father had pulled some strings and arranged his step-daughter a non-funded civilian job on base at Aviano. The pay was not generous, but Hay-wan lived with her parents and so had few overheads. She had remained an only child and had attended the University of Arizona when her step-father was stationed at Davis-Monthan in Tucson, Arizona. However, she'd quit her Fine Arts course virtually on a whim, saying that she didn't want to spend her life teaching kids who didn't want to learn about Botticelli and Beethoven. In the meantime, her step-father and mother had been posted to Italy and she opted to join them as Italy sounded like more fun.

Hay-wan had worked in the Aviano Recreational Services and the previous year she had been offered a similar job on transfer to Patch Barracks with better pay and on-base housing. Her family was being transferred back State-side, and Hay-wan felt ready for a change, so she accepted the posting at Patch.

'Life will just have to wait for a couple more

years,' she had once giggled to Polly. Well, it was Hay-wan who had convinced her to sign up for the trip to Milan over the Veterans weekend. For this Korean lady, Milan was her old stomping ground.

Aviano was located not far from Venice, and a short train ride from Milan, and as Hay-wan had taken that train ride often, she was much enamoured with Milan. While at Aviano she had studied Italian, and was quite proficient, although the proliferation of vowels still gave her some problems. With her fluency in Spanish, Polly could manage to decipher an Italian menu, but it would be handy to have someone like Hay-wan along when they were walking and shopping in the streets of Milan.

Hay-wan was short, barely reaching Polly's shoulder, but she had a beautiful porcelain-skinned face and meticulously coiffed raven-black hair. She always dressed her slender body stylishly, which left little wonder for Polly why this Korean fashion-freak loved shopping in Milan. Hay-wan had breathlessly described the beautiful *Duomo*, a Cathedral that looked more like a structure 'created for fantasy fiction than as a place of worship' as she had put it. Nearby was the *Teatro Alla Scala*, the world-famous opera house which, unfortunately, she apologized, was currently closed, undergoing a major reconstruction and renovation. These were sights to be seen but the Korean's genuine enthusiasm focused on *Via Montenapoleone* and *Via Della Spiga*, where world-famous fashion houses showed off their wares. However, most of the serious products on these two streets carried four or five-figure price tags, Hay-wan had warned – and that was *Euro* not *Lire*.

For fashion at a more affordable price, Hay-wan had advised they do their shopping in the *Galeria* and on the *Corso Vittorio Enamanuele II*. The *Galeria* was a shopping mall which stretched half a mile, or so she guessed, and it was covered by a high skylight of stained glass, while underfoot they had laid richly tiled walkways giving tourists the feeling that they were shopping inside some immense church, a cathedral of fashion.

'In the *Galeria*,' Hay-wan had promised breathlessly, 'you're going to see the most elegantly artistic McDonald's in the world, it'll blow your mind,' she had giggled. 'It feels like you're taking your communion with a cheeseburger!' Polly was so looking forward to this trip, she just couldn't wait, all the more so because she would be taking it with Hay-wan.

After a hard run and several minutes of recovery, the endorphins in her head would start dancing. It caused her to feel horny, and so as she drove back to her apartment for a shower and change before going to work, her thoughts turned to Sam Lumumba. She wouldn't have minded finding him waiting in the street outside her door sitting in his shiny yellow sports car. The late working hours of the previous night had given her a plausible excuse for coming to work late. However, she doubted if Sam would come back again before her trip, although lately his visits had been more frequent and his attentions more ardent. She was still enjoying the relationship but thought she might get to feel a bit claustrophobic if Sam started to get too heavy and visit too often. Just at the moment he served her needs admirably.

Sam was an interesting fellow and a good bed partner, but for her that was as far as she was willing to take it. There was something incongruous about the man. His story about being an illegitimate son of Patrice Lumumba rang with more than just a hollow echo of deceit. She knew it had to be a lie and would have to confront him with it one day. Moreover, she suspected from titbits of information he had carelessly dropped now and then that he was not in an entirely legitimate line of work. Nonetheless, she didn't care so long as he never confessed this to her or started coming around too often. She wasn't ready for a serious affair. Truth was, she wasn't sure she ever would be.

She wasn't at all sure what she was looking for in

a man, but she felt certain that when she came across
him, she'd know it. She also knew that she tended to
compare prospective suitors to her Dad. Was she
looking for another Rupe? Was that necessarily bad?
Mom had done alright by her choice of man. This
reflection caused her to remember that she must e-
mail to her Dad a copy of 'Intellectual Terrorism',
her opinion piece, before she went to work. She'd
value his critique.

****

THE HIT AT AL NUR

Dieter Brückner finally decided that he would make his decision on whether or not to forward his report to his superiors when he'd had one last conversation with Andrei, and assessed the credibility of his promise to hit Ahmed. If he believed, him then Dieter would have to further consider whether or not he should even submit the report. With Ahmed dead, it would serve little purpose. The Russian hadn't called back with his plan, thus eroding the scant confidence Dieter had harboured for a final resolution of this problem. It was 6.35 in the morning when he finally concluded that he'd had quite enough waiting and dialled up the Russian.

He had expected a sleepy baritone voice to answer; however, Andrei answered promptly and alert. 'I was just about to call you,' he quickly blurted out.

'I saved you the trouble; what did you have to say?' replied Dieter, unconvinced.

'It's going down at 9.30 this morning,' the Russian exclaimed in a tumble of words.

'What's going down?' asked Dieter.

'Ahmed.'

'Where?'

'Al Nur.'

'Outside the mosque?' Dieter asked with a tone of incredulity.

'Inside the mosque, better than in the street, don't you think?'

'Yeah, but just how're you going to muscle your way inside the place, and how do you know he'll be there?'

'We have an insider.'

'Who?'

Andrei drew a long silence before finally answering, 'My *Neger*.'

'Him? Since when did he become an insider?' Brückner enquired suspiciously.

'Since he killed your tea merchant.'

Dieter was an old hand at interrogation technique

and saw the implicit question in what Andrei had said, '*your* tea merchant.' So he ignored it.

'How, specifically, is he going to get your thugs inside?' he asked instead.

'They are expecting him at 9.30. He will shoot whoever opens the door. My boys will jump out of their cars and rush through the door that the *Neger* will keep open for them.'

'How many are you sending?'

'Six,' Andrei replied confidently.

'Are they're already in Berlin?'

'Yup.'

'Who do you have in charge?'

Again Andrei paused. 'Basil,' he finally disclosed.

Dieter chuckled with gallows humour. There was certain intelligence in the Russian's decision. Basil had the most to lose if his hit on Ahmed failed.

'Can you keep those Berlin Bulls off our backs?' asked Andrei.

'You know I can't do that,' Brückner responded in a monotone, 'How long do you figure this hit is gonna take?'

'Two or three minutes.'

'Then you don't need my help. Nobody's gonna alert *GSG9* over some dead Muslim *Ausländers*. Let me know if you hit any snags, and Andrei, don't disappoint me. That would be very bad for me, and I will dedicate the rest of the shreds of my career to making what's left of your miserable life hell. Let me know when it's over.' He disconnected with a flick of his thumb. For the time being his report would remain in the desk drawer.

He had no intention of being a third party to the news; he wanted to be imbedded. At 9.15 he'd post himself in view of Al Nur. He had parked in the same alleyway down the street from Al Nur as he had used the day before when he'd waited to intercept Black Knife. He was alone, he had no backup and his presence was strictly unofficial. Well, he certainly didn't look like he belonged there, not on this particular street. If one were to suddenly recover from total amnesia and find they were standing in his shoes, they'd have never have guessed they were in Europe, except for the chilly weather. The policeman could have done with some global warming this morning. As he stood in the shadows, the alley acted like a wind tunnel, the cold air burning his cheeks and forehead. His eyes kept watering and his nose had turned numb. The skies had cleared during the night which at this time of year, any Berliner could tell you, will usually bring in wind and cold.

There were several gaggles of kids all moving up the street in the same direction with no adults accompanying them. They wore scarves, mittens and knit caps with ear flaps. They didn't appear affected by the cold. Weren't they supposed to be in school. he wondered. He remained on the corner of the alley where it joined the pavement, leaning against the wall so he could peer down the street in the direction of Al Nur. He had no direct line of sight to the mosque, but he could see the traffic travelling past the door or stopping outside. When the Hamburg gang drove by him or stopped near the mosque, he'd be able to see them. They would have to double park, as there were no gaps along the kerbside. In any event, they would want a clear getaway after the hit. Dieter had decided that once he spotted them, he would venture out into the street for a better view.

One piece in this puzzle which did not seem to fit was Herman Namlos. How could he be working for Ahmed, and still be trusted by Andrei? This brought up a second imponderable for Dieter: what had been going on between Andrei and Ahmed? The Russian seemed to consistently avoid this issue. Black Knife had approached Al Nur using the mask Dieter had created courtesy of poor Mahdjoub. His unanswered question was precisely what deal Andrei had cut with the Arab.

Well, the *Hauptkommissar* had learned early in his career to follow the crime trail clue by clue, and make no unwarranted presumptions. Heroin was high on his list of contenders. He knew Andrei's Hamburg gang distributed blow, X and amphetamines, so why not smack? Al Nur was supporting itself on something besides Allah's good will. A lot of the Muslim extremists were involved in the heroin trade, much of which came in directly from Afghanistan. So there remained a possibility that Andrei was lying and might claim to have made a hit that he never really had. That's why Dieter stood in this alleyway this cold windy morning freezing his arse off. He wanted to see the alleged hit first-hand. If they took care of Ahmed inside, the news would be up and down the street in minutes.

He glanced at his watch, 9.26, four more minutes to show-time. If he'd been a betting man he would have put his money on a 'no-show'. He'd developed a negative expectation of events, finely tuned by experience. Something along the lines that if it can go wrong, it will go wrong. Somebody had once told him it was called 'Murphy's Law' whoever 'Murphy' was, probably a New York cop. He hated disappointment and failure but always prepared himself for it. He was still ruminating on the possibilities of this potential disappointment when he saw the yellow Mercedes SLK crawl by; Black Knife had just made his appearance. He edged forward for a clearer look and saw that right behind the Mercedes there followed a queue of three more cars. Black Knife was alone in his SLK, but as the other three cars drew up opposite, Dieter he saw there were two men in each of them. The yellow Mercedes continued another fifty metres and double parked in front of Al Nur and Dieter felt the electricity of the moment as if he were watching a scene from an action movie.

Herman turned the ignition key off, swung his legs out through the open door of his Mercedes, stood up and casually looking up and down the street. The fact that he was violating traffic regulations by double parking in this street didn't occur to him; he was, after all, on his way to break a whole lot more serious set of statutes. As he walked across the street, he pushed the electronic car key into his front pocket, and then casually gave the small of his back a quick pat to ensure that his handgun remained secured under his jacket. He cast a glance down the street where three black BMW's were slowly inching their way towards him. Other than this entourage, nothing on the street looked out of place; in fact the foot traffic seemed sparse for the time of day. He had noted the children at the end of the block but they appeared to be heading away and absorbed in their own conversations. He decided that the wind and cold was deterring most people from walking outside.

Standing before the locked grate at the entrance to Al Nur, he took in a deep breath as he took a last visual sweep of the street, and then jabbed the buzzer with his gloved index finger. The wait seemed interminable. He was tempted to pull up his sleeve and glance at his watch when a click of the door lock sounded, and the door opened. The little old man who had brought him a wash basin the night before peered at him. The bent and withered fellow neither smiled nor registered recognition, but his gnarled hand inserted a key into the grate lock and gave it a gentle shove. Herman stepped aside and then grabbed hold of the grate in order to swing it wide open. The little old man shuffled back a couple short steps to make room for the visitor. Herman took two quick strides and in one fluid motion drew the weapon from the small of his back, pointed it at the head of the little bent man and fired off a round directly into his wrinkled forehead. The old Arab was dead before he hit the tiled floor, and blood and brains were splattered on the wall behind where he had stood. Herman turned and waved at the three cars which had now crept into a line behind his Mercedes. The Hamburg gang catapulted out of them, each carrying a Kalashnikov, and dashed across the street towards the open door while

Herman held the grate open, signalling for them to hurry. They all duly noted the little Arab with half a head lying on the floor near the entrance, all hopping over the bloody bundle of rags except for Basil who used him as a stepping-stone.

Basil was the last in line, having stopped at the entrance to wave his men through the door.

'Where?' he breathlessly asked Herman, who was still holding the grate open.

'Second door on the right,' he replied, 'it's called 'the women's room'.

'Second door on the right,' Basil commanded, 'Go, go, go!'

The first of the gang to reach the door, cautiously tried the knob. He discovered no resistance and pushed the door open a crack. Glancing over his shoulder he saw the other four grouped up behind him while Basil remained about halfway to the door, covering their backs. They looked at him for direction and he gave them a nod. There was a split-second hesitation, and then the bunch of them burst into the room.

That was Herman's cue, he raised his pistol, pointing it directly at the back of Basil's head and fired. The bullet found its mark, passing through the back of Basil's skull cleanly, but flattening out slightly as it shattered its way through the bone. Still possessing enormous kinetic energy, it continued its destructive path through the brain, bursting out through the right eye socket in a spray of bone fragments, brain material and a mist of atomized blood. Pitched forward by the initial impact of the bullet, Basil crashed to the floor only momentarily rising himself on one arm as the nervous system reacted for the last time. Herman hit the floor next; he hadn't been shot but he knew what was coming next. Inside the women's room there erupted a cacophony of automatic weapon fire and the last two gunmen though the door staggered back out. The door next to the women's room opened and the two body guards with which Herman was familiar open fired on the two Hamburg hoods. They were both hit several times before they had a chance to return the fire. Several of Ahmed's men had been waiting inside the women's room for the gang and literally cut them to pieces in a murderous crossfire.

What was now being acted out had been Herman's scheme. He had pre-empted that asshole Andrei and, in so doing, he would earn yet more respect from Ahmed. The Arab had already demonstrated his trust in Herman's scheme, as well as his own cold bloodedness, by conceding that Herman should shoot the little old man in order to reinforce the Hamburg gang's confidence in Black Knife and he, in turn, had proven his commitment to Ahmed's cause. He would have loved to brag about his cunning to Polly, but of course that was out of the question; the only applause he would receive was from his own pair of hands.

On the subject of cunning, he had also further developed his plan for smuggling the 'package' into Patch Barracks and wanted his full hundred thousand dollar advance from Ahmed. His betrayal of the Hamburg gang, he now felt, deserved the benefit of the doubt from these black-asses and his just reward. In fact, he had made that a condition of his cooperation with the Arabs when he had spoken on the telephone to Ahmed the previous night. As it turned out, his concern for money seemed to present strong evidence in his favour. Upon hearing his demand, the attitude of the Arabs seemed to have shifted in his favour; they seemed to understand naked avarice.

Herman needed the money. After this delivery job for Al Nur, together with the recent catalogue of killings, there was no way he could remain in Germany or anywhere in the European Union for that matter. But, with a total of the three hundred thousand promised by the Arab added to his bank account, he'd have over half a million sitting safely in Switzerland. It would provide a modest income if wisely invested and he already had some ideas.

He had a fair idea of what Ahmed had in that 'package' and his warrior pride was tickled by the prospect. If it was what he anticipated and, furthermore, if he succeeded in carrying out the mission, the result would definitely be worth a poem and a song. That aside, with half a million bucks he could live like a king almost anywhere in Africa. So, as he witnessed the last Russian fall to the floor, Herman mused that maybe he ought to take up politics in Africa – Sam Lumumba, son of Patrice.

Outside on the street Dieter nervously glanced at his watch again. Five minutes earlier a shot had been fired inside Al Nur and then, moments later, the Hamburg gang had rushed into the mosque followed by the crackle of gunfire. The muted sound had carried into the street and caused the few pedestrians to duck into whichever storefront was closest. Now a few brave men cautiously peered from doorways in the direction of Al Nur. The police would be there in a few moments and he'd expected to see the Russians re-emerge and race off in their cars. Instead he saw four Arabs come out of Al Nur, one of them opened the door to the yellow SLK as the others proceeded to the three BMWs still idling in the street. Each Arab took a car and followed the Mercedes down the street. Dieter sucked in a deep breath and slowly exhaled as he watched and waited.

'What's gone down inside that mosque?' he wondered and it was more than the chill wind that made him feel cold. He fought off the temptation to telephone Andrei. Certainly at this point the Russian knew less about what might have happened than he did, so what would be the point? Right now he needed to leave the scene, since too many questions would be asked if he just happened to be passing as all hell had broken loose in Al Nur. He turned and thrust his hands deep into his pockets and pulled his head down into the collar of his coat, and braced himself against the bitter wind that howled down the alleyway. Heading back to his parked car he reasoned that there must have been a set-up and, further, that one Herman Namlos would have been a key player. Had Andrei's *Neger* betrayed the Russian? That was his initial assessment, bolstered by years of criminal investigation experience. Motive was often the most elusive component of an investigation, and more often than not it was money. He guessed that was the driver in this crime as well.

Given his experience with street criminals, he reckoned that for a soulless hooligan like Black Knife, money was a more likely candidate than ideology, but he'd wait for the police report before making a final judgement. One thing that wouldn't wait was his report concerning the information disclosed

to him by Mahdjoub about the shipment of radiological material into Germany for use by the Al Nur terrorist cell. He decided to go directly back to the
office and dispatch it through his chain of command.
That *Neger* Herman had better be counted among the
casualties, he thought to himself as he opened the
door of his car. If not he would definitely be added to
the policeman's shortlist along with that Russian asshole, Andrei.

****

PRESENT WHEREABOUTS UNKNOWN

So please explain what's so new about suicidal heroism, it has been practiced by brave men and women since biblical times, and before. Yes, these modern suicide bombers are brave, they sacrifice their very lives for their convictions, but always keep in mind that it is their convictions which must be scrutinized with suspicion, not their bravery. Furthermore, those apologists who rationalize radical Islamic convictions and only take umbrage at their sacrifice are enablers of terrorism, because it is this conviction which propels Islamic terrorist acts, not some quirky death wish.

Apollonia Johnson

Polly sat at her office desk in Patch Barracks deep in thought. The previous week, after her Friday morning run with the Special Ops contingent, Polly had half-wished that Sam Lumumba might be waiting for her, sitting smugly in his yellow sports car, parked on the street in front of her apartment. She had got her wish, albeit slightly belatedly, the next day. On Saturday afternoon she had returned to her apartment with Hay-wan after they'd been shopping and had done lunch in the Königstrasse district. Polly had driven her car, as Hay-wan didn't like to drive in downtown Stuttgart due to all the one-way streets and hectic traffic. She still wasn't completely familiar with the area and was afraid she'd lose her way.

They'd returned laden with fresh fruit and vegetables, condiments, fish and bakery goods, which they had purchased at the *Markthalle*, a huge bazaar of vending stalls housed in a building the size of a football stadium. She and Hay-wan had planned on cooking dinner together at Polly's apartment, and then go to see *21 Grams* which was playing at the downtown movie theatre, the one that showed American films with the original English soundtrack. Most theatres showed American films dubbed over with German voices. In fact, they would consistently use the same German voice for a given well-known American actor in whatever movie he or she participated.

However, Americans and Germans fluent in English preferred the original Hollywood soundtrack, so this particular theatre did a brisk business. Polly still marvelled over the popcorn each time she went there. Instead of butter and salt they sprinkled in sugar. On the plus side of the ledger, the movie theatre served beer and wine, not unusual in Germany.

Hay-wan had never been to a local movie theatre. She lived at Patch Barracks and the Americans had a theatre on base which featured the latest releases. They also had a video rental store with a fair selection of DVDs for Zone One players. Well, going to the movies may not have been the most exciting agenda for two single girls in Stuttgart, but it suited them just fine. Of course, the prospects of an exciting evening suddenly turned odds up when she drove with Hay-wan to her apartment that afternoon and saw Sam's yellow sports car parked at the curb. He was patiently sitting inside playing rock music with the heater blasting.

She had mentioned Sam Lumumba to Hay-wan in the past – nothing concrete, just a few titbits of girl-talk, enough, however, for Hay-wan to feel that she might be in the way. So she opted for a gracious exit, rather than playing gooseberry.

'We'll do dinner and the movie another time,' she had insisted.

However, as he helped them carry in the groceries it was Sam who remained adamant that Hay-wan should not leave. He exuded enthusiasm over the prospect of going to the movies and seeing *21 Grams*. From his comments, it was clear to Hay-wan that Sam was a genuine movie buff and his extrovert enthusiasm pleased Polly. So it was that the trio ended up standing in the kitchen where Polly was putting away the groceries and making initial preparations to embark upon the culinary chores which would lead to their meal – salad, steamed broccoli, four-grain farmer's bread, and fish fried in batter. The batter was spiked with a secret mix of herbs and spices Polly had got from her Dad. He used it to fry up his catfish and she used it on any old fish that was destined for her frying pan. If the subject of dessert came up, she intended to suggest that they go out after the movie for something sweet.

Hay-wan stood a full head shorter than Polly, although not really short by Korean standards, Sam judged. Truth was that this was the first time he had ever gotten up close and personal with a Korean. He'd bedded down one time with a Vietnamese but didn't remember that being anything special. She'd had a diminutive body and tiny tits with dark nipples but everything else seemed to be standard-issue size. Sam saw that Hay-wan had a torso almost as long as

Polly's, but the Korean's legs were much shorter. He noted that her breasts were about the same size as Polly sported but he didn't find her sexually attractive. Maybe it was because he had a concrete alternative who really did turn him on.

Sam had brought Polly a bottle of wine, a Montepulciano.

'A little taste of Italy to celebrate your upcoming shopping trip to Milan,' he had announced with a broad smile as he presented it to her. Sam had brought her wine before, but the reason he had just given for bringing this bottle seemed totally out of character. She and Sam had only one common interest, and that had solely dominated their hours together. If they could have entered the sex Olympics she was sure they could have walked away with the gold for mixed doubles. When, the previous week, she had told him about her planned shopping trip to Milan he had seemed totally disinterested, only complaining that he wouldn't be able to see her. His newfound interest in the trip, she thought, must just be an affectation to impress Hay-wan. Certainly, he now demonstrated an interest in the planned trip which had been totally absent a week previously.

'Are you going to Milan, as well?' he asked. The reply was a flurry of excited chatter from Hey-wan, whose enthusiasm for the trip was apparent. Polly watched with interest as she continued to prepare the fish for the pan. 'Boy, he sure knows how to press the right buttons,' Polly marvelled as she listened to Sam go on and on with Hay-wan about the shopping trip. His change of attitude was quite incredible. He wanted to know the smallest details, itinerary, routes, what kind of bus, how many people were going, were they all ladies, and so on. Sam had never struck her as the kind of guy interested in these details. 'What's got into him?' she wondered, but her only conclusion was to return to her first thoughts on the matter; he was probably angling to get into Hey-wan's panties, and she'd have to think about how she might feel if he did.

The alternative seemed to be that he was simply trying to make polite conversation with Hay-wan – put her at ease – but that didn't fit either. Polly had never seen Sam as the kind of a guy who would be that considerate. He had always revealed himself as a self-absorbed individual with little patience for events or problems which did not affect him personally. The one exception to that was in bed where he had adequately demonstrated that he knew how to give as well as take.

Polly's kitchen comprised a small space, certainly not designed to hold a committee of three if one of them needed to perform some serious food preparation. She took pride in her cooking and these two chatterboxes were getting in her way. She had cheerfully indulged them at first, because as Sam pumped Hay-wan he also busied himself uncorking the wine and poured them all a glass. Nevertheless, the overcrowding was slowly getting on her nerves.

In addition to the congestion in her kitchen, this endless gush of questions and interest which Sam displayed for the Milan shopping spree finally began to irritate her. Her reaction was not based on Sam's preoccupation with Hay-wan and it wasn't jealousy. In fact, she was comfortable with this threesome and she had indulged a fleeting fantasy that they might indeed extend it to her bedroom. However, whilst confident that Sam would be enthusiastic she had no idea how Hay-wan would feel. No, experiments like that could wait for another day. It was Sam's conversation that bothered her. It seemed so utterly contrived as, she had found, were certain other aspects of *Mr Sam Lumumba*!

After her first date with Sam, she had done a search on the Encyclopaedia Britannica web-site for *Patrice Lumumba*. The story Sam had related concerning his origins had bothered her. Somehow, it hadn't quite rung true with her recall of African history, sketchy as it was. What she learned from the site she had never shared with Sam but now, in this moment of bristling annoyance, she decided to have it out with him.

Interrupting Sam's conversation with Hay-wan by touching him on his arm, she cast a quick wink to her girl-friend. Hay-wan caught the wink and waited to see what was coming, she always enjoyed a joke. Polly flashed a mischievous grin to put Hay-wan at ease and then addressed Sam who had now turned his face towards her.

'Sam, where were you born?'

'Huh?'

'Where were you born?' she repeated softly.

'The Congo,' he answered after a moment of hesitation. 'I've already told you that. Why are you asking?'

'I know,' she urged impatiently, 'but where in the Congo were you born? You've never told me that.'

He eyed her suspiciously, 'You never asked.'

'Okay, so now I'm asking,' she said as she folded her arms.

'Why now?'

'Just indulge me, Sam; where in the Congo were you born?' She glanced quickly at Hay-wan who stood with a puzzled expression on her face.

'I don't remember,' he shrugged. 'I was very young at the time. However, they tell me it was in Kinshasa. You ever heard of it?'

'Yup. But your Daddy, Patrice, never heard of it.'

Sam cocked his head like a dog listening to a strange sound, 'What're you talking about, Polly?'

'When your *Daddy* was there, they called it *Leopoldville*.'

'Well, nowadays they call it Kinshasa,' he replied as he looked at her long and hard then glanced back at Hay-wan, who continued standing immobile and appeared less than comfortable by this turn of events. Finally he cast Polly a nonchalant shrug of the shoulders and chuckled, 'So, you've been doing some serious research on me. That's a good sign.' This time it was Sam who winked at Hay-wan, 'It means you've got a real interest in me. I'm flattered.'

Polly took a few seconds to collect her thoughts, 'Nice try, Sam-bo,' she granted him in her own mind.

'How old are you, Sam?' she asked bluntly.

Sam now saw the little red light flashing in his mind's eye and went on the defensive, trying not to show his unease.

'I've told her before, I'm thirty,' he said coldly. He really was beginning to go off this conversation.

Polly held his eye contact and measured her words, 'Thirty looks about right, Sam, it's the arithmetic which is tripping me up.'

Sam was now getting irritated by her indirect questions and raised his voice a notch to show his annoyance, 'What is your point, Polly?'

'Your Daddy was assassinated in January 1961. So when I do the arithmetic, it comes out about twelve years short! With the best will in the world, if you were the last thing the late lamented Patrice Lumumba did, you'd still have to be a very well preserved forty-two!'

'Polly!' Hay-wan protested, 'you're being cruel!' She could see that Sam was struggling.

'No, it's okay,' Sam assured her in a quieter, resigned tone. 'She's right, I lied.'

'Why did you lie to me, Sam?' Polly quickly challenged more aggressively than she'd wanted.

'I think the wine's getting to you, Polly,' Hay-wan tried again to intervene and take the heat out of the situation.

Sam held up both hands and smiled at Hay-wan, 'It's okay. I lied. She has a right to ask these questions.'

Polly had worked herself up and was in no mood to let go.

'Are you going to answer them now? Are you going to tell the truth?'

'You want to know why I lied?' he asked lamely.

'That'll do for openers,' she agreed, having stopped work on the broccoli but continued to squeeze the kitchen knife, clutching it so hard that her knuckles turned white.

Sam saw the knife and read her body language. He said, 'You don't look very happy, Polly.' and turned to Hay-wan for a light-heartedly confirmation. 'Does she look happy to you?'

Polly would brook none of his diversionary tactics; she was dammed mad and wanted some answers.

'What's your real name, Mr. X? Show me your driver's license.'

'I think maybe I should go,' said Hay-wan who was now obviously uncomfortable with this turn of events and the atmosphere.

'Not yet, Hay-wan,' Polly insisted. 'I want you to hear this too.' Then, turning back to Sam she asked flatly, 'Well, will you show me your driver's license, or not?'

'If I show you my license, will it satisfy you? Can we get back to being a happy family?' He turned and gave Hay-wan a playful wink but saw it was lost on her.

'Depends on what it says,' Polly said haughtily, 'Does it say Sam Lumumba?'

'No.'

'May I see it?'

'You don't have to show it to us if you don't want to, Sam,' Hay-wan suddenly broke in, 'Polly, your mood has turned downright ugly. Why don't you go in the other room and collect yourself. Sam and I can prepare dinner.'

Polly studied Hay-wan for a moment, then softly addressed her as a mother who gathers her patience before scolding her child.

'You've only just met Mr. X who I've fucked at least a dozen times. I like to know the real names of those I fuck.'

Sam held up his hands to signal surrender. He then reached into his trouser pocket and pulled out a wallet. From the wallet he extracted a piece of paper and handed it to her. She had to unfold it twice before it was fully opened, which proved a bit clumsy since she had not relinquished grip on the kitchen knife. The license was dog-eared and partially ripped at one of the folds. German drivers' licenses were issued once for life. No renewals necessary unless the driver committed a gross violation.

She read the name and birth-date. Then she read the birth-place. 'You're Namibian ... Herman,' she exclaimed. 'Herman Namlos, is that a Namibian name?'

'No more questions, Polly,' Herman said. 'Now you know the name of your fucker. That's as much detail as you need.'

She carefully laid down the knife she had been

clutching, and then with that same hand she shook her finger at him.

'This is my house, Mr Herman Namlos. In my house I make the rules, and I will ask any damn questions I choose before I let someone back in my bed, or to my dinner table for that matter!'

'Then I guess I'll skip dinner,' he said as he motioned for her to return his license. She carefully folded it and handed it back. As he tucked his wallet back into his trouser pocket, Herman turned to Hay-wan.

'Would you like to go out with me for dinner?'

Hay-wan looked at Polly for guidance. It was clear from her expression that she wanted to go with Herman. Polly realized that she had worked herself up into a state where she no longer had any desire to go to the movies. She actually wanted to be alone. She especially wanted this Sam/Herman character to get the hell out of her house. He was right. There was no point in any further questions. It was over.

'You're welcome to join us, Polly,' Herman chimed in, his tone sincere.

'No, you two go on. You're right, Hay-wan. I'm in an awful mood. I'll talk to you tomorrow,' she said as she wrapped Hay-wan in a hug, deliberately avoiding looking at Herman. As Hay-wan left the small kitchen Polly poured herself a generous measure of the wine and turned her back on Herman as she went at the hapless vegetables with the razor-sharp Sabatier kitchen knife. She ignored his farewell and gritted her teeth as she cursed in her own mind, 'Fuck you, Sam Lumumba or Herman Namlos or whatever your fucking name is, fuck you and the fucking stupid car you drive!' As a couple of huge tears ran down her face she heard the door of her flat close and blurted out loud, 'Damn! Damn! Damn!' She didn't notice that she'd sliced into her finger instead of the broccoli.

Polly had reflected upon this scene as she now sat at her office desk in Patch Barracks. A week had passed since this event. It was now Friday, and this evening they would be getting on the bus and heading for Milan. The prospect excited her, but at the moment she had a more urgent matter upon which to reflect, so she allowed her mind to sink back into private thought.

As noon of the previous Sunday had passed, she had grown increasingly apprehensive for the welfare of her girlfriend, Hay-wan. She and Sam/Herman had driven off in their separate cars. She could only presume that they went out together for dinner or whatever. She didn't mind. Sam or Herman or whatever his name was, was now a relic of the recent past as far as she was concerned. Her apprehension centred on the notion that she felt responsible for having put Hay-wan in possible harm's way. In truth, she was ninety-eight per cent sure that her girlfriend would be okay; but that last two per cent continued to haunt her. Thus, she had finally surrendered to her anxiety and called Hay-wan. If nothing else, she had felt compelled to reassure the Korean that she harboured no hard feelings over what had transpired the previous evening. Maybe, Polly considered, she ought to apologize and decided to play that one by ear. She wasn't quite certain why she should apologize, but thought she might just have been out of order.

The Korean answered her telephone. When Hay-wan grew excited, she spoke in a breathless stream of words, offering no more respect for punctuation than did Jack Kerouac. Polly had to interrupt her girlfriend several times in order to slow her down and try to bring some organization to her message. At last Hay-wan's tempest of words had spent itself and Polly arranged it in some sort of order. Hay-wan and Sam, she continued to refer to the Herman guy as Sam, had gone to downtown Stuttgart and left both cars in an underground parking lot near the Königstrasse area. Then they had gone to *Churrasco*, an Argentinian steakhouse. Polly had eaten there once and hadn't been too agreeably impressed. Most

German beef, she had long before concluded, was slaughtered after it had dutifully given milk for at least ten years and was exhausted. She bought her beef at the Patch Barracks commissary; it was all imported directly from the States.

After dinner they didn't go to see *21 Grams* because, Hay-wan had said, she didn't know how to get to the movie theatre; she didn't even know the name of the place. So, Sam suggested they go have a drink somewhere and around eleven he would take her to a local Disco and they could walk. 'It was a huge disco,' Hay-wan had enthused, 'but, my God, the music was loud! There was no way you could even talk to each other!'

Then the sobering part of her tale began to unfold. She kept hedging around it until Polly forced her to come clean. 'He called it X,' she said sheepishly.

'In the States we call it Ecstasy,' said Polly, really annoyed that her former lover had ready access to hard drugs. She wondered how many more skeletons Herman Namlos had residing in his cupboard. Hay-wan's version of events was that she didn't realize he had offered her a hard drug until after she had taken it and began to feel its effects. She'd developed a headache after they had left the restaurant and Sam had given her what she thought was an Advil or something. 'Yeah, right,' Polly had commented to herself.

'Anyway,' Hay-wan continued lamely, 'I don't remember a whole lot more about the evening.'

Polly figured that was more bullshit, but did not challenge her girlfriend. Instead she had softly inquired, 'How did you get home?'

Hay-wan explained that she was in no condition to drive, so Sam offered to drive her back to Patch. They drove in her car, and he left his car in the underground parking garage. She recalled that when they got to the sentry gate at Patch, he argued that they should let him drive her to her apartment in the housing area, but with Security still being a touchy issue, the MPs would have none of that. '… so the MPs drove me home,' she had sighed.

'How did Sam get back to his car?' Polly had asked suspiciously.

'I think the MPs called him a cab,' Hay-wan had quickly replied.

Last weekend's adventure in which Hay-wan had indulged would have been considered a non-event from Polly's perspective had it not been for what then transpired that morning. She'd come to the office a few minutes late because of her Friday morning's run with the Special Ops people. She went through her e-mail messages and finally came to one which, as she read it, caused feelings of nausea. She printed it, and had it now laying squarely in front of her on the desk. She'd read parts of it several times, each time hoping the previous read had been in error – no such luck.

This report was sourced from the Germans through the *BKA* in Berlin. An informant had disclosed that a load of radiological material sufficient to create a dirty bomb had been smuggled into the area of Florence, Italy, for onward deliver to an Al Qaeda terrorist cell based in Berlin. Although there was no specific information regarding the actual point of delivery into Germany there was a list of names associated with the Al Nur mosque. One name leapt out from the list, one *Herman Namlos*, a known associate of the Russian Mafia in Hamburg, probably a hit man, now apparently acting in a mercenary capacity with the Arabs. Present whereabouts unknown.

Polly dropped her head into her hands and rested her elbows on he desk, 'Oh, Dad,' she said to herself, 'what should I do?'

****

THE BUS TRIP BEGINS

Hauptkommissar Dieter Brückner was once again watching things go from bad to worse. Ahmed had been spotted boarding a commercial flight to Milan on Wednesday morning and the decision was made to let him run and have the Italians tail him. The logic was that it was the best chance to get a lead on the makings of the bomb, and those who would assemble and transport it. However, the devil was in the detail and somewhere between the airport and the city of Milan, about a fifty kilometre drive, the Italians had lost him. The car that had come to the airport to collect him did not have Ahmed inside when it arrived in Milan. The police tailing him only discovered this when three Arabs got out in front of a mosque in Milan and none of them was Ahmed.

Further bad news was to follow. Herman Namlos's distinctive SLK had been seen in the Stuttgart area early on the same day, heading south before he, too, was lost. The border crossing point at Singen had been alerted and there was a short sigh of relief when, two hours later, the yellow Mercedes passed over the border into Switzerland. The Italian authorities were alerted and had a surveillance team ready to pick him up when he emerged on their side of the Swiss border, but by late afternoon he hadn't appeared and hadn't re-appeared at a German crossing point. The best that could be said was that he was still in Switzerland, 'Got a meeting with his fucking bank manager,' Dieter had raged.

However frustrated he was, Dieter was quick to realize the focus was moving away from his zone of influence and that he had too much invested to let go. So when his boss remarked that he was looking tired she was stunned by two aspects of his reply. First, he agreed with her, something he'd hardly ever done before and, second, he called her *Chef* (Chief - Boss). Dieter had always observed the correct formalities when addressing his supervising officer but he'd never in his own mind respected her enough to use the familiar term. She was flattered but should have been alerted by such a change in stance; Dieter would have been. He had then gone on to say that he thought the Italian operation, such as it might be, was out their direct control and that he'd take some leave and go to see his brother. 'Family business,' he'd said. Thus it was he left his Berlin office on 'leave', fuelled his BMW and started the long drive south, keeping in touch with events through a trusted colleague whose only comment had been, 'You sure you know what you're doing?'

Even though he felt appallingly tired, Dieter pressed on and had covered two-thirds of the four hundred and fifty miles before he was suddenly jolted awake by the blaring of a heavy lorry horn as his car slowly drifted in front of it. It had only been a micro-sleep, maybe three or four seconds, but enough to have been fatal if he hadn't been lucky. He switched off the heating in the car, lowered the driver's door window and used the cold air to blow the cobwebs from his tired mind. At the next service point he saw the sign for a motel and checked in. Whilst looking through the menu card in his room he fell asleep and woke cold and hungry at 6.30 in the morning. A scalding hot shower and a shave made him feel slightly more human but his head still throbbed. Grabbing a pack of sandwiches, a large polystyrene cup of coffee and a bottle of coke at the fuel point he was soon back on the road. There was someone he needed to meet, and the sooner the better.

This was the 'big day' when the operation would begin and Herman felt very pleased with himself. Earlier in the week, the Swiss bank had confirmed that one hundred thousand dollars had been wired to his account. The following Monday, Ahmed had assured him, the Al Nur cell would wire him two hundred thousand dollars more. He'd devised a good plan and even Ahmed could not disguise his pleasure with the arrangements. During the middle of the week the Arab had flown by commercial airline to Milan to set the mission in motion.

This morning, Friday, Herman had rented a BMW, using his alternate identity papers and license. He had refused to leave his car in Berlin and had reluctantly compromised when the Arab agreed he could drive it to Zurich on Wednesday and leave it there. If the Germans were keeping him under surveillance, going over the Swiss border would suggest that he would come back out on the Italian side, and thus they would alert the Italian border guards to look for a yellow Mercedes SLK with his license plate.

To play it safe, the Arab insisted, they had to assume that Mahdjoub had shared his knowledge of the radiological shipment with the German authorities. For this reason Ahmed was adamant that

Herman should not tail the bus with his sports car.

'For one thing,' Ahmed had argued, 'two of the women on that bus know your toy car by sight and, secondly, the Bulls knew your registration number. Aside from the possible leak through Mahdjoub, there was no escaping the fact that Herman was probably on the *Innenministerium* suspect list for the massacre of those Russians at Al Nur. Six guys don't suddenly evaporate without leaving a vapour trail. By now, somebody would have talked to the police, maybe even Andrei. Herman took a singular delight in having for once up-staged that arrogant piece of Russian shit. He pictured for a moment the ranting, red-faced Russian angrily throwing his empty vodka bottle against a far wall while his ladies sat by silently, fearfully waiting to see how he would next vent his boiling anger.

The bodies of the Hamburg gang casualties had been quickly, almost miraculously, spirited away and Herman knew that Al Nur had disposed of them. They could fire up their furnace and practice with those six Russian bodies, he mused, until their glorious day when they could start burning Jews. The police had been met with a wall of silence and with no weapons, empty cartridge cases or bodies it was hard to get excited. The hastily cleaned up bloodstains on the floor of the women's room were explained as being the product of the ritual slaughtering of some chickens and goats for a religious festival. In the absence of anything else to go on, none of the Bulls was going to start forensic sampling. Even if there had been a shootout, what did they really care that some imigrants might have been killed in some sort of internecine turf war. They completed their notes and left. However, Ahmed suspected that the police knew much more than they had shown and that he must assume that they knew Herman had gone freelance and was cooperating with Al Nur.

'They will stalk us and patiently wait for the right moment to pounce,' he had warned Herman.

So, he had driven from Berlin to Zurich and rented the BMW from a Swiss agency in order to further confound the German police. Actually, he felt a certain comfort in knowing his Mercedes was safely ensconced in Zurich, close enough to keep his money company. Early Friday afternoon he had driven his rented car back through the same border crossing at Singen and into Germany. It was an easy two-hour drive from the border to Stuttgart, although Friday afternoon was unpredictable when it came to traffic jams.

It was now late Friday evening as he tailed the tourist bus at a respectable distance back towards the Swiss border. As they were on the autobahn, the exercise was no challenge, and so he allowed himself to reflect. Three hours before, he had begun tracking the bus outside Patch Barracks Main Gate. As Hay-wan had innocently informed him, the bus went to Böblingen where it made a second pick up at *Panzer Kaserne*. According to Hay-wan, there were seventeen people scheduled on this trip, all women except, of course, for the guy at the wheel, who would be a licensed German bus driver.

It wasn't until they had stopped in Da Pippo, the Italian restaurant in Dagersheim, that he actually confirmed Polly and Hay-wan to be among the gaggle of women. Obviousl, he hadn't been able to follow the bus when it went on base but now it had drawn up in the street near the restaurant and Herman had taken up a position about two hundred metres away. It was pitch dark, but the street lights and light from the restaurant illuminated the group. He didn't bother to count them as they strung out of the bus and crossed the street to Da Pippo, but seventeen appeared about right.

While he waited for the ladies to eat their dinner, he made his first mobile contact with Ahmed since having left Berlin and, of course, Ahmed answered from Italy. He confirmed the bus was in Dagersheim, on schedule. He also wanted to ask the Arab if everything was a 'go' from the Italian side, but he never got the chance. Ahmed cut the communication short with a quick acknowledgement followed by an immediate disconnect. Herman considered such caution to be a bit overdramatic, but he wasn't about to take the Arab to task over it.

Herman needed the delivery to go according to plan so he'd have his payday. Let the Arab play his cunning counter-surveillance games. He needed this mission to succeed for reasons which reached beyond a two hundred thousand dollar payday. He also relished the glory this project would bring him. He smugly reflected that he felt like a warrior again. Finally he had embraced an enterprise worthy of poems and songs. Energy surged through him as if he had been struck by a bolt of lightning that filled him full of power and glory. Such ruminations were a pleasant distraction to wile away this boring trek on the autobahn.

An hour and a half after entering the restaurant the giggling gaggle of women emerged and clambered back onto the bus. The tail lights dimmed as the driver restarted the big diesel and the bus moved off on the second leg of its trip. Herman kept the red tail lights of the tourist bus in view as he relished the unfolding adventure. Polly had taken a seat on the right side in the first row of the bus at the suggestion of the driver. That was where the tour guide would sit and there was a pull-out table on which she could site her laptop and work. This was an ideal solution because she didn't want to be cosseted with the other giggling girls down the bus, many of whom had imbibed what was probably more than a sensible amount of the light Italian red wine. But she felt she should explain herself to Hay-wan who was clearly disappointed at their not sitting together. It seemed to Polly that she presumed that she was being shunned by her friend because of the incident with 'Sam'.

'I have some homework which I must get off my mind and out of the way,' Polly apologized, promising to join Hay-wan and the other girls just as soon as she had finished – not more than a couple of hours, she pledged. The truth was that she needed some quiet time to sort things out in her mind. It had also occurred to her that after all the rich Italian food at Da Pippo's, it was going to start reeking back there like a waste disposal plant, especially once the ladies began dropping off to sleep.

She still hadn't decided on what her proper response should be to the information she'd received on Herman Namlos. She had uncomfortably written a report concerning her relationship with this Nambian mercenary, but she had stuffed it into her desk drawer. She had resolved that when she returned on Sunday she would e-mail it to her father and get his advice on whether or not to submit it. She was fairly certain he would tell her to hand it in, but maybe there were certain elements which she didn't need to include. Anyway, she had reconciled herself to follow Dad's counsel.

Also, before completing the report, Herman Namlos was a topic she had wanted to pursue with her friend, but she couldn't come right out and tell Hay-wan her concerns because the material she had received was classified. Nevertheless, she needed to know in the greatest detail possible what the man had discussed with her, and what she might have told him. At dinner, she had tried prying more information out of Hay-wan concerning what 'Sam' had said or suggested. The Korean doggedly continued calling him Sam and Polly also sensed that Hay-wan interpreted her questioning to be resentment over having been snubbed by him.

Moreover, Sam had taken Hay-wan to dinner and a disco which made the Korean an accessory to the misfortunes of the previous Saturday evening. She sensed that Hay-wan felt guilty for having gone out with him instead of remaining with her friend. She'd done nothing explicitly wrong, but all the same it had been a bit of a cheek. Was this also a factor in her self-imposed isolation from Hay-wan here inside the bus? No, she genuinely did not believe so. At that moment, she was wading up to her ass in troubled waters and a dark mood gripped her; she needed to be alone.

She had recognized, soon enough, that this line of questioning about Hay-wan's evening with Sam was only raising suspicion and making her friend uncomfortable and so she had dropped the inquiry. The problem remained that she had no firm basis for assuming that Sam/Herman had visited her the previous Saturday for any other reason than sex. Yet, deep in her mind, there was a gnawing suspicion that Herman Namlos had been up to no good when he visited.

'He's listed as an associate of suspected Al Qaeda terrorists, for Christ-sake, and you've been fucking him!' the voice in her mind screamed. It wasn't something you would want signalled back to Langley unless it had relevance. Try as she might, she could not imagine how this drawing would come out when and if she joined all the dots up.

On the previous Saturday the guy had shown a very uncharacteristic curiosity about her shopping trip to Milan. What was that all about, she wondered? On the other hand, he may just have been attempting to appear congenial, especially given a third party was present. Her Dad had always upbraided her for being such a worry-wart. 'Life doesn't have to be a chess game, Polly', he had said on more than one occasion. 'Sometimes you just gotta sit back and let shit happen!' She'd got her obsession for control from her mother, and she sensed that Dad recognized it.

So here she had been sitting for the past hour with her laptop on the tour guide's table randomly typing in case Hay-wan took the trouble to look. What she was really doing was just turning the facts over in her mind, knowing there was a connection she just wasn't seeing. She was also beginning to put another journalistic piece together in her mind, a companion piece to 'Intellectual Terrorism', should it ever be published. She had brought a copy of *The New Republic* with her that she'd picked it up from her dad's collection last time she had visited the folks. 'My God,' she thought, 'that was over a year ago.' He was a subscriber and kept all his old issues for reference. She had picked up this particular back issue because it contained a book review by Omer Bartov. She had thought it might be useful with her new article.

In the bus interior, her laptop screen afforded enough light for her to distinguish the print of the magazine page; it was like reading by the light of a full moon. She had to prop the page just right in order to get sufficient light onto it. Thus, she laboriously copy-typed a passage from the book review that cited the Reuters reporter, Christian Eggers. It concerned the trial in Germany of Mounir el Motassadeq, a founder member of the Al Qaeda cell in Hamburg, which had planned the 9/11 attack on the World Trade Center. What was most shocking about Egger's account of the trial had to do with how little of a stir it raised in the Western media. One of the witnesses, Shahid Nickels, a member of Mohammed Atta's (thought to have piloted the first airliner to hit the twin towers on 9/11) core group, gave evidence. 'Atta's worldview,' he had said, 'was based on a National Socialist way of thinking. He was convinced that *the Jews* were determined to achieve world domination.' He also went on to testify that Mohammed Atta considered New York City to be the centre of world Jewry, which was, in his opinion, Enemy Number One.

There seemed to be a tacit sense of 'political incorrectness' in Western Europe for exposing linkages between Nazi doctrine and extremist Muslim pronouncements. Such mention would be insensitive to the modern *Bundesrepublik* of Germany and its citizens, even though explicit references to *Mein Kampf*, or admiration for Adolf Hitler and his insight, had been repeatedly expressed by the Mufti of Jerusalem, Yassar Arafat, and nearly the entire leadership of Islamic terror, including Osama bin Laden. Similarly, the witness Ralf Göttsche, who shared the student dormitory with Motassadeq, testified that the accused had said, 'What Hitler did to the Jews was not all bad', in conjunction with many other anti-Semitic pronouncements.

It was the manner in which the Western European media appeared to shun the recognition of how Nazi doctrine had helped to shape extremist Islamic thinking in the 1940s and 1950s right down to the present day which fascinated her. She wanted to know why. No, more than that, she wanted to take these Euro-Socialists to task!

****

THE CHASE

Once Herman had passed over the Swiss border into
Italy, Ahmed began pestering him routinely for status. Everything was going like clockwork, Herman
continued to assure him. The night was cold and the
Italian border guards had waved him through from
their window, not even bothering to step outdoors.
Evidently, the tourist bus had encountered no resistance at the border either and he was about a hundred
and fifty metres behind it, always trying to keep one
or two vehicles between them. He needed to stay in
closer proximity because the bus was using national
roads as opposed to taking the *autostrada*, probably
because it required a toll. At this time of the morning,
a little after five o'clock, there wouldn't be much
traffic. Herman estimated they'd hit the outskirts of

Milan in an hour or so, and Ahmed had advised him it would be another twenty or thirty minutes for them to get into the centre of town. So the current ETA was for no later than 6.40 a.m.

'But the stores don't open until ten o'clock,' Ahmed had remarked, 'what do you think those women will do until then, stay on the bus?'

'How would I know,' Herman retorted with impatience.

'This is your plan, Black Knife! These are details that you must know! If they stay on the bus, it will not be good. At ten o'clock our operation will be much harder to carry out than at seven in the morning. It will be much riskier.'

'They've been sitting on that bus for ten hours,' Herman offered. 'I don't think they want to remain sitting there. Besides, they're Americans. They must eat breakfast – you know, pancakes, fried eggs, English muffins, bacon and sausage. No doubt they have a place arranged to go for breakfast.'

Herman presumed that the revelation had satisfied Ahmed, because he broached his fears no further. Instead, the Arab replied, 'Yes, the Americans are fat. They have learned their eating habits from those Jewish apes and dogs that control them.'

After dozing off once, Polly realized that she needed to sleep. Chewing the same thoughts over in her mind wasn't helping her resolve the problem. There was still something she wasn't seeing and thought that some rest might just ease it the fore. So she closed down her laptop and packed everything back into her computer bag. She then spent a moment passing small talk in German with the driver in order to assure herself that he was alert. His cold-as-ice expression melted into a broad smile when she spoke to him and his responses were animated, so she concluded the bus was in good hands.

He seemed like a nice guy. She learned during this exchange that he'd been married for twenty-seven years and raised two children. His son had studied EU law at the University of Strasbourg and his daughter, the younger of the two, had studied Hospital Administration in Bayreuth. He proudly disclosed that his daughter had spent last year studying through an exchange program with a US hospital in St Louis.

'She loves America,' he commented. He was clearly a proud father, and that went a long way towards capturing Polly's affection. It was only after she had got out on her own, and listened to the 'horror tales' of so many others concerning their family life that she had truly come to appreciate her Mom and Dad. She'd been really lucky.

'Are you also going to drive us back,' she had

asked.

'Of course,' he had responded.

'Won't you be tired?' she had objected.

He had laughed. 'While you ladies are shopping, I will be sleeping.'

She left the bag up front, and with quiet and careful steps made her way back to where Hay̆-wan occupied her row. The opposite row was vacant, and Polly presumed that her friend had saved it for her. The Korean appeared asleep, but when Polly sat down and was about to shut her eyes and attempt to recapture that doze she'd forsaken at the front of the bus, Hay-wan sat up and looked over at her.

'Where are we?' she asked in a sleepy voice. 'What time is it?'

'We're in Italy,' Polly whispered. 'It's five in the morning. Go back to sleep. We have plenty of time to talk after we get there. You'll need your energy.'

'Are you going to sleep?'

'Yup.'

Hay-wan slumped back down and closed her eyes. The short conversation with her friend reminded her that she had an exciting shopping trip ahead. This prospect suddenly flushed away the gloom which had been gripping her. She shut her eyes and almost immediately re-captured sleep.

****

Ever since they'd entered the city, Ahmed had remained on the mobile phone with Black Knife, who now followed closely behind the bus, which he couldn't afford to lose in traffic. He had never driven in Milan before, but he'd heard about the notorious Italian drivers. So far, the traffic wasn't bad.

It was twenty minutes to seven when the bus entered a square very near the *Duomo* and then abruptly parked. Herman had been relaying their progress to Ahmed every several blocks and, presumably, the Arab was directing the assault team on another phone, or was Ahmed part of the team? Herman didn't know. He parked away from the bus on the other side of the square and scanned the area for any names that Ahmed could relay to the team so they could find the place. He was sure that they were close by.

The first name he saw was twenty metres from where he had parked. 'Grand Albergo,' he whispered into the phone as he squinted to make out the rest of the sign. It was at an oblique angle to his line of sight, making it difficult to read. The strain caused his eyes to burn and suddenly forced Herman to concede that he was very tired. Then he spotted the signs that would pinpoint his location. 'Piazza Armando Diaz. The bus is parked between Via Guglielmo Marconi and some narrow street with a neon sign that says Venus Night Club.'

Herman waited several moments. He could faintly hear the Arab jabbering, probably into another mobile. Finally Ahmed spoke to him.

'They will be there in a short time. Are the women getting off the bus?'

'A few have just got off,' he said as he squinted to make sure. The first pair off the bus was unmistakably Polly and Hay-wan, followed by the driver. He hoped to hell they weren't intending to walk his way.

'They must all get off!' Ahmed ranted on the 'phone.

'Hey, relax,' replied Herman, more relaxed than he actually felt. 'They've just started to leave the bus!' He felt relief as he watched Polly and Hay-wan head into Via Guglielmo Marconi which would carry them in a direction away from him.

****

The cold morning air hit Polly's face in a refreshing way. The bus had been overheated, at least for her comfort, and it made the air inside stuffy. Her sinuses felt full and she felt her eyes tear from the cold and dabbed them with a handkerchief.

'Are you crying?' Hay-wan asked. She had followed directly behind Polly as they got off the bus and now walked beside her. They were in the lead. The group accorded that Hay-wan was the most knowledgeable to guide them.

'No. It's the sudden cold; it makes my eyes water. So, where're we going for breakfast?'

'Biffy's.'

'Will they be open this early?'

Hay-wan cast her a smug little smile.

'Recreational services at Aviano arranged for them to open early, 'specially to serve us breakfast. I used to be posted here, remember?'

'So you know the way to this Biffy's joint, huh?'

'Like the back of my hand,' replied Hay-wan. 'And on the way you'll get your first glimpse of a fairy-tale cathedral, the *Duomo*. It's so beautiful that it's almost eerie. You'll see.'

Polly had left her laptop on the bus. She had been so distraught the previous evening that she hadn't given any thought to the security of the computer when she had impulsively decided to take it along. She had just resigned herself to lugging it around with her all day when, to her enormous relief, the driver promised that he would guard it personally.

'I will take it with me when I go to eat,' he had assured her.

'How about when you sleep?' she had asked, ever cautious.

'I sleep on the bus. I sleep in the back row. I will take it back there with me. And the bus is locked when I'm inside,' he had reassured her.

****

Herman heard the motorcycles as they drew up and stopped in the narrow street directly in front of the Venus Bar.

'Scheiss!' he cursed as he recognized the uniforms and held the phone to his ear, the line was still open, 'Hello, Ahmed?'

'Yes?'

'Bad news. We've got two Bulls who've parked their bikes just off the square, just a few metres from the bus.'

'Have all of the women left the bus?'

'Yes, I think so. The driver's standing in the street.'

'Are you sure all the women have left?' Ahmed repeated.

'I don't see anybody at the windows. You understand that there are two Bulls surveying the square?'

'Yes, I understand,' Ahmed replied with an uncharacteristic chuckle, 'Is anyone else in the square?'

Herman took another look, 'Nope. Nobody.'

Now his attention was taken by the bikes again as they were started up and eased out into the square. One swept around to stop in front of the bus whilst the other parked at the rear. Both riders dismounted and approached the driver from opposite directions.

'Ahmed,' Herman spoke into the phone, trying to keep an even tone, 'big trouble, now the Bulls have pulled the coach driver.'

'I know,' came the bored reply. 'Now go over there and provide them some backup.'

'Huh?'

'Go to the bus and keep an eye out for any possible witnesses.'

'Are they our team?'

'Don't ask questions,' Ahmed replied curtly, 'just do as I say.'

'Oh, shit,' said Herman, 'a van just pulled onto the square. It's creeping along, looks like it's heading for the bus. Doesn't seem natural. My guess is they're Bulls.'

'Describe it,' Ahmed calmly responded.

'Black Mercedes van.'

'Yes. Go help the team. Hurry up!'

By the time Herman had reached the bus, the driver had unlocked the door and climbed inside, leaving the laptop in its case standing on the sidewalk. He was fumbling for his papers and tacho discs; both Italian Bulls had entered the bus with him. One of them stepped past the driver and suddenly produced an implement resembling an ice pick. He grabbed the driver from behind, his hand wrapped over his mouth as he stabbed the implement into the base of the driver's skull, holding until he collapsed and lay motionless.

A third man arrived on the pavement by the door of the bus, dressed in slacks and a shirt. He was about the same height and build as the now dead driver but with jet black hair. He acknowledged Herman with a curt inclination of his head. His name was Nhadi Hussein and, although born in Saudi Arabia, he had attended university in Italy. With his dark good looks and fluent Italian, he could easily be confused for a Sicilian. For the purposes of his new assignment as a coach driver he had been given the name Marco Fanucci and that's what his papers now said. The two policemen got off the bus and made a show of going through some papers with 'Marco' before he got on board. Then, with a hiss of compressed air, he closed the doors. Stepping around the body of the driver, he pulled down a travel rug from the overhead racks and covered him. It wasn't out of consideration, he just wanted the body covered from prying eyes. With that he dropped into the driver's seat and started the engine, the bus was needed to be elsewhere as soon as possible.

As the bus pulled away Herman was left standing on the curb. He looked across to his car where he saw Ahmed leaning casually against the front wing, gesticulating for him to go back to the car. Looking at the laptop in its case he wasn't sure what to do with it. As Ahmed became more insistent, his frugal nature took over and he snatched it up and jogged, tossing it onto the back seat.

'What now?' he asked Ahmed.'

'Follow the bus,' he ordered.

Looking up, Herman could see that the bus had, in fact, stopped further down the Piazza but was already indicating that it was about to pull out. Herman turned the key in the ignition and a few moments later they were passing through Milan as it slowly came to life.

'What's that on the back set?' Ahmed enquired.

'Laptop,' Herman replied.

'Whose?'

'I don't know,' Herman answered honestly. 'Seemed a shame to leave it lying around.'

'We'll see about that,' replied Ahmed thoughtfully.

Working his way south through the nearly empty streets, Marco drove the bus to an industrial estate where the hangar-like doors of a factory unit were opened for him as he approached. As the bus and car entered, the doors were pushed closed and a group of people appeared from the side offices, some carrying tools and some carrying cleaning equipment. Within seconds the lower luggage lockers had been opened and work had begun. Inside the bus, the dead driver was stripped of his uniform and rolled up in an old blanket. Weighted down, his body would slide beneath the slimy surface of a hopelessly polluted lake outside Milan during the course of the following night.

In a side office, the driver's uniform was being cleaned and his identification badge copied. Within twenty minutes Marco had a laminated copy of the driver's company badge with his details substituted, together with his own personal papers which identified him as a coach driver. As Herman waited, he sipped on a cup of scalding hot cappuccino and watched with idle curiosity from the office window as a long box was brought from storage, to be almost reverently placed in the luggage lockers. It took the whole length of the lockers, but was only some twelve to fourteen inches wide. He knew his brief was to take the coach back to Germany where, he was told, the box was to be removed and its contents used to create an incident to punish the Americans or the British.

His misplaced assumptions were twofold: first, he thought he was just a delivery boy and, second, he thought he was carrying a ground-to-air missile that would bring down a jumbo jet. What else would be so slim and long? In fact, what had been re-fabricated in a miraculously short time was the RDD.[52] It had previously been configured in an entirely different shape when the cell had assumed it would be carried to its destination in a van or small truck, but as Herman's plan had been approved it had to be reshaped to fit in the coach.

The bomb had been designed by Midhat Mursi, an Egyptian-born chemical engineer who had adopted the alias of Abu Khab. He was Al Qaeda's expert and answered to Ayman al-Zawahiri, bin Laden's second in command. He had been responsible for what the security services called 'very innovative and effective designs' and it was thought that he was sharing his expertise with many other groups including the Palestinian Hezbollah. He had not been present at the initial construction, and the original design and the subsequent rapid rethink had been done via the miracles of modern communications. It was accepted that Mursi had been responsible for hardware used in the Bali nightclub bombings and it appeared that, in terms of technology, he accepted the time-proven maxim, 'If it ain't broke, don't fix it'. The requirements for this bomb were the same, requiring remote detonation, rather than relying on the fanatical commitment of a suicide bomber who might bring attention to himself before the vehicle could enter the target area. It was therefore decreed that a mobile phone would once more be employed and the micro-circuitry was altered to the required specification. Dialling the correct sequence would actuate the phone and initiate the bomb.

The new bomb contained a massive charge of C4 which had come from stocks systematically hived off from engineering projects and stolen from the military worldwide. It formed the core of the RDD, and was wrapped in the Cordex that would actually detonate it. Packed in thin slabs around the explosive core was the collection of radioactive material, again collected over many months and from many sources, mainly in the old Soviet States: plutonium, iridium and uranium from hospitals, universities, and military sources, but mainly from food processing plants in the old USSR where a surprising quantity of extremely 'dirty' material had just been abandoned. There were always entrepreneurial individuals who could fulfil a wish list, given enough of a cash incentive.

The case containing the dirty bomb was secured in place lengthways in the footlocker and then suitably 'distressed' panels of plywood were screwed into place on either side of it. These new panels were then trimmed with wood to give the impression that the lockers were not designed to be open right through, but that they were used from each side. New wood would have raised the suspicions of the most inexperienced policeman or customs officer but the scored and marked panels gave the impression of considerable use and time in place. With the new secret compartment being just fifteen inches wide it would take the application of a measuring tape to ascertain that there was anything untoward in the arrangement. To the naked eye it shouldn't ring any alarm bells. Several modern designs of coach had the main luggage area segregated by baffles to avoid the shifting of the load on tight corners on mountain roads. It was hoped that this modification would be accepted as a retro-fit for safety.

Herman felt surplus to requirements and just interested himself in observing the elements of his plan coming together. In the early afternoon it was clear that work was more or less finished and the last touches were being applied. Ahmed was standing off to the side of the bus with other members of the team, principally the three who seemed to have had most to do with the supervision of the whole operation. Faxed copies of plans and circuit diagrams had been spread out on a work bench and they were clearly giving him the last technical details. Then came what seemed to be the exchange of mobile phone numbers as Ahmed entered them on his Nokia, the last of which caused some obvious amusement. The next moment there was much embracing and kissing of cheeks as the doors of the unit were opened and Marco started up the bus and began the first stage of the journey back.

****

At ten o'clock Dieter Brückner parked his car in the car park of an imposing police station in downtown Stuttgart, his *BKA* ID had been enough for the attendant on the barrier, that and the fact he knew who he wanted to see. He'd been there before and knew his way to the offices occupied by the *Kripo* on the second floor. It was a large open-plan office which took up most of the floor width of the building, and down one side were five offices which were occupied by some of the more senior officers. Dieter strode down the length of the office and peered through the glass panel of the last but one door. He saw his friend, Rolf, seated at his desk, elbows on the desk, supporting his chin whilst he read through a document. Without knocking, he slipped the door open and stuck his head through, asking, 'Is this where I join the real police?'

Rolf Stein was plucked from his concentration and looked up a little confused until he saw Dieter's grinning face. Standing up and automatically closing the file on his desk, he greeted him in their native Schwabian dialect.

'Ja, wen hot's denn do og'schwemmt?' * The two of them had been at school together and went their own ways when they began full-time employment, only to find some years on that they had both made the same career choice. Dieter made a reply in the same vein and strode into the office to shake hands. Rolf offered him a coffee and the two men sat down in a couple of easy chairs in front of the desk.

'Now while it is always a pleasure to see my cousin from the big city,' began Rolf, 'I doubt you're here on holiday or taking the waters.'

'Well,' Dieter responded, 'I am actually on leave but there is a certain something I wanted to keep an eye on whilst I relax.'

'Relax!' laughed Rolf. 'You? Relax? You were born with a Bull's whistle up your ass, Dieter, it's just a case of how hard you're blowing it.' He knew

*Literally, 'Look what the sea's washed up.' Similar to the commonly used English expression, 'Look what the cat's dragged in.'

Dieter was a dedicated and extremely capable police-man but he also knew how capable he was of 'bending the rules' and even, on occasion, completely ignoring them. It had always been a dilemma for him when Dieter hove into view, for he knew of his dedication but worried about his methods.

'So tell me the story,' Rolf asked as Dieter duly sketched out the substance of what they knew about the RDD and the plan to detonate in Germany. He carefully circumnavigated complications like the shoot-out at Al Nur and his negotiations with the Russian Mafia.

'So the Italians lost this Ahmed character between the airport and Milan and then they couldn't spot that homicidal black bastard, Namlos, entering the country. No wonder the cell decided to bring this bomb in through Italy,' said Dieter bitterly.

'So what's the situation now and what are you going to do?' asked Rolf.

'Well, the *BKA* will be looking for either Ahmed or Namlos re-entering the country but, hopefully, the Italians will make contact again and be able to deal with the bomb before it leaves. Even if it goes off it's got to be a better option for us than having it happen in our back yard,' commented Dieter cynically. 'I have a colleague in Berlin who's going to keep me up to speed on what head office are up to and I'm just going to freelance.'

'Freelance?' Rolf queried, more than a little suspicious.

'If they're going to get the damned thing over the border it's going to be through a crossing point here in the south, so I want to be on hand. Can you sort me an office and a phone for a couple of days?'

Stein thought for a moment before answering. 'Yes, we can, but here's the deal. It's a chair, a desk and a phone. I'll do what I can if you need some help, but we can't provide backup unless and until it's within our jurisdiction. And that, my friend, means staying on the right side of the law. No cutting corners. Agreed?'

'Agreed,' said Dieter as he checked his watch and took a sip of coffee. 'You going to buy your old pal lunch?'

****

As the bus swung out of the factory unit in Milan, Ahmed made for the car and indicated that Herman should follow. Opening the door, he reached over to the back seat and hefted the laptop computer out in its bag. Beckoning over one of the group of workers he offered him the computer.

'Hey, that's mine,' remonstrated Herman.

'Not any more,' commented Ahmed then spoke to the delighted recipient in Arabic.

'Now where's your gun and I want that knife of yours,' Ahmed continued, 'we've got to travel clean.' Herman reached inside the car and brought out the pistol but was reluctant to surrender his Black Knife.

'Just hand it over,' insisted Ahmed, 'with your payday coming you'll be able to buy another.' Herman argued a little longer but in the end he slid up the sleeve of his jacket and tugged at the Velcro fixings.

'Now get in the car, we've got things to do before that bus leaves tonight.'

****

The shopping ladies had congregated at Biffy's for dinner and all were accounted for, although a great deal lighter in the wallet. That weight loss was more than compensated for by the bags they carried, laden with fashionable booty. Polly had bought her Dad a to-die-for matching shirt and tie. Her Mom was always a more difficult choice for gifts, as she had very specific tastes which seemed to shift with her moods, so she'd opted for a Gucci purse. What the hell, if she didn't like it Polly wouldn't mind keeping it for herself.

For herself she had done something that, had it not been for Hay-wan's enthusiasm, she simply wouldn't have dared. The business suit was on special offer at 1,799.00 Euros... more than 2,000.00 US dollars! But it was absolutely dreamy, the cut, the material, the red lining and it was *Yves St Laurent*. She had always thought this designer to be a French fashion house, and originally it had been, but the Italians had bought them out. She had no time for the alterations but the shop on Via Montenapoleone made a call to Stuttgart and made an appointment for her to get fitted and altered there, complimentary. They even offered to ship the business suit to Stuttgart, but Polly would have none of that. She trusted no one with her newly acquired treasure.

Now they had gathered at Piazza Armando Diaz ten minutes early. Hay-wan had anticipated the bus would already be waiting there, but it wasn't. No matter, Hay-wan had certainly been right about most other things. The shopping had been the absolute best Polly had ever experienced and, during dinner, it became apparent that all the other ladies shared this view. For most of them, it had been their first visit. They were mostly enlisted servicemen's wives, and she understood they didn't have much of a budget for spending on fashion. Thus, she had made Hay-wan promise that she would make no mention of the Yves

St Laurent purchase which she had made; 'Not a word of it,' she had insisted.

The bus arrived just five minutes late and parked where it had let them down in the morning and the group made for it. Laughing and struggling with their bags they all teetered forward on their heels, the cobbled surface of the Piazza not being ideal for some of their footwear. Striding ahead on her long legs, Polly was a little in front and saw the driver, his back to her and head down, apparently reading something.

'Do you have my computer please?' she asked anxiously while she was still a couple of metres away. She stopped dead in her tracks as the driver turned to face her, realizing immediately it wasn't the German who had driven them out.

'Where's the other driver?' she asked blandly.

'He sick, *Signora*,' replied the handsome young man who now confronted her, making a gesture of vomiting and holding his stomach.

'He have some bad chicken for lunch and had to go to *L'Ospedale*, they *pompare il suo stomaco*, they pumpo his belly,' he continued in his fractured English.

'So they send Marco to take you lovely ladies back to the Germania – to Germany,' he corrected.

The rest of the group had now formed a semicircle around 'Marco' and all were smitten by the new

342

driver's broad smile and very Italian nature, all except Polly. Her instincts told her something was badly wrong. There was still something nagging at the back of her mind that wouldn't come through. The more she sought the answer, the more illusive it became, like a moth fluttering on the edge of a pool of light, drawn to the source but reluctant to expose itself until it is ready.

'Do you have my computer?' she asked again.

'Computer, *Signora*? I don't have no computer. Was, er, was she on the bus?'

'I left it with the other driver. He said he'd take care of it.' Marco raised his arms in a kind of gesture which invited her to search him.

'I don't see no computer, you look on the bus, huh?'

Still ill at ease, Polly mounted the steps to the bus and placed her purchases reverently on the overhead rack, then made a perfunctory search of the bus with no success. Through the windows she could see the ever charming Marco helping the other women pack their treasures into the lockers, further obscuring the newly fitted compartment. At last, everyone was back on board and he closed the door and dropped into the driver's seat, flicking various switches to the 'on' position and starting the big diesel engine at the rear. As he tapped information into the GPS system he glanced over his shoulder at Polly who had resumed her position in the guide's seat.

'I think the German driver, he look after your computer for you, *Signora*,' he tried to reassure her, 'When I get back I make talk with him and the company and we find her for you, yes?' Polly nodded her agreement since there wasn't much else she could do.

As the bus climbed up towards the Swiss border, the girls chatted animatedly about their trip and showed each other some of their wares. Polly, however, remained detached, slightly remote in the courier's seat and deep in thought. Still the moth fluttered on the edge of the patch of light in her mind as she tried piece together the events of the last few days that were still causing her some anxiety. In the end she began to dismiss it as being a reaction to her shock of discovery that Herman Namlos had duped her. She couldn't get the thought out of her mind that she'd been sleeping with someone who had some unspecified connections to international terrorism, and she was still uneasy about Marco; the ever smiling, ever helpful Marco, driving the bus and flashing his winning smile every time she glanced over and caught his eye.

He, himself, couldn't be happier. He was at last actually doing something for the cause in which he believed. He silently speculated about the rush of pride he would feel when the news came on the TV that a US or British airliner had been shot down – maybe even Airforce One?! That, he felt sure, would secure him the appropriate stock of virgins and supply of virility in the next world without the necessity to be a suicide bomber and to get blown to atoms. Just to be responsible for the delivery of such a weapon must surely be the ideal contribution. Approaching the Swiss border, he began to feel the first real churnings of nerves.

****

Five hundred metres back, Ahmed and Herman watched as the big brake lights on the bus flashed on as it came to a halt. There were only a few vehicles at the crossing and there were two main lanes, one for HGVs and coaches and one for cars. Herman slowed and then headed for the car lane. Looking across, they could see a uniformed officer go to the door of the coach and board it. Seconds later he was off and the coach crossed into Switzerland as an idle border guard in his heated post casually waved Herman and Ahmed through. Not more than half a metre from his elbow was a fax copy of an alert for two such men travelling in an unspecified vehicle.

By the time he could be bothered to read it, the significance of what he'd seen would be lost in the number of vehicles he had passed through on that shift.

The passage through Switzerland was uneventful and Marco relaxed, having cleared his first hurdle. However, the entry to Germany might be a little more regulated, he speculated. He hated the Germans and their bloody rules and regulations. Behind him, the women had quietened down and some had already nodded off to sleep, all except the tall black bitch sitting to his right. Every time he glanced over she was staring at him and sometimes trying her mobile phone but thus far he didn't think she'd managed to contact anyone.

Indeed, Polly had been trying to contact quite a few people but nobody was answering. She thought that if she could just talk things through the moth might flutter into full view. At the third attempt she managed to contact the guard commander at Patch Barracks who agreed to meet her at the gates on her arrival, but found herself floundering for a reason.

'I'd just like a few things checked out,' was all she could come up with. With that, the battery on her mobile gave up the ghost and she rummaged through her bag for the charging lead to plug into the cigarette lighter in front of the driving position. She couldn't find it and slapped the flap of her bag shut angrily and let it drop to the floor. She remembered that she'd packed it in the cable pouch of her laptop. Still deep in thought, Polly sat back in her seat and tried to relax as she stared at the headlights of the oncoming traffic.

****

Back in the office he'd been loaned, Dieter Brückner sat in the in the pool of light thrown out by his desk lamp. He too felt he had a moth fluttering at the edge of it. Somehow Herman had eluded him and was probably in Italy, and might even have hooked up with Ahmed, but why? He was a hit man for a Russian thug, not a terrorist. His only conclusion was that Herman had left his car in Switzerland and hired another. Hence, his rather garish and highly visible toy had not been spotted by any of the border patrols. Or, maybe, and more likely, they simply hadn't been arsed to read the alerts or to look for it. He was plucked from his reverie as the phone on his desk rang.

****

Approaching the Swiss side of the German border at Singen, Marco again began to feel nervous.

Essentially, this and the entry into Germany were his last hurdles. After that he could not see why anyone would want to stop and inspect the coach, 'Unless,' he wondered to himself, 'that black bitch was suspicious and had alerted someone to the fact they were on their way.' But his worries seemed to evaporate as first the Swiss officials waved the bus through without any form of intervention and the Germans just made a cursory inspection of the papers. It was more than sufficient for them that it was a German-registered bus with a cargo of people who were either US personnel or related to US servicemen. This was part of the simple genius which Herman had unwittingly offered in his plan.

It was not the same story for Herman and Ahmed. Again they had chosen a different lane from the bus and watched as it was waved through by the Swiss. However, as Ahmed casually waved their passports at the Swiss official, he was instructed to stop. After examining the two passports they were asked to pull through the barrier and park in a segregated area and wait. This particular guard did take his work seriously and had read the fax sheets posted at the beginning of his shift and had seen the photos of the two men. Inside his small office he checked the passports and scanned the photos, Herman was an immediate and unmistakable match but Ahmed was less clear because he had shaved. However, within a few minutes, he knew the driver of the car was one Herman Namlos and that the German authorities were very interested in his whereabouts. Picking up the phone, he called his colleagues on the German side, no more than a few hundred metres away, and passed on the information, asking if they wanted the two suspects arrested.

Earlier in the day the telephone number of the office in the Stuttgart Police station had been passed to the southern border crossing points on the fax alert. The guard commander had called the Stuttgart number and Dieter listened to him and decided to take a small chance. It would only complicate things if Herman and Ahmed were detained on the Swiss side of the border and so he asked the border guards to call their colleagues on the other side and request they let the car pass. He then spelt out in graphic detail what he would do to the rather junior officer at the German border post if he did not arrest and detain the two suspects.

He estimated that he could get to the border crossing in about two hours. Opening the plastic aspirin pot he dropped the last few into the palm of his hand and washed them down with a cupful of very bitter, very cold coffee. It was going to be a long night.

****

On the Swiss side of the border Ahmed was losing his cool in a big way.

'How the fuck are we going to catch the bus if these shit-head clockmakers hold us here?' he asked of nobody in particular. Herman just shrugged; he was more concerned that they had been recognised and that they were about to have their collars felt.

A small pool of light spilled out from the small office as the Swiss officer came out.

'It's you they've spotted,' hissed Ahmed through clenched teeth, 'I knew it was a mistake to travel with a *Neger* – they always stop *Negers*!'

Herman was about to suggest that these days it was more likely that they'd stop Ahmed than him when he was encouraged to see that the guard was still on his own and that he had their passports in his hand.

'Shut the fuck up, you stupid rag-head,' he replied quietly, whist smiling at the approaching guard, 'I think we just got lucky'

Passing the passports through the window, the guard waved them on without another word. Glancing at Ahmed, Herman started the car and moved off to cover the short distance between the Swiss and German posts. Ahead he saw a guard directing them into a lane and followed his instructions without suspicion. Halting by the glazed booth,

Herman lowered the window and handed the two passports over to another uniformed officer. As he did so his attention was taken by a noise and a cold draft of air as the passenger door was opened. What he saw next induced an instant tightening of his sphincter muscle as he saw the unmistakable muzzle of a Heckler & Koch machine pistol being aimed at Ahmed, as he was quietly but firmly asked to get out. A second later he felt the cold pressure on his neck as a Glock 17 was pressed against it and the suggestion made that it would be best all round if he, too, were to get out of the car.

In the cold night air he was required to 'adopt the position', where he found the bitterly protesting Ahmed facing him over the roof of the car. After a thorough external search, his wallet, phone and keys were taken away and he was allowed to stand up. He was then encouraged to walk towards a block of buildings. The rather nervous but efficient guard commander had obviously taken very seriously Dieter's threats to mutilate certain areas of his body if he fucked up.

Two hours and five minutes later Dieter arrived at the border crossing, his head still throbbing. For a few moments he sat in the car and gathered his thoughts. For a second his illusive moth fluttered into his consciousness, but he couldn't quite grab it before it merged back into the darkness. If only he could get rid of the headache, he knew he'd be able to think more clearly. For a few minutes more he massaged the acupressure points on his hands to see if that would bring any relief, but as he stepped out of the car his head swam and the pain returned even more viciously.

What Dieter could not have known was that, some sixty minutes earlier, he had passed, in the opposite direction, the coach as it cruised its way closer to Stuttgart and its destination. Inside, Polly still wracked her brain, trying to find the detail that she thought was still missing, the piece of the jigsaw that would show her the whole picture. Perhaps she was looking too hard, she wondered, and tried to relax. They were about an hour short of Patch Barracks, where at least she would be able to talk things through with colleagues. Glancing across the bus, her stare was once more met by the broad smile of Marco. He couldn't be happier; his part in historic events was nearly over. The story he'd be able to tell the men when he got back home. He would be a man amongst men, a hero.

Dieter was shown to the detention room by the guard commander. Stepping inside he immediately recognised Herman as he sat studying his shoes. Ahmed saw Dieter's appearance as an opportunity to

begin another verbal assault, rising from his chair
and complaining that he had been dragged from his
car at gunpoint and wanted to place a call to the highest authority. On a nod from Dieter a guard placed
his hands on Ahmed's shoulders and sat him down
firmly, telling him to shut up at the same time.

'Were they associated with any other vehicle?'
asked Dieter.

'Nothing obvious,' replied the guard commander.
'We've looked at the CCTV tapes, using a fifteen
minute bracket either side of them arriving at the
Swiss post. We have some fifty cars, about ten heavy
lorries and a coach. No vans.'

'Coach?' queried Dieter.

'Yes,' confirmed the guard. 'We get three or four
an hour, even at this time of night. Cheap trips, skiing, city breaks, that kind of thing. It was German
registered, to Grünebaum Reiser, a small travel company based in Böblingen, just outside Stuttgart.'

Dieter's curiosity had been aroused. As the coach
was mentioned he thought he saw Herman glance up
but he couldn't be sure.

'Call Stuttgart, use this number,' he said as he
handed Rolf Stein's number over on a slip of paper.
'Tell them I want to know who's hired that coach,
where it's been and where it's going.'

Turning to a young sergeant he asked, 'Anything

on them?' The border officer pointed to a few items on a table, Herman's wallet and mobile and some change, together with Ahmed's mobile and a similar wallet and a wad of Euro notes, all high denomination.

Sitting opposite Ahmed, Herman slowly shook his head from side to side a couple of times, and let out a slow, quiet sigh. Everything had been going so well. He was just beginning to believe that his Swiss account was about to grow, right up to the moment the Bulls dragged him out of the car.

Dieter stood up and walked over to the still protesting Ahmed.

'What were you doing in Switzerland with that piece of dross?' he asked, nodding his head in the direction of Herman, 'or had you two strayed further afield?' Predictably, there was no reply, just another protestation of wrongful arrest. The young sergeant had picked up Ahmed's mobile and was turning it over in his hands.

'Quite a piece of work,' he commented, 'first one of this model I've seen. You can't afford luxuries like this on a policeman's pay.' He switched off the keypad lock and idly scrolled through the functions as the screen lit up.

'That's private!' protested Ahmed, rising from his chair again. 'Leave it alone.' Again he was firmly encouraged to resume his seat, but clearly remained agitated.

'That could be evidence,' said Dieter but stopped short of telling the young officer to put it down because his attention was taken by the desk telephone as it jangled noisily.

****

At last the coach turned off the motorway and, after rounding a few corners, the entrance to Patch Barracks came into view. Polly felt relief as she saw the familiar uniforms outside and the US flag painted on the sign that said, 'Stop Here'. With a hiss of compressed air the coach came to a halt and the sleeping company at the back began to wake up and stretch. As the door swung open a draft of cold air enveloped Polly as she slipped down the steps to meet the guard commander. She still didn't know what it was that was so terribly wrong. Flashing her EUCOM ID she began to walk to the guard post as she tried to formulate her suspicions without introducing such embarrassing facts that she had been sleeping with the enemy. It was during the process of trying to string her words together that the small pieces of information slipped into line and for the first time it hit her: Herman – terrorists – RDD – Italy

– Transport! She covered her mouth with her hand as she silently mouthed, 'Oh my God! What have we done!?

****

Seventy miles away to the south, in Singen, the border patrol officer who'd answered the telephone listened for a few moments and jotted down a few notes. Looking up, he spoke to Dieter.

'Your people in Stuttgart got lucky. They phoned the coach depot and the manager was there booking out an early departure. Our bus is on hire to a group of American wives for a shopping trip to Milan. Return destination, Patch Barracks. In fact, they say it should be back there by now.' Again Dieter thought he detected a reaction from Ahmed, who continued to watch with a fixed gaze as the other policeman thumbed the buttons on his mobile.

'Wonder who he's got in his address book?' the policemen asked nobody in particular. 'Bet he ain't got George Bush,' he speculated. Then he laughed out loud, 'Hey, *Kommisar,* you won't believe this, but he's got a number here for bin Laden!'

'Give it to me!' protested Ahmed, but he was ignored.

'I just got to ring this one,' joked the sergeant as

he pressed the 'call' button. Dieter saw Ahmed move as though to rush forward then he seemed to relax and sat back in his chair, the smallest vestige of a smile spreading across his face. At that second Dieter's little moth that had fluttered around so annoyingly all night flew into the bright lights and he saw the whole picture.

'Nein!' he shouted as he launched himself across the room, grabbing the mobile phone from the startled sergeant and knocking him off his feet. Dieter desperately thumbed the 'cancel' button but the signal had left the phone on its journey to the nearby communications tower.

****

In the secret compartment under the coach at Patch Barracks the screen on a mobile phone suddenly illuminated the cramped confines of the box which contained the device. Microseconds later it had received the message it required to make one more connection. At 05.37 (local time) the coach, its contents, the guard post, twenty-nine human souls and everything within a thirty-metre radius was virtually vaporized, producing a huge dirty cloud of dust and particles. It left a crater nearly five metres deep and the whole rear axel assembly from the coach was found on the roof of a barrack block three hundred metres away. All that remained of the people who had died were some unidentifiable pieces of flesh and bone, the twisted remnants of a couple of rifles, a Kevlar helmet and a shred of red lining material with an Yves St Laurent label attached to it.

Five minutes later, in the detention room at the border post, Dieter Brückner felt his mobile vibrate in his inside pocket. He didn't even need to look at the screen to know who it was or what had happened. The prevailing wind was already carrying the radioactive cloud over the barracks and onward toward the city centre of Stuttgart. There was nothing anyone could do; it just spread a fine, filthy dust of contaminating particles. Ten months later the first of thousands of cases of cancer began to be reported.

****

EPILOGUE

Rupe Johnson received the news from one of the Agency guys from Langley. Herman Namlos and Ahmed had been detained and the Americans had demanded that the Germans extradite the pair to the United States for questioning and possible indictment as accomplices to the bus bombing which killed twenty-eight Americans, but the German courts refused. They had declined, based on insufficient evidence being produced against these two men. Even the evidence implicit in Ahmed's mobile phone was deemed inconclusive. The number lifted from his phone book which had been filed under 'bin Laden' was traced to a unit which had been bought in a market in Milan. The fingertip search of the explosion site by a specially trained team in full NBC

(Nuclear Biological & Chemical) kit had not found sufficient of the actuation mechanism of the RDD to link it to any specific SIM card or number.

The CIA claimed to have a piece of evidence incriminating Herman Namlos apparently a report which may have linked him to the ill-fated bus. They had found it in the desk drawer of the CIA liaison officer to EUCOM, but refused to release it to the German judge. It would 'compromise assets', they contended. That irritated the judge and the court acquitted both men and released them. The Agency guy apologized to Rupe. 'Nothing we could do, old buddy. Sorry.'

Rupe slowly hung up the telephone. As he had done often before when his daughter, Polly, had captured his mind, he reached into his desk drawer and once more clutched the sheets of paper he'd printed out from her e-mail attachment, now dog-eared from his repetitive reading. His wife, Alejandra, had refused to read Polly's piece; they each expressed their sorrow in different ways.

Alejandra assuaged her hurt with anger. Polly had got some of that quality from her mother, he mused. Rupe knew that Alejandra had never wanted her daughter to work for the CIA, although she had never really come right out and said it in so many words. Rupe had taken satisfaction from Polly following in her old man's footsteps and, unlike Alejandra, he nursed his grief with reminiscences. When he read Polly's article, he could hear her voice saying the words. He engaged his mourning once again by reading the manuscript she had e-mailed him.

Intellectual Terrorism
By Apollonia Johnson

In her book, The Rage and the Pride, *Oriana Fallaci got it right. When we in the West think of Islamic terrorism's most horrific act, frightful images gush into our minds: those of the airliners as they struck the Twin towers and the hapless victims, some hand in hand, jumping from smoke-belching windows. Yes, this was horrific, no question! But Ms Fallaci remarks that six months earlier there occurred another terrible act, also perpetrated by these Islamic terrorist: the senseless destruction of the two millenary Bamiyan Buddhas by the Taliban. On the Arab streets they watched with a cruel pleasure apparent as Western scholars and diplomats pleaded helplessly for mercy, for compassion towards these antiquities which, by virtue of their history, should have transcend their indictment as a mote in Allah's eye.*

As a raging Ms Fallaci points out, it is even more terrible because this desecration was not carried out by a skulkin,g clandestine group of reprobates; it was approved and executed by a nation in the name of a religion that dominates an entire region of the planet. The world watched with repugnance as clumsy attempt after attempt by artillery and explosives failed to carry out the sentence that had been handed down on these hapless ariefacts. It was like witnessing a botched execution in the electric chair, one requiring several attempts as the burning, smoking, stinking felon refuses to surrender his last breath or heartbeat. In the very same way the Buddhas spitefully endured for several days until a successful demolition was finally achieved by these henchmen of Allah.

I live in Germany. I've lived here before September 11, 2001, and I still live here. I travel throughout Europe and I'm fluent in three European languages, so listen to me. With due respect to Ms Fallaci, the Twin Towers was a modern horror and the destruction of the Buddhas terrible, but there is a more sinister, more pernicious evil right here in the heartland of Germany and in many other parts of Europe. The perpetrators do not wear beards and tribal headdress; they do not read from the Koran or carry a prayer rug; they do not live in squalor or suffer the illusion of oppression from global capitalism; they do not feel the deprivations of freedom under despotism, or the denial of opportunity by an economic cabal of nepotism; their women do not suffer house arrest behind black curtains and are not forced to wear totally enshrouding clothes and are not forbidden an education. These supporters of Islamic terrorism are the

Euro-pacifists. They serve as enablers and apologists for Islam's jihad and anti-Zionist mentality as they burn with rage at America for smugly challenging their European narcissism.

They relax in their Levis, drink Budweiser, sip Californian chardonnay, watch Hollywood films and eat fast food with relish; they listen to rock 'n' roll, the blues and jazz as they point with sneering self-absorption at Mozart, Goethe, Diderot, Van Gogh, DaVinci; they memorize a list of hundreds of other historical European people of arts and letters, few of whom they have listened to and few of whose work they bother to visit in their museums of fine arts and, ironically, hardly any of these snobs have read the literature they apparently cherish. Still, nose in the air, they scoff at the Declaration of Independence and the longest living democratic Constitution in the world today. 'After all,' they sniff, 'look what it created: a money-grubbing, racist, exploitive government.' That's what those Euro-liberals who care to bother about politics will say. Frankly, most Germans, most Europeans, won't bother. The majority find politics depressing, so they read the tabloid

*newspapers and view their televisions like
amoeba ingesting through osmosis as liberal
socialist and pacifist views softly and indelibly
mix into their protoplasm.*

*One could quibble over exact numbers
and the relative merit of various public opinion polls, but there was an absolute consensus
in all the polls during 2003: that a majority of
Germans held Israelis far more responsible
for strife in the Holy Lands than they did
Palestinians. Further, that they held the
Americans far more responsible for Islamic
terrorism than they did Libyans, Syrians,
Saudi Arabians, Yemenis, Egyptians or
Iranians. In fact, that was a ubiquitous
European perception. Moral relativism had
achieved an a priori intellectual respect. If
you're Islamic, you comfortably bask in the
sunshine of world opinion, but if you're Israeli
or American, then you are forced to ask: Why?
Why are we to blame?*

*The fact is that 'why' is not an important
question; here is the point: this Islamic counter-crusade is a natural dialectic of human history, and their pitiless employment of terrorism conforms to basic human behavior. Their
hate is as natural as cancer, or the plague, or*

locusts, or anthrax, or the exploitation of women, or slavery, or war. The Islamic counter-crusade comprises a bunch of guys from the wrong side of the tracks who resent our fine neighborhood and flaunting manners. Is that behavior something new? Is the sacrifice made by suicidal zealots something new?

How many people have given up their lives to make a political, religious or moral point and how many have died to gain a military advantage? Witness the Buddhist monks who poured petrol over themselves, lit it, and died without a murmur. The IRA hunger strikers who quietly wasted away in British prisons; the suffragette who dived in front of the British King's horse for women's rights; the students who linked arms in Tiananmen Square to face the troops and tanks and died in their hundreds. Not forgetting, of course, the Japanese kamikaze pilots or the German Hitler Youth who were prepared to pilot V1 flying bombs to specific Allied targets. The charge of the Light Brigade; 'Going over the top' in the trenches of Belgium and France; climbing into a Second World War fighter or bomber knowing each time you do so the odds of coming back diminish exponentially; run-

ning up the beaches of Normandy into wither-
ing machine gun fire— those who read history
could compose an encyclopedic list of suicidal
Westerners dying for God and country. Read
the accounts of the war heroes who managed
to survive; each had their moment when they
considered death with certitude, but they
forged ahead, often soiling their trousers or
vomiting in the stark terror of those moments.

So please explain what's so new about
suicidal heroism. It has been practiced by
brave men and women since biblical times and
before. Yes, these modern suicide bombers are
brave, they sacrifice their very lives for their
convictions. But always keep in mind that it is
their convictions which must be scrutinized
with suspicion, not their bravery.
Furthermore, those apologists who rationalize
radical Islamic convictions and only take
umbrage at their sacrifice are enablers of ter-
rorism, because it is this conviction which pro-
pels Islamic terrorist acts, not some quirky
death wish.

Sacrifice for religious or ideological con-
victions certainly pre-dates written human his-
tory. Suicidal killing is probably a gene we
inherited from Pithecanthropus erectus. On

the other hand, democracy is a relatively new and unprecedented human enterprise (as opposed to a concept).

Whether jihadists fight a hopeless battle against uniformed infidels, or blow up 'innocent' civilian infidels, or murder heretic true believers, what must be understood is that this suicidal endeavor is not something new. It is an age-old act of human desperation, motivated by a singular delusion embraced by these perpetrators in order to seek relevance in the same way that Christian martyrs, or Buddhist monks who burned themselves, or the pitiful gesture of voluntary human shields are grasping for some higher purpose than their otherwise tedious journeys from the table to the toilet here on Earth.

The dream of one world is an opiate to which Germany and other European states are addicted. World peace would be at hand if only we could get the Zionists and the Americans to start acting sensibly. Give the world a full stomach and a fair share of pride and world peace can become a reality. War will become an ancient relic of that Neanderthal world from which we are emerging. The one-world Europeans dare not look *the Islamic counter-crusade straight in the eye; the view would be sobering. Coming down from their 'high' would simply cause too much pain and distress. So they look the other way, they cuddle these Islamic counter-crusaders, and pop another happy pill. This is the third tragedy which is now unfolding before our very eyes – the demolition of Western values.*

These Germans, these French, these Euro-landists, these fifth-columnists, these fellow travellers of the counter-crusade, these socialist liberals are committing the most perfidious form of terrorism – intellectual terrorism. Never legitimize socialist liberalism with the notion that it is an ideology. It is not! Socialist liberalism is an art of convenience; it is a modus of behavior. These socialist liberals have not killed 3,000 innocent victims, or pulverized archeological treasures; they have done something even more heinous. These cowering pacifists are shamelessly soiling truth with their blurred parallax of moral equivalency seen through the one-world lenses. They squander the future of Western culture for a safe and comfortable present (and they are doing it for the sake of the children, so they unabashedly remind us, even though they refuse to have any!). I do not know if Oriana Fallaci would agree with my allegation, but I suspect that she might.

COMING SOON FROM
CITATION PRESS

GRANITE RIDGE INITIATIVE

KARL VINCENT

ISBN-978-0-9551238-0-1

PROLOGUE
CIA HQ Langley, Virginia.

'He's doing a "Jeremiah Denton"!' Morty Frank suddenly exclaimed.

Ed Cummings stood, resting his forearm on the back of Morty's chair, peering over his shoulder, watching the low resolution video playing on the monitor.

'Jeremiah Denton?' Ed queried. 'Name sounds vaguely familiar, but I can't place it. Another hostage?'

Morty shook his head while the rest of his body remained motionless in the chair. He kept his eyes glued to the screen as he replied, raising his voice to compete with the audio complementing the video.

'In 'Nam Denton was a POW at the Hanoi Hilton. During a Jane Fonda-inspired filming of American prisoners, the North Vietnamese forced them to make apologies for their war crimes. One of them was Jeremiah Denton. As he confessed, Denton used his eyes to blink out in Morse code the word T-O-R-T-U-R-E.'

'And you think that's why this poor bastard, Perry Norman, is blinking his eyes that way? I don't know Morse code, do you?'

'You young whippersnappers don't know shit!' Morty sucked on his lower lip thoughtfully before continuing, 'Bit rusty, but I'm gonna go back to the beginning of this clip and write down the dots and dashes.'

He punched a couple of keys on the console and the display halted then flashed to the beginning of the video. It was a short segment of the previous night's Al Jazeera broadcast, with an English voice over translation courtesy of the Central Intelligence Agency. Morty muted the sound and ran it again. The video was prefaced by CIA 'boilerplate' and dated 6 Sep 2004. He presumed the video itself had been shot a day earlier. That would be Sunday. According to the briefings, the abduction had taken place early Saturday evening. Perry Norman had been jumped by four men and unceremoniously bundled into a black van as he walked through the parking lot at Empire Oil. Helplessly, his administrative assistant, Mrs MacDonald, had watched the scene from behind the glass doors of the foyer.

As Morty waited to get to the part where the hostage on the video started his eye-blinking message, he reached for a ballpoint and a discarded Manila envelope lying within reach. 'C'mon, c'mon,' he muttered impatiently, his eyes fixed on the screen.

'You really think there's a message he's blinking?'

Ed Cummings scoffed, 'It just looks like they're shining bright light into his eyes. He'd probably have been blindfolded before they rolled camera and his eyes ain't used to the light. That's my impression. Sometimes you can overdo that thinking-outside-of-the-box crap.'

'Naw,' Morty insisted, 'it don't look natural. Gimme a chance to take down the dots and dashes, and see if there's any sense in it.'

'Well, if he is, maybe he's trying to give his location. The Brits in MI6 would find that mighty helpful,' suggested Ed, now not so sure of his ground.

'He won't know where the fuck he is,' snapped Morty, a little more sharply than he'd intended.

'Well sorreee,' replied Ed in a fawning voice, but Morty's attention was riveted to the screen and he probably didn't hear.

'Those jihadists are clever sonsabitches when it comes to hostage-taking. All he knows for sure is that he's in a world of shit and maybe about to have his head hacked off with a carving knife,' he mumbled as he made ready to start jotting on the envelope.

Cummings leaned a little closer to the monitor as he wisecracked, 'Stay tuned to Al Jazeera for neck-breaking news! You think the Brits are gonna deliver on these demands?'

'Nope.'

'So I guess we're gonna witness another beheading. How long d'they give... seventy-two hours? You really figure they're serious?'

Morty shrugged, 'These assholes have shown no reluctance in the past to follow through on their promises. Of course, this guy is Chief Executive of Empire Oil. He's not just some military grunt, truck driver or contract worker like they usually pick up. He's a valuable asset. They have some clear leverage with this one. They might show flexibility on the time frame.'

'When was he reported missing?'

'Saturday.'

'That makes it a pretty tight schedule. They're one short night's sleep and a wake-up ahead of us, so I calculate that the poor bastard has used up half of his remaining lease on life. He better hope to hell they're flexible.'

'Five hours ahead too,' said Morty.

'Whatever,' shrugged Ed. 'Pardon me for asking, but doesn't he look a bit young for being the CEO of Britain's largest oil company? F'Christ'sake, you could be his uncle. He seems to me like maybe early forties?'

'Fifty-two years young, married the boss's daughter. For the record, it's the largest privately held petroleum concern in the UK,' Morty corrected. 'Largest British petrol provider was an embellishment by the Arab news network. They don't let facts or technicalities get in the way of a good story. It's a family business that Daddy started from scratch, so it says in the background briefing. Do you ever bother to read the briefings?'

'Sometimes,' Ed responded lamely. 'From what you just said, it sounds to me like the Brits might cave in on this one.'

'You mean like rank has its privileges?'

'Yeah, something like that.'

'Maybe… maybe not,' he said with a shrug of his shoulders. 'Those jihadists are asking the British government to release that crazy cleric and eleven other Islamic terrorists and transport them to Syria. At the moment they're locked up somewhere called "Belmarsh" awaiting trial in the UK. No-negotiating-with-terrorists is the government's official line.'

'Yeah, and as I recall they didn't bend those rules when the IRA made similar demands.'

Morty hesitated a moment before softly responding, 'That's not entirely true.'

'Oh? You sure about that?' He didn't wait for a reply. The question was out of line. He didn't have a need to know. 'So where do you think they're holding this poor sonovabitch?'

'They grabbed him in Aberdeen, Scotland. That's where Empire has its headquarters. Chances are they're still somewhere in the vicinity. It's not the same as operating in the Middle East where you're surrounded by friendlies and can move at will.'

'Then how did they get their video to Al Jazeera?'

'Dunno, probably a digital file through the Internet. If they don't change servers maybe the Brits will get a handle on them.'

'Have our Cousins asked us for any help?'

'Dunno.'

'How would Mr Norman know Morse code?'

'You really must read the briefings. That's what they're for, to bring office juniors like you up to speed.'

'I cherry-pick,' Ed defended. 'You can't read them all and still get your work done. I took the Labour Day weekend off.' He quickly added, 'I'd planned to give the family a little quality time down in Fort Lauderdale. Had tickets and reservations, but Hurricane Frances put the kibosh on that plan. So I've got some catch-up to do.'

Morty heaved an admonishing sigh. 'Perry Norman was in the Royal Navy, qualified clearance diver and worked on Special Ops with the SBS and Marines. Earned a chest full of medals in the Falklands War. Then he got out and put together a bunch of ex-navy divers to plumb the depths for profit... mainly on the North Sea oil rigs and pipe swimming in the Persian Gulf...' Stopping his briefing he pointed to the screen. 'Okay we're there,' he announced as he put the envelope on top of a case file and got ready to write down the code - if there was one. As Ed watched, Morty's eyes flicked from the screen to his improvised note pad and a line of dots and dashes began to appear. Finally he laid down his pen and exhaled slowly as he pushed the 'pause' button. 'That's it!'

'Make any sense?' asked Ed over Morty's shoulder. 'Where we gonna find a copy of the Morse code?'

Morty didn't answer. Instead he picked up his pen again and began to slowly separate the string of code, scribbling and sometimes changing the words above the line. Occasionally pausing with a frown, the tension in his face would ease and he would jot down another letter of the alphabet.

'Make any sense?' Ed pressed again.

'Yup,' Morty finally responded as he sat back in the chair, 'It's a simple enough message.'

'You decoded it?'

'Yeah, not that many characters... see.' He indicated with his ballpoint at the jumble of letters he had hand printed over the string of dots and dashes.

'No deal,' Ed read out slowly, 'that's it?' Morty nodded in reply as he checked the translation.

'In other words,' said Ed, obviously taken aback, '…let the bastards chop off my head? Is that what he's saying?'

'Seems so,' confirmed Morty.

'Jeezuz, gotta hand it to that Brit… he's got balls!'

'Yeah, or no brains.'

'I mean that's what's going to happen if nobody's gonna make a deal,' added Ed. 'So… what'cha gonna do with this discovery?'

'Do? Do?' repeated Morty. 'What we analysts are paid to do: pass it up the Intelligence chain. Fact is I'd bet the Brits at MI6 already have this one figured out. The interesting question is what they'll do if they have.'

****

GRANITE RIDGE INITIATIVE

ISBN - 978-0-9551238-0-1

DUE FOR RELEASE
FEBRUARY 2008

MEET THE AUTHOR

You can hear and see Karl Vincent talking about Black Knife on:

www.meettheauthor.com

Go to the web site. Click on the British flag and then search for Karl Vincent.